A
PLANET
OF
ECCENTRICS

Ven Begamudré

A PLANET OF ECCENTRICS

1990
oolichan books
LANTZVILLE
BC, CANADA

Canadian Cataloguing in Publication Data

>Begamudré, Ven, 1956-
>A planet of eccentrics

>ISBN 0-88982-100-3

>I. Title.
>PS8553.E342P6 1990   C813'.54   C90-091363-0
>PR9199.3.B43P6 1990

Publication of this book has been financially assisted by The Canada Council, the Saskatchewan Arts Board, and Multiculturalism Canada.

Published by
OOLICHAN BOOKS
Box 10
Lantzville, BC, Canada V0R 2H0

Printed in Canada by
MORRISS PRINTING COMPANY LTD.
Victoria, British Columbia

for Shelley

Acknowledgements

These stories were written between 1982 and 1989. During this time, I received advice and encouragement from people too numerous to name: writers-in-residence at the Regina and Saskatoon public libraries, colleagues at the Saskatchewan School of the Arts, members of The Bombay Bicycle Club prose group, readers in the Saskatchewan Arts Board's literary script reading service, and editors of magazines and anthologies. I also received generous financial support: individual assistance grants from the Saskatchewan Arts Board and a project grant from The Canada Council.

Five of these stories have appeared or will appear elsewhere. "Vishnu's Navel" in *Tesseracts³* (Porcépic Books, 1990). "A Planet of Eccentrics" in *West Coast Review* (now *West Coast Line*), vol. 22, no. 4, Spring 1989. "Honestly, as in the Day" in *Canadian Author and Bookman*, vol. 64, no. 4, Summer 1989. "A Promise We Shall Wake in the Pink City After Harvest" in *The Old Dance* (Coteau Books, 1986) and as "A Promise We Shall Wake" in *Special Report: Fiction*, August-October 1990. "Mosaic" in *More Saskatchewan Gold* (Coteau Books, 1984); adapted as "Mosaic for Radio" for upcoming broadcast on CBC Radio's "Ambience."

Author's Note

Many characters in these stories feel at home in more than one language. That is why, in general, I have not italicized words from languages other than English — unless the main character does not understand the words or unless the narrator regards the language as somewhat foreign. When pronouncing Indian names and terms, it may often help to accent the first syllable, for example, *Vish*-nu, *Nan*-jan-gud, *man*-go (but si-*tar*).

Contents

Vishnu's Navel

Garuda, the king of birds, could mock the wind with the speed of his flight; yet he circled lazily outward from earth. He stopped twice: once at the moon to rearrange metallic artifacts left there by men; once more to ride the rings of Saturn. When at last he caught sight of Lord Vishnu, Garuda considered turning back, but he had already come a long way and he planned to go much farther. Upon reaching the primordial sea, he alighted on the great serpent Sesha, on whom Vishnu reclined.

Vishnu the Protector, beloved of gods and men, looked bored. He gazed so intently at his navel, he did not notice Garuda until the king of birds declared, "Evening, Lord."

"You," Vishnu sighed. "Of course. I heard a passing comet chuckle."

Garuda joined his golden human hands before his golden human breast. He bowed his white eagle head over them. After folding his red eagle wings upon his back, he sat with his human legs crossed beneath him. He sat carefully, so his talons would not hook under Sesha's scales. At last Garuda said, "Comets are easily amused."

"Even you cannot cure boredom," Vishnu scoffed.

"If I were perfect," Garuda said, "I would be you."

"Perhaps," Vishnu murmured and turned away. He propped his head on the knuckles of the hand with which he gripped a club. With his remaining three hands, he held a discus, a conch shell, and a lotus. He cocked his fourth wrist as if he meant to drop the lotus into the sea, then waved off a gnat. The lotus reminded him of Brahma the Creator, who had long ago emerged from another lotus. It had grown from Vishnu's navel, the source of all creation.

Suddenly, Vishnu felt piqued. This very night, all the gods would gather to divert themselves with tales about men. Brahma often smiled, sometimes even chuckled, but he refused to allow anyone to see him laugh. Of his four faces, he kept three — the one in front, the ones facing left and right — as stony as all the statues carved by men of gods. If he laughed, he did so with his fourth face — the one behind. Just once, Vishnu wanted to make Brahma laugh openly.

After Vishnu asked, "Is there some reason for your visit?" Garuda said: "North of Mysore City, in the land now called India, lies the town of Srirangapatna on an island in the Cauvery River. South of the town, west of the trunk road to Mysore, lies—"

"Do you never fly directly to a spot?" Vishnu demanded. "First you take us north, then back toward the south, and now west. Might we consider a diversion to the east?"

"Flying directly to a spot is for crows," Garuda snapped.

Sesha's coils contracted. He raised his thousand heads in warning — the thousand serpent heads which formed a jewelled canopy above Vishnu.

"Forgive me," Garuda sighed. "Frequent interruptions make me forget myself."

"Go on, please," Vishnu urged, "or you might forget the tale itself. Brahma will sneer if I lose its thread when I retell it."

Vishnu again waved off the gnat, now from his ear. "If I choose to retell it."

Garuda sat back. He rested his hands on his knees and continued, uninterrupted:

As I was saying, south of Srirangapatna, west of the trunk road to Mysore, lies the Ranganathittu Bird Sanctuary. Near it lived a man whose name was also Ranganathittu, called by his family Thittu. His parents were like pheasant-tailed jacanas, for like the female jacana, his mother deserted his father after bearing four children. To Thittu, the family sounded birdlike when they called: his elders like raucous crows — "Thit-tu! Thit-tu!" — and his siblings like exasperated geese: "Thit-tu? Thit-tu?" Before long, they stopped their calling, for he refused to respond with anything but grunts or single words delivered hoarsely.

His elders blamed a cuckoo called the brain-fever bird. During his birth, it had joined its unending cry with his mother's. They decided young Thittu had thus succumbed to brain fever even as he had entered the world. Since they mistook him for an idiot, they never sent him to the local school and never arranged a marriage for him. Cut off from the world of men, he spent much of his time in the sanctuary, in the world of birds — so much time that he even learned to speak their language. He slipped out of his hut long before the goddess of dawn, in her crimson robes and golden veil, wakened birds in their nests.

He enjoyed being ignored by his elders. They addressed him in gibberish as though he understood little else. Yet it pained him to be ignored by the sanctuary's few visitors. Though employed by no one to do so, he greeted visitors with the mating dance of the common peafowl. He approached with mincing steps, then hopped from foot to foot. Just as the peahen affects indifference to the peacock's dance, most visitors also affected indifference. A few laughed, for he frightened them with his loud shrieks, imitations of the peafowl's warning call. Most waved in that backhanded manner men have of dismissing beggars, a manner of seeing without taking note. He did beg, it was true, but not for alms; he merely begged to be noticed.

He followed them from the gate along the wooden walk to the picnic area. Past it stood a ticket booth above a landing. Here people hired boats to ply the waterways which swirled about the islands of the sanctuary. Even the ticket seller and the boatmen ignored Thittu, though he tried to earn their praise — not only by greeting visitors but also by preventing their stay from being spoiled by crows.

He despised those crows. They gathered in the bamboo and acacia and cawed so loudly, they drowned out the calls of birds nesting on the islands. Often the crows gathered on the islands themselves and spoiled the serenity. At night the boatmen chained their boats to the landing and locked their oars in the ticket booth, so he had no means of reaching the islands. He contented himself with keeping the picnic area free of crows. He did this by flinging bits of coconut shell or lumps of cow dung. These last he stole while they dried, pressed flat on the whitewashed sides of the huts.

What angered him most was the way the crows clamoured for
attention. The other birds rarely did; they had no need. People
sought them out to marvel at their markings and at their myriad
shapes. Yet even keeping the picnic area free of crows earned him
little notice. And while he grew past youth into manhood, a man
deprived of both the cares and the bliss of a householder, he feared
he might grow invisible.

One day, a foreign watcher of birds pointed a strange camera at
Thittu. It clicked and whirred, then spewed a white rectangle.
While a coloured photo magically emerged, Thittu drummed with
his fingertips on his lower lip. "Heh, heh!" he exclaimed. "Click,
click!" To his surprise, the visitor handed him the photo. When he
tried to return it, the visitor waved his hand as if, again, dismissing
a beggar. "Keep it," he said; so Thittu did. Over time the colours
faded until it became a pale yellow shadow. He decided this
happened because he had kept it; that it would have remained true
to life only if the visitor had taken it away. Unable to bear the sight
of his self fading, Thittu buried the photo near his hut. But even as
he grew past manhood toward old age, so did his fear.

Two lovers visited the sanctuary one day toward the end of the
cold season. They seemed to him like saurus cranes, whose devotion to their mates inspires legends. No such female would ever
leave her mate. The woman looked like a madanakai, one of those
damsels of the hourglass shape beloved by Hoysala sculptors. Her
hair, though dark at its roots, glinted like white gold. The man
looked like a bronzed pelican: barrel-chested and short-necked.
He seemed unable to turn his head without twisting his trunk.

They wore similar clothes, as foreign visitors often did: rough
blue trousers and white pullover shirts marked in front with the
letter I, a red heart, and the letters LA. The woman followed the
man at some distance after they left their hired car at the gate. That
is why, when Thittu saw the message on the man's shirt, he
decided her name was La. The man passed without looking Thittu
in the eye. Mincing on her high-heeled sandals, the woman
approached. Her walk reminded him of the mating dance of the
common peafowl, but it also confused him, for it is the peacock
that minces toward the peahen. To hide his confusion, he greeted
her by chanting, "La, La, La. La, La."

She stopped and exclaimed, "*Ein clown!*" She said it as though accompanied by some invisible admirer. Then she tapped her chest and said, "*Nein, nein. Ich liebe L-A.*"

He decided L-A must be the man's initials, but Thittu turned and saw HELMUT on the back of the man's shirt. Before Thittu could address the woman again, she passed him, so closely that he could smell her skin. It smelled like lavender. On the back of her shirt, he saw HEIDI. When she called, "Helmut!" the man turned to say, "*Ja*, Heidi?" and Thittu realized these were their names. Helmut shrugged as though he saw little reason to hire a boat during the off-season. They returned along the walk.

Thittu hopped from foot to foot. Panic rippled his throat. How could they leave so soon? A splendid foreign camera dangled from Helmut's shoulder; yet he had taken no photos. Thittu pressed his grizzled cheeks and grinned. "Heh, heh," he suggested. "Click, click." When Helmut frowned, Thittu asked, "Heh, heh? Click, click?"

Helmut laughed. "*Hier nichts zu click, click,*" he said loudly. "*Click, click nein.*"

Thittu pointed at himself and tried to explain. If they took his photo, a memory of him would lie in their house, and he would never grow invisible. He thought Heidi would understand. When she passed him, he closed his hand around her forearm, one covered with hair as soft as down. "Click, click!" he cried. Her scream so startled him, he tightened his grip and found her arm suprisingly muscular.

She snarled, "*Braun schwein!*" and pushed him away.

He fell into bamboo that clutched him like a dozen rattling arms. The ticket seller came running. So did the boatmen, who freed Thittu from the bamboo. Instead of sending him on his way, perhaps with a kick and a cuff, they held him tightly. Helmut shouted at the ticket seller, he shouted at the boatmen, and they shouted at one another. Then everyone except Heidi shouted at Thittu. While she minced her way back to the gate, he chirped for her forgiveness. He pleaded with roos and coos.

"Crazies like him lock away you should!" Helmut stormed. "In Vienna with them that's what we do!"

"Extremely sorry, sir," the ticket seller whined. "Sorry in the extreme!" He followed Helmut past the gate to the car. "The fellow has no official business here. He is a madcap."

The last Thittu saw of Heidi, she was rolling up her window. Then Helmut climbed into the car, and it drove off. Moments later, the ticket seller returned. He held a switch. While the boatmen held Thittu, the ticket seller whipped him — whipped him across the shoulders and face and chest until he fainted, not from pain but from fear the men might kill him. When he woke, he found himself at the gate. The goddess of night had lowered her dark robes across his world. He crawled back to his hut. There he lay for days in a fever. It pained his body far less than it pained his mind.

When he finally returned to the sanctuary, the boatmen chased him off. Much later, they once again allowed him to resume his duties, but he no longer had the strength to either greet visitors or battle crows. He found himself unable to remain awake through the long day. Visitors often encountered him curled on the walk like a chick in its egg. No one woke him, not even the boatmen. This proved a blessing, for he dreamt he had been transformed into a bird.

At times, he became an acrobatic sultan tit. He climbed a tree and hung upside down from twigs while he hunted for insects and grubs. Other times, he became a tailor bird. Using his pointed bill as a needle and shreds of cotton wool as yarn, he sewed leaves into a nest for his young. Always, though, clouds darkened his skies. Then he dreamt he was a bird which had woken from a troubling dream, one in which it had lost its wings and been compelled to walk the earth as a man — a man who could not even find refuge in a sanctuary for birds.

One afternoon, toward the end of the wet season, he woke to find visitors tumbling from a van. Like other watchers of birds, they had arrived with a purpose. He saw this in the way they strode through the gate, in the way they carried small, thick books in their numerous pockets. They reminded him of the bird called "seven sisters," the jungle babbler. It is always found in flocks of six to eight, and it chatters while rummaging for food. Though he could no longer hop, he delighted them with his peacock dance, now a mere shuffle of the feet. They followed while he led them onto the wooden terrace. From here, one could look out across a narrow channel for a tantalizing glimpse of the sanctuary's inhabitants.

An elderly woman in a canvas topi leapt onto the terrace and raised her binoculars. They were smaller than others he had seen; hers snapped shut into a thin, gold case. "I say, chaps," she calmly announced, "I do believe I saw one. Was it, though?" She flipped through a book and slapped a page. "Yes, it was!" She snapped open her binoculars and peered. "Oh my Lord," she gurgled, calling upon her Christian god, "I do believe I saw a striated weaver. Look over—" She began to experience trouble breathing.

"Y'all just pullin' ma leyg!" a man insisted. He wore boots made of crocodile skin. "Where'baouts?"

"In those reeds," she gasped. "It may be a male, and—Yes, it's weaving a nest!"

"Ah see it!" he cried, then doubled over. Instead of merely struggling for air as she did, he clutched his stomach. He clenched his teeth and groaned, "If thayt ain't the gradest thaing since washed gravel!"

Utterly bewildered, Thittu backed away from the visitors. Still they intrigued him, and each bore a camera.

A second woman, younger than the first, carried a parasol. It tilted over her shoulder when she tried to raise her binoculars. They were silver and etched with pink feathers. Upon spotting a white-breasted kingfisher, she dropped the parasol. "*Fantastique!*" she whimpered. She began to weep.

A second man, older than the first, elbowed his way to the railing. One side of his brown hat was pinned to its crown. He eased a leather tube rimmed with brass from a pocket, then pulled the tube into a telescope. He squeezed one eye shut and scanned the island. "A pa'doise floy-ketcha!" he shrieked. Even as the first woman inquired, "Must you be so dramatic?" he sank to the terrace and began to twitch. "Tike me, Lohd!" he cried. He spread his arms as though to keep the earth from quaking. "Oi'm re-eady!"

Thittu approached the one visitor who hung back. His skin was neither as ruddy as the red junglefowl nor as white as the egret. He

appeared to be a guide, for he carried a map. Thittu frowned at the
others with concern.

"Twitchers," the guide explained. "I took them to Srirangapatna, yet they showed no interest. None whatsoever. They
are making a tour of bird sanctuaries. Each and every single last
one."

Thittu mumbled, "Twid-jhers?"

"Twit-chers," the guide repeated. "They live and breathe for
birds. Upon encountering one they have never before seen, they
experience such joy they take ill. I, too, feel ill at such behaviour,
but I recover quickly." The guide cupped his hand. He grinned
while rubbing his thumb over his middle two fingers.

After the first four twitchers recovered from their strangely-felt
joy, the guide led them and their companions to the ticket booth.
Even as he hired boats, the twitchers stumbled down the landing.
The boatmen shoved off.

The twitchers disturbed the birds more than the crows did. The
sanctuary echoed with, "Oh my Lord!" and, "If thayt ain't the
gradest thaing since—!" It echoed with, "*Fantastique!*" and, "Tike
me, Lohd! Oi'm re-eady!"

When the twitchers returned, they could barely walk. They
tumbled out of the boats and lay exhausted on the landing. They
staggered to the stone picnic benches and collapsed. The man with
stomach trouble, the one in crocodile-skin boots, appeared to have
shrunk to half his former size. The weeping woman clutched her
parasol and wept. Another woman stared in front of her and
babbled, "A racket-tailed drongo, I saw a racket-tailed drongo, I
heard its tail feathers hum."

Thittu slowly drummed with his fingertips on his lower lip. Was
he, himself, not like the drongo? He squatted on his haunches in
the middle of the picnic area and, like the drongo, began imitating
other birds. First he gave a series of sharp, whistling screams.

"I'd say it's a night prowler," the gasping woman gasped.

Grinning, he bobbed his head. Next he made a shrill, piping
call.

"Thayt there's uh avocet," groaned the groaning man.

"*Ce n'est pas*—Not close enough," said the woman who wrung out her kerchief. "*C'est un*, black-winged stilt." She asked Thittu, "*Vrai?*"

He frowned at the guide, who nodded.

"I just knew!" she said and burst into tears.

Thittu made some harsh, nasal sounds.

"Taow easy, mite," said the twitching man. "That's moi pa'doise floy-ketcha."

Thittu made a high-pitched bubbling call like the sound of air blown through a reed into water. Silence followed. After he repeated the call, a fifth twitcher cried, "A masked fin-foot!" The others applauded.

After that, he stared eagerly at the cameras. "Heh, heh?" he asked. "Click, click?" The twitchers frowned at one another. "Heh, heh!" he insisted. "Click, click!" When no one responded, he gave them his best imitation: the loud melodious call of the shama.

Two of them guessed correctly, but the guide shrugged when they questioned him. "There are no shamas here," he said. "They are too shy. I myself have never seen a shama, not in all my years as the number-one guide in Mysore District. I would pluck out these very eyes if I could find a shama for you."

The twitchers rose and reluctantly followed him back to the van. Each of them dropped a coin at Thittu's feet. He gazed dully at the seven coins. He did not need money to be happy; the twitchers had made him happy with their attention. All he asked now was that they ensure he never grow invisible, and they could do so seven times over.

That night, after all the birds except the night prowler and the drongo had fallen silent, he crept back to the sanctuary. He cut down a bamboo thicket and lashed the poles with dried coconut fronds. He floated his raft to the nearest island and hid the raft among dense reeds. Then he hid himself behind a babul tree, well away from the silvery white thorns about its base. In the morning, after the goddess of dawn wakened birds in their nests, he began the loud melodious call of the shama. He sang all day and all the next until his throat began to knot. Soon after dawn on the third day, the twitchers and their guide returned. Even from the island,

Thittu could hear them chatter like the jungle babbler. He could almost hear them gasp and groan and weep. He could imagine them—side by side on the terrace—twitching.

When he heard them run toward the ticket booth, he pulled his raft out of hiding. The ticket seller and the boatmen, the guide and all the twitchers waited to welcome him. He spread his arms and performed his repertoire: the shrieks of a common peafowl; the screams of a night prowler; the call of a black-winged stilt; even the unending cry of the brain-fever bird. Oh, how the twitchers applauded. Thittu felt like a king—a king of the birds. While his raft neared the landing, he continued his performance with the bubbling call of a masked fin-foot; the nasal sounds of a paradise flycatcher; and, finally, the melodious call of the shama.

"You!" the guide exclaimed. Even he now bore a camera.

The twitchers turned to leave. "We want our payment re-funded," they told the guide. "The bonus, too."

"Of course," he said. "Certainly, why not?"

"Heh, heh?" Thittu called after the twitchers. "Click, click?" The ticket seller growled, "We shall give you click, click!"

The boatmen pulled Thittu off the raft and up the stone steps of the landing. The ticket seller ran to see off the van. When he returned, he held not a switch but a length of stout, green bamboo. Then, while the boatmen held Thittu, while he chirped and twittered and roo'd and cooed, the ticket seller beat him to death.

At this point in Garuda's tale, Vishnu sat up — so quickly, the great serpent Sesha bobbed upon the primordial sea. "Ga-ru-da," Vishnu warned, "if I relate this tale of yours, the gods will shed tears. Brahma will sneer until his lips twitch like those foreigners."

Garuda tilted his eagle head until it brushed his human shoulder. "Have patience, Lord," he pleaded. "Once, when we discussed why men amuse us so much, you told us comedy is the sum of tragedy and time."

"The only comedy here," Vishnu scoffed, "will be the gods' laughing at me — for a sorry tale about a man whose life had so little purpose. It is barely tragic at that. What is the loneliness of one man compared, say, to the foolishness of the many who war? That is tragic. Even gods can learn to laugh at that over time."

"You know best, Lord," Garuda said. He made to rise.

"And where might you be going?" Vishnu asked.

"To find another tale," Garuda said. "This time I shall not try to be amusing." He smiled coyly.

Vishnu raised his club.

When Garuda flinched, Sesha lowered his thousand heads. Garuda nodded at the silent reminder: Vishnu the Protector would never strike unless the fate of heaven or the world hung in the balance. Even when bothered by gnats, he threatened them half-heartedly.

"Do you expect me to wait here with an unfinished tale," he demanded, "while you search for another? This tale is clearly unfinished. I can see by your smile. Every tale deserves to be told at least once, to an audience of at least one. I doubt this tale will be retold, but here is your audience of one."

Garuda again took his place on Sesha's coils.

"Finish quickly," Vishnu commanded, so Garuda did:

Yama, the king of justice, called Thittu to the lower world, where he hurried past the insatiable dogs of death. He entered Yama's palace. While a councillor thumbed through the great register, Thittu's soul hovered in the form of a quivering, white light. The account of his deeds took little time to relate. He did not deserve to be dragged through any of the twenty-one hells, for he was guilty of so little. Thus Yama set aside his noose and, naturally, sent for me.

"It seems clear this man should be reborn as a bird," I said.

Yama hefted his mace and allowed it to fall at his feet. The lower world trembled. "I did not summon you to tell me what is clear," he growled. "What kind of bird?"

"Something wondrous," I suggested. "Perhaps a fabulous partridge who feeds on moonbeams."

Yama snorted. "Would it not be better if he became an ordinary bird? Then he could have a mate."

"An ordinary bird then," I agreed. "But what kind?"

"If you please, Lord Garuda," Thittu said. When Yama glared at him for speaking, Thittu's voice trembled like his soul. "I-I would like to be a bird no one could ignore."

"A fairy bluebird?" I asked. "A scarlet minivet, or even a brahminy kite. You could always become a common peafowl, though as a peacock you would hardly be common."

"None of them," he said and then announced his choice.

When Garuda fell silent, Vishnu once more raised his club. He lowered it quickly for this time Garuda did not flinch. "Am I to remain in suspense forever?" Vishnu demanded. "What did the man choose to become?"

"Can you not guess, Lord?" Garuda asked. "What is the one bird that can never be ignored?" Garuda spread his hands. "Thittu chose to be reborn as a crow."

Vishnu's laugh began as a smirk, then became a chuckle. Soon he guffawed, "A crow!" He slapped his thigh with the hand bearing the lotus. He laughed with his back arched, with his head thrown back. Sesha bobbed until the primordial sea threatened to swamp the earth.

"Would a tale like this force Brahma to laugh openly?" Garuda asked.

"Never mind Brahma," Vishnu said, "that stony-faced spoiler of others' sport! The rest will laugh."

A satisfied smile crinkled Garuda's beak. This time Vishnu did not stop Garuda when he rose and unfurled his wings. "If I may, Lord," he said, "it is comforting to know you are only mistaken over small things."

Vishnu looked askance. "What now?" he asked.

"You were wrong twice," Garuda said. "Once when you called Thittu's life a life with no great purpose—"

"I said that?"

"And once more when you called my tale sorry."

"Ah, I see."

"Not yet," Garuda said. "A life lived with no great purpose leads to another life, so it is not completely wasted. And just as the purpose of a man's life, even one like Thittu's, lies in its living and in little else — so the purpose of a tale lies in its telling. If it accomplishes more, so be it. Even if this one does not force Brahma to laugh openly, it has already accomplished more."

"Oh-hoh!" Vishnu exclaimed. "Pray, how is that?"

Garuda tensed his wings for escape. "Must I reveal everything?" he asked. "Think, Lord: you are no longer gazing at your navel."

Long after he left, Garuda could hear Vishnu's laughter, could hear him gasp, "A crow!"

Garuda circled out from the primordial sea toward earth. This time he stopped only once: to ride the rings of Saturn. A passing comet chuckled. And while Garuda spun, rocking with his head thrown back, his wings unfurled and his arms uplifted, even Brahma, who was not above disguising himself as a gnat — even Brahma laughed.

A Planet of Eccentrics

Like a satellite unable to escape the gravitational pull of the earth, my life continues revolving about my father's district of Nanjangud. This is not meant to be a complaint; it is merely an observation. Indeed, an American tour operator told me, while reminiscing about his quaint midwest town, "You cannot go home again." Why anyone would wish to do so, I cannot guess. And yet I know it is foolish to attempt to leave the past behind, for however long ago or far away that past may feel, it remains with us always. My daughter reminded me of this earlier in the evening, when I returned from piloting a charter for a party of European travel agents. During my absence, my wife had taken our children on an extravagantly brief visit to Nanjangud. While I approached our house, I heard the swish and slap of a skipping rope accompany my daughter's reedy voice. She sang:

> Doctor Das from Bang-a-lore,
> Dressed a wound he could not cure.
> Mother, if you mind our noise,
> Doctor Das will steal your boys.

As with any district, Nanjangud boasts a regulation complement of characters. Take for instance Mahodyamma, the beggar. Every day for sixty years, she rode the morning train to Mysore City and at night returned to Debur Village. My mother said after Mahodyamma died, the police uncovered a fortune in her hut. Among its lowest bricks, they found a hundredweight of coin, some dating to the reign of Queen Victoria, while the remaining bricks hid crumpled notes in no denomination lower than ten. Why she had remained in a village with neither electricity nor

running water, no one could imagine; nor could they fathom what
became of her fortune. Or take Katthiappa, the blind boy who
insisted on throwing knives. He claimed he could sense auras and
so knew precisely where to aim: at that edge where the warmth of
one's body mingles with air to form perspiration. He claimed it
was, in fact, condensation, formed by the soul trying to escape a
body not yet accorded the privilege of death. He injured only one
person, and that early in his career, when a landowner lost an ear
lobe because Katthiappa misread the landowner's aura. "It was the
fellow's own fault," my father said, "for being so cold-blooded."
Or even take Thanthiappa, the arthritic telegraph operator, who
remained at his post long after he began stuttering in Morse code.
But that is enough, and though the district never tired of clucking
its communal tongue, it reserved for such characters a special place
in its communal heart, for they were locals.

Dr. Das, on the other hand, attracted more than his fair quota of
attention, for he was an outsider. By that I do not simply mean he
hailed from outside my father's district. No, he hailed from outside
Mysore State, all the way from Bengal. Many southerners claim
Bengalis consider themselves too good for other Indians: too
proud, especially, of their part in the freedom struggle, a roman-
ticized affair fueled by men like Surendranath Banerjea, a moder-
ate despite his nickname, "Surrender-not." Consequently, those
who encountered Dr. Das vacillated between respect and scorn.
No one knew his first name, only that his initial was B, and so at
first the people of Nanjangud Town referred to him as Bengali
Das. After his practice spread to outlying areas, villagers who had
little use for geography took to calling him Bangalore Das. Then,
even townspeople who knew the state of Bengal lies a thousand
miles farther north than the city of Bangalore also began referring
to him as Bangalore Das. My father supposed it was their way of
making the doctor an honorary citizen of the south.

Dr. Das arrived in Nanjangud Town the year my parents
enrolled me at Bishop Cotton School in Bangalore. I never saw the
doctor, but I followed his rise and fall through my mother's weekly
letters. During my parents' monthly visits, my father commented
on the news she had relayed through the post. It was his way of
implying that, while her letters may have been as truthful as

teachings from the *Bhagavad Gita*, both were indecipherable without the commentary of a modern man.

Dr. Das was not the first man trained in allopathy, or western medicine, to move his practice to Nanjangud, but he quickly became the wealthiest. His patients began by visiting him out of curiosity; then they visited him more for his credentials, framed on the wall of his dispensary, than for his skill. My father supposed they liked frowning at the Old English script, for it seemed a hybrid of British stodginess and South Indian flair, or so he likened it. On the wall behind the door hung a certificate in homeopathy from Temple University in Philadelphia. He wondered once why an Indian would travel all the way to America to study a form of medicine more widely practised here than abroad. We had to wait a number of years to solve that particular riddle.

Before long, Dr. Das's patients visited him because he gave them a choice of cures. At the end of each examination, he asked, "Do you want an injection or a compound?" People like my father, who took only minor complaints to him while hoarding serious ones for doctors in Mysore City, accepted the compound. Sometimes it was a corked bottle of bitter tonic, sometimes a newspaper cone of tablets, which blackened from the printer's ink. Both these remedies were dispensed by the compounder, Vaidyappa, who faithfully guarded his employer's secrets until shortly after the end. Most uneducated patients replied, "Oh, injection only, Doctor Sir," and he sent them home proudly rubbing their buttocks. After all, tonic or tablets were little enough to show for the standard rates he charged — up to eight annas — for treating complaints as varied as eczema and infertility. My father supposed one man could never solve root problems like undernourishment; so particularly to the poor, whose diet varied as seldom as the weather in the dry season, Dr. Das gave injections of glucose. His fellow allopaths never lodged a complaint against him, for they had often resorted to such expediences in earlier days. Moreover, as long as he charged rates higher than theirs, his competitors remained assured of steady, if uninteresting, practices.

By the time I entered Tata Institute to study aeronautics, Dr. Das's patients visited him not because he offered them a rare choice in a largely pre-ordained life, but rather because he built the finest house in Nanjangud Town. They trusted success. The house was not large, but he had it faced with pale green tiles, all the more exotic since the builder had imported them from Italy. Even better, its compound was so vast, it could have fed the entire population of a village; yet since no one in the district starved, the new house — like his cures — lifted spirits. It allowed him to become Nanjangud's first patron of the arts. A stage rose at one end of the compound to balance the two-storied house at the opposite end. On Saturday nights, in exchange for a paltry four annas, men, women, and children could spend sundown to sunup listening to veena and tabla players or watching yakshagana actors caricature dramatic heroes.

Dr. Das reserved Saturday afternoons for open-air salons on the visual and literary arts. Young men who fancied themselves artists, both the arrogant and the shy, exhibited or recited their creations for criticism by their peers. Others, who fancied themselves bards of a new age, one sprinkled with terms like "five-year plan," debated themes in the works of E. M. Forster, Maxim Gorky, and Victor Hugo. While lounging on a French Empire sofa, Dr. Das looked on and listened. My father said he often expected a dancing girl to press peeled grapes between the doctor's lips, but women were not allowed to attend these afternoon salons. He rarely spoke during them; he merely encouraged the timid with a raised eyebrow or reassuring smile. After rumours about his romantic inclinations took root, these Saturday afternoon artistes came to be known as Dr. Das's Boys.

Even my father, who prided himself on his liberal-mindedness, snickered about the non-speaking roles Dr. Das played during the all-night performances. Sometimes he played the heroine's sister and pillowed her head in his lap while she sighed about her absent lover and picked the petals of a lotus one by one. Sometimes he played a groom's mother with such scowls and sneers that young brides howled when they recognized their mothers-in-law. Once he powdered his hair with rangoli to play an aged widow awaiting death. On that night, my mother confided, my father lost his superior smile and allowed the shadow of guilt to cross his face over not having done more for his own widowed mother.

I said nothing of this during their subsequent visit, but I did say, as I often did, "What of this new doctor?"

My father supposed Dr. Das enjoyed dressing like women for it allowed him to lampoon both his own passion for the arts, a passion shared by all well-to-do Bengalis, and also to lampoon the latent distrust of women in a society that feared their power. My father could afford to be generous on this point because, of late, rumours had begun spreading like banyan shoots about Dr. Das, namely that he enjoyed dressing like a woman not only in public — which was acceptable during a performance — but also in private, which was not. He had been seen more than once, by men hired to guard ripening fields at night, twirling among tomato plants or traipsing through the sugar cane while dressed in the red silk sari of a bride-to-be. My father could afford to be generous, for he had drawn his own conclusion about these moonlit transformations, namely that Dr. Das emulated Radha's love for Lord Krishna.

"Ondu," my father said, pressing his index finger to his knee. "Bangalore Das, as we well know, is from Bengal. Eradu," my father continued, pressing his middle finger to his knee. "The fellow is more than likely a Bengal Vaishnava."

My mother wagged her head in agreement.

I remained superficially disinterested. I knew — despite having attended a Christian school and having absorbed my teachers' distaste for Hindu spiritualism — I knew from my private reading that Bengal Vaishnavism had been revitalized by the medieval saint, Chaitanya. He had sung publicly in praise of Lord Krishna, the eighth avatar of Vishnu the Protector. Chaitanya had even chanted the lord's name throughout the night, a practice that had not endeared him to his neighbours. By identifying himself with the cowgirl Radha, who had adored the cowherd Krishna, Chaitanya — and thus Dr. Das — became the unswerving devotee of a fickle god. It remained to be seen whether, like Chaitanya, Dr. Das would also renounce the world to become a sannyasi. One thing seemed clear to my father: with the exception of Dr. Das's Boys, no one in the district would weep and faint if the doctor left Nanjangud. Such had been the case with Chaitanya's followers when he had left them, and such had been the case with Radha each time Krishna had left her.

"Muru?" I asked, but my father made no third point. "Could it not simply be," I suggested, "that Bangalore Das—"

"Bengali Das," my mother insisted. Her parents had been from Bangalore, and while she found the doctor quaint, it irked her that others in my father's district might think all Bangalorians acted like madcaps.

"Could it not simply be this doctor is eccentric?" I asked. When my father scoffed, I raised my hands to calm him. "What, after all, does it mean to be eccentric?" I asked rhetorically. I was full of my newly discovered talent for debating, my only extracurricular activity aside from learning to fly. I now reached into my knowledge of physics to be profound. "To be eccentric," I said, "is to mean one is not situated in the centre, as an axis would be. To be eccentric is to mean one deviates from a perfect circle, and so the earth's motion around the sun is eccentric. Are we not, then, a planet of eccentrics? In short," I concluded, "to be eccentric is merely to obey nature's law."

"In that case," my father declared while rising, "I shall be eccentric also and obey nature's call. You may continue displaying your elocution to your mother." He told her, "Why your son wants to perfect oratory in order to pilot aeroplanes, God only knows!"

"Do not worry," she said after I sighed at his exit. "I know why you want to pilot aeroplanes. It is for the same reason he has devoted his own life to constructing canals: for the sheer beauty of it."

"Only, I have no intention of coming home with muddy feet," I declared.

"Perhaps," she conceded. "Then again, I never once worried about his falling from the sky. But never mind," she insisted. "Can you guess what your aunt is saying about this latest girl she has found for you?" Apparently this latest girl was perfect but for her narrow hips, which my aunt feared would make childbearing difficult. And so it went.

One day, perhaps shortly after I married — the girl with the narrow hips, as it turned out — Dr. Das tempered his mostundoctor-like behaviour. Even the least astute people of the district realized his change coincided with the arrival of a middle-aged widow named Saraswati.

From the postmaster of Debur Village, whose duty included noticing postmarks, the entire district learned Saraswati hailed from Calcutta, the capital of Bengal. Dr. Das closed his dispensary early on Saturdays and rode his bicycle to Debur in order to treat her for cancer. People guessed her ailment — and his compounder Vaidyappa later confirmed it — because her hair had not been shaven like that of an orthodox widow; rather, it grew in tufts. Such were the unpleasant effects of the chemotherapeutic treatment she had endured in Calcutta. But why, people wondered, had she decided to spend her last of days in a South Indian village? Why not farther north than Calcutta, perhaps lounging in a houseboat on Dal Lake in the magical Vale of Kashmir?

My favourite aunt, she who had arranged my marriage, offered a plausible explanation. She recalled that during her childhood, a woman named Lakshmi had lived in Nanjangud Town. It was said of this Lakshmi her complexion was exceedingly delicate — for she had been born during a nearly total eclipse of the sun — so delicate that if she remained outdoors for too long, the sun burned the patterns of her skirts and long-sleeved blouses onto her skin. My aunt swore she had traced, with her own fingertip, swirls and squares and the petals of flowers that glowed on Lakshmi's alabaster limbs. Her family had subsequently moved to the north, for it had been unable to find anyone willing to marry a girl who welcomed a life in purdah. My aunt concluded this newly arrived Saraswati must be that long-gone Lakshmi's daughter.

No one expressed surprise when Dr. Das stopped allowing his patients to prescribe their own cures, or when the Saturday afternoon salons moved to the local toddy shop, or when the all-night entertainment ceased. Yet strangely enough, he appeared to place less faith in allopathy than he once had. Dredging up his long unused skills as a homeopath, treating Saraswati's body itself rather than merely its cancerous cells, he kept her alive for over a year. My father supposed that, although Dr. Das had learned homeopathy in a place as exotic as Philadelphia, he had never practised it, since he had sought the prestige accorded by Indians to allopaths. One night, even as he twirled in moonlit fields while dressed like a woman, Saraswati died in her sleep. Within a fortnight, he was, himself, no more. Given the apparent coincidence of this second death, the district medical officer ordered a post mortem, the first to be performed in Nanjangud Town since the mysterious death, years before, of a landowner. The DMO discovered Dr. Das had waged a long and secret battle with cirrhosis of the liver and concluded only the challenge of keeping Saraswati alive had helped him postpone his own impending death. Under police questioning, Vaidyappa confessed to having spent many a moonless night throwing gunny sacks of empty Johnny Walker bottles into the Kabini River. The district clucked its communal tongue and would have allowed Dr. Das to fade quietly into legend had his will not renewed its concern for his state of mind.

He left the bulk of his estate to establish a charitable hospital, aptly named the Dr. B. Das Clinic, and the remainder to erect a temple to honour Goddess Saraswati, the goddess of poetry and music. Through Vaidyappa, once more, the district assembled the reasons. It seemed Dr. Das and his last patient had lived in the same district of Calcutta, had frolicked in the same playgrounds and had attended the same schools; yet her parents had considered her playmate unsuitable for her despite his plans for a worthy profession. They had deceived him. They had offered to bear his expenses if he would supplement his education by studying abroad. During his sojourn in America, they had matched her to a bank officer. Upon returning to Calcutta, Dr. Das had learned of Saraswati's marriage, had accused her of having betrayed him, and had fled to the south to become an itinerant allopath. He had eventually settled in my father's district, no doubt drawn there by its connection with Saraswati's mother. He had once claimed to having chosen it because he enjoyed eating the stubby Nanjangud banana named for the place, and everyone had believed him. The explanation had seemed no less absurd than many which unmarried men give for living far from home.

By the time I earned my licence as a commercial airline pilot and found myself the father of two, the Dr. B. Das Clinic had closed, for public funds could no longer support it. The town council renamed the two-storey building, with its compound ideal for grazing goats, the Nanjangud Home for the Poor. On the wall of the main feeding area, so named because the poor have no use for dining rooms, hung a coloured picture of Dr. Das drawn from memory by one of his protégés. Onto the glass over the brow, Vaidyappa had pasted a red dot to represent a tilak. He had been allowed to remain as watchman, a demotion certainly, but my father supposed Vaidyappa was content. He told people who recalled his former occupation, "Life is not so bad, sir. I have merely exchanged one type of compound for another."

The Saraswati Temple, located on the bank of the Kabini River downstream from Nanjangud, has survived years of neglect. While most of the aged townspeople except those like my parents have forgotten Dr. Das, children who never met him preserve his memory in their own version of "London Bridge." The eldest two stand with their arms forming a pointed arch, and the remainder pass under the arch while the leaders sing, as my daughter now does:

> Doctor Das from Bang-a-lore,
> Dressed a wound he could not cure.
> Mother, if you mind our noise,
> Doctor Das will steal your boys.

As in "London Bridge," the arch collapses on the final word to trap one of the children, whom the leaders then take aside. Instead of whispering, "Do you want cake or ice cream?" they ask, "Do you want an injection or a compound?" To which the boys reply, "Oh, injection only, Doctor Sir," and so the game continues.

And so Dr. Das himself faded from my own memory until this evening, when I heard my daughter sing while I quickened my step toward our gate. Each time her skipping rope slapped the earth, a fountain of dust rose to coat her feet. While washing them, she gave me news of my parents. My father makes no secret of his dismay that instead of failing to earn my licence, and perhaps becoming an engineer with Hindustan Aircraft Company, I pursued my ambition at the cost of having to accept a post in North India, in Patna of all places. Even northerners momentarily hold their noses while describing Bihar State — little more than a junction, situated as it is between Uttar Pradesh to the west, Bengal to the east and the Kingdom of Nepal to the north. Those who make my existence here worthwhile come from Delhi by train, and from Patna I fly them to Kathmandu. It has become a mecca for westerners bent on finding a narcotic Shangri-la amid squalor that long ago ceased troubling us.

After my wife coaxed the children to bed, she returned to serve my late evening meal and chatted while I ate. Toward the end of the meal, she declared, "Can you guess what people are saying about this latest woman the police found dead in the railway station?"

Something about the tone she used, perhaps that manner my mother still possesses of making even important news sound trivial, caused me to take more than usual notice of my wife's tale. It had been relayed to her by our cook, who in turn had heard it from her brother, a fitter at the Patna Junction Railway Station.

"She finally died," my wife said. "The woman who lay on her rickety charpoi in a corner of the station. She had been there some twenty years. Can you believe that? She never spoke, and she grew thinner and thinner until finally, this morning, she was no more. The police are searching for a one-eyed sadhu who cared for her these past few years. I think they have little hope of finding him. Strange, but he did not take the money. She must have been from a well-to-do family once. She was dressed finely, though her ornaments were out of fashion. The police found over five hundred rupees in her street trunk. They have already consigned her body to the Ganga River. What they did with the money, I cannot fathom. The one-eyed sadhu might just as well have taken it for some temple offering pot."

I began growing impatient, for my wife unwittingly reminds me that I have inherited both my mother's tendency to pass on tales and my father's propensity to comment on them. To recapture my attention, my wife said, "But here is the best part of the story:

"The police found some yellowed scraps of paper in the street trunk, and do you know what the notes said?" She pronounces the Hindi words with less difficulty than I do. "One said, 'Kah awoge ji?'; another, 'Kahan ho?'; and the third, 'Intazaar karti, bahoot din ho gaye.' That means, 'When will you come? Where are you? —

I have waited for you so long.' The police think she was to have met
her lover there, at the railway junction, but somehow they missed
one another, and she waited all these years for him to return to her.
Imagine anyone waiting for a lover for twenty years!" She laughed
nervously before saying, "I would not wait here so long if you failed
to return from Kathmandu. I am not that foolish!"

She sensed my unwillingness to listen much longer, but she
mistook the reason for it and spread her cool fingers on my
forearm. "I was only jesting," she said. "You know that. If you did
not return, I do not know what I should do. Perhaps your mother
was correct when she said I might prefer you tracked mud into the
house, as your father often did."

While I filled my pipe, she went on. "Do you not think it is
frightening sometimes what eccentric people do? Still, I suppose
they serve their purpose. I suppose they exist to remind the rest of
us what we ourselves are capable of becoming if we have no one to
look after us. At the very least, I suppose they provide us with a
source of tales, for who would pay much notice to the life of one
much like himself? Still, to wait like that for twenty years!"

She began removing my dishes, and I wandered up to sit on the
rooftop terrace. The setting sun illuminated Golghar, built — but
rarely used — as a granary. It overlooks the new area of Patna,
which surrounds Gandhi Maidan. Steps spiral up Golghar's bee-
hive exterior, and its interior offers tourists wondrous echoes. I sat
in the fading light and squinted at details greying among shadows
on the ghats. The ditty about Dr. Das appeared to echo among the
cries of vendors hawking wares in the next street. I imagined a
widow named Saraswati huddled in a corner of the terrace while
she awaited whomever came for her first, her lover or Death, and I
resented the melancholy which threatened to spoil my latest home-
coming. Like my daughter, who has learned a new skipping song
while visiting a town I have not seen these twenty years, I too have
become one of the children who preserve Dr. Das's memory.

Though we never met, I had been correct in calling him eccentric. I had merely chosen the wrong words to convey my true
meaning to my father, namely that there is nothing improper with
being eccentric. The question is one of degree. To a man who
builds canals, after all, a man who flies aeroplanes may be eccentric.

Whether Dr. Das had merely filled a void in his life by dressing like a woman, or whether he had lived so far from his true home that he had not cared what people thought of his behaviour — whatever the case, he had been nothing more than a harmless eccentric. I am certain of one other thing. If men like him did not exist, the remainder of us would invent them in order to feel natural by comparison. And yet to be eccentric is to be natural, and to fear our eccentricities is to fear our humanity. No wonder we sometimes wish the earth could deviate from its present orbit and describe a perfect circle about the sun. Such an orbit would contain neither apogee nor perigee. It would not be natural, but it would allow us the comfort of pretending God is more than some fickle cowherd; that He is truly with us always.

Gardens Apart

Tormented by his allergies, both genuine and contrived, my father could not tolerate plants. After he left, my mother Amma assembled a garden on our balcony. In the evening she sat in her eighteenth-floor concrete garden and watched single-engined planes give the CN Tower a wide berth. I in turn watched her through the sliding glass door. The darker it grew, the less distinct she appeared while the more distinct my own reflection grew. She sat surrounded by thumbergia, ivy geranium, and a single fuchsia. My brother Laurie pronounced it *few-shi-ya* as though gagging, much as he did when I experimented with Amma's lipstick. That fuchsia became my favourite. The plump red and white blooms looked like hummingbirds and often pulled away to hover and flit about the foliage. I found comfort in the illusion, but that garden was too precarious, too much part of a concrete world for the blooms to remain hummingbirds for long. When Amma moved her garden indoors to shelter it from the chill night air, I helped.

She also tried to shelter us during the divorce. My father had already sold most of our furniture without consulting her, because he had needed the funds for his rural health foundation in South India. When Laurie and I bickered, our voices echoed as if trapped in a cave. In my diary I called that spring *The Spring of Irreconcilable Differences.*

That was also the spring I began filling out, in every direction. It's not that I was fat — big-boned was more accurate, imposing sounded better — but a joke circulated among the older boys at school: "Lorna's so big, in her class picture she's the whole back row."

Once, while Amma and I watered the hanging baskets, she let me ramble about boys who thought they were men, men who

34

acted like boys. "Oh, Lorna," she finally said, "can you not see your father never meant to harm us?" Even at home, she spoke as though lecturing her undergraduates. "He simply could not face living here knowing those villagers have so little hope of proper medical attention."

I grimaced at the fuchsia. "The name's Lou," I reminded her. I didn't look like a Lorna, certainly not *Lorna Doone*. Amma had been reading it when she first became pregnant. Later she had named Laurie for Laurence Olivier, and she was proud of us both: a boy she called Laurie and a girl who called herself Lou. When I finally said, "You planning to drown those thumbergia?" she snapped: "Do not condescend to me, young miss. Are you the only one here who has been hurt? Do you not think I lie awake wondering if only I had listened to my brother, I —" Her voice dulled, and she admitted, "— I might have foreseen this and discouraged your father from also wanting a family."

"How?" I asked. "Did Uncle Jagadish say something?" He lived in Geneva with his Japanese wife and their son.

Amma looked relieved at the change in my tone. "In those days," she explained, "I knew little about foreshadowing or about the cruelty of hindsight."

My diary contains this: *Uncle Jagadish was a ship's engineer on the Calcutta-Yokohama run. One day he read a newspaper account of another Indian. There'd been a flood in Japan, and the powers-that-be had appealed for food and clothing. A foreign medical student had donated everything he owned except the clothes on his back. Jagadish wrote to Amma, "Saint Francis of Assisi lives." He meant, "A man like this might make you an ideal husband." She'd given up on finding a proper match and left India to study in England. Thanks to fate, Jagadish met my father when he booked a second-class berth on the same ship. Jagadish had arranged a transfer to a desk job in London, so he invited my father to visit him and Amma there.*

Her wry smile brought me back to the garden. "While both are valuable," she said, addressing me as though I were about to convocate, "an MA creates more possibilities than an MRS."

She finished her linguistics degree, my father interned, Laurie and I were born, and life began seeming predictable. Then York University hired Amma on the strength of her thesis, published as

A Lexicon of Indianisms in English. True, my father sacrificed his growing practice in Notting Hill by moving to Toronto, but how could she dream he would one day sacrifice all three of us? She found herself with me, anxious about puberty; with Laurie, growing withdrawn; with a concrete garden.

She remarried so quickly, to a Parsi named Joseph Daruwallah, that I worried she wanted him only to rescue her from that garden. I didn't trust him, but everyone who bought insurance from him did. Laurie guffawed each time he overheard Joseph phoning prospective clients. "Daruwallah means drug seller in Hindi," he would say. Then he would pause. "As in pharmacist, not as in pusher."

Amma being Amma, she did ask for my opinion, but not until after the wedding. "I'm glad you didn't do it for me," I said. "Laurie? He needs more than some local saint who can't mail birthday cards on time."

"Thank you for your understanding," she said.

She bore Joseph twins. When he eventually suggested moving to Regina, both she and Laurie agreed. I cared little where we lived by then. London, Toronto, Regina — they were all the same to me. Geneva — now that would have been different, but I wasn't my Uncle Jagadish's daughter.

*   *   *

In the fall of our move, Amma began work on her doctorate. The following spring my diary would say, *It's not enough Amma has four children and a career. She has to have a garden. Simply has to.*

She expected consensus to rule our home, so we discussed everything, even what to do with the back yard.

"A pool?" the twins yelled. "A water slide?"

"A deck for parties," Laurie said. He turned away to hide his grin, made metallic by braces. He felt so conscious of them, even I sometimes consoled him.

"A shed for my workshop," Joseph suggested.

"Lou hasn't voted yet," the twins complained. "Come on, Lou. A pool, a water slide."

I pretended to scoff. Their real names were Cyrus and Darius, but Laurie and I called them Frank 'n Stein after the doctor people confuse with his creation. Still, after they had been born, I would pretend they were my own babies. During long walks, I showed them off in their double baby carriage. If they fell ill, I felt miserable for days. Now I remained silent, fortunately, since Amma declared:

"No, no and no. This entire area will be my garden."

Joseph, Laurie and the twins looked at me as though only I could change her mind. "If Amma wants a garden," I announced, "Amma gets her garden."

Joseph ambled off to his study. Soon we could hear his humming with Glenn Gould and Bach's *Well-Tempered Clavier*. It drifted through the house, fugued across the hardwood floors.

"Party poop," Laurie sniped. He added that, if anyone should happen to want him, he would be doing his homework.

The twins pouted until a cabbage butterfly wove into sight. It lured them past lilac bushes and out the back gate. Before long, we could hear their voices from the park bordering the nearby creek.

"Tell me one thing," I asked the wispy clouds. I hadn't yet learned to call them mare's-tails. "Just why does Amma want a garden? Amma doesn't know the first thing about gardening."

She laughed and said, "That, as your friends enjoy reciting, is for me to know and for you to discover. Will you help me plant my garden, dear?"

I crossed the yard to the hummingbird feeder I had given her for Mother's Day. The feeder was still empty and that was why, for now, the lilacs in which it hung lured only bees. At last I told her, "Do hummingbirds hum?" I had little to do besides plan my upcoming trip to Europe. It was a graduation gift from Joseph. While he and Amma watched "The National" and "The Journal," I pored over maps and travel books. My first stop would be Geneva, where I hoped to learn what demon in my father had lured him away.

It took me a week of June evenings to dig out the patchy lawn; to fork peat moss and sheep manure into the newly exposed soil. Regina soil is clay, a gumbo so dense that, when I looked back, I could see patches of earth packed at intervals. I clawed up my footprints with a rake. *That way,* my diary said, *Laurie can't improvise a soliloquy about the gardening habits of Sasquatch.*

Amma did not choose her plants by their names or by what she imagined they would look like. She simply peered at the white plastic stakes and ignored those calling for full sun. People stared at the woman in the sari, a woman with a diamond stud in her nose, who looked out of place in a greenhouse. Their smirks drooped when they shifted their focus beyond the pallets of bedding plants and found me glaring. I balanced a cardboard tray on the palm of one hand. I gripped a four-cubic-foot bag of peat moss with the other. When Amma said, "Come along Lou," I did. I strode, with my elbows bent and shoulders hunched, like a caricature of the Incredible Hulk.

Once home, Amma carefully squeezed the plants out of their rigid cellophane pots. For ten-inch spacings, I spread my hand, marked the earth with my thumb and little finger. For twelve-inch spacings, I used my foot. I planted my heel beside the last mark and made the next with my big toe. I dug the holes with a soup spoon from the twins' sandbox. The cones of dark soil, their white roots densely packed, nestled perfectly. In one evening, three borders of impatiens — super elfin coral — appeared as if by magic.

"You should take a more relaxed attitude," Amma said. She nodded approvingly at the dark and light green clumps. "Gardening is meant to be recreational."

"Amma wanted a garden," I told the sky. "Amma is getting her garden." I pointed a bare foot, grimy, at a patch beside the door. The patch was six feet long and three feet wide. "What goes in here?" I asked.

"Oh," she said, "that is my graduation gift for you."

"A grave?" I asked. "Laurie would just fit."

"Madcap," she said, "that is your very own garden. You may plant whatever you please."

"Swell," I said even as she went inside. "Swell," I repeated and sat on the step. I thought of geraniums first. They would look fine in the boxes Joseph had built under every window — geraniums red, pink, and salmon with trailing lobelia licking the breeze like tiny purple tongues. But geraniums reminded me of that first garden. Worse, they reminded me of Mexico. Joseph had taken us there, after the wedding, on his version of a honeymoon. *Wandered off to see how real Mexicans live,* my diary said. *Found some real ones, all right — families in boxcars on sidings. Abandoned. The boxcars, that is. Each car's got window boxes with red geraniums. Every time a train goes by, the boxcar houses get the shakes till petals fall on the gravel and the rusty tracks. Bet tin cups rattle inside, in cupboards made of Coke and Pepsi crates.*

I decided Laurie would like to tease snapdragons, would softly pinch their mouths open. But he might suspect my motives if I said, "I planted them for you." The twins would like pansies, all puppy dog grins. Joseph liked raspberries. My hairdresser claimed they did well in clay, and I trusted her. She understood why I wanted my hair cut, not done. But I didn't want anything practical in my garden. I settled on a row of snapdragons — pixie mix — and a mass of pansy-violet hybrids — Johnny-jump-ups — both edged by unassuming purple alyssum — royal carpet. I chose something for nearly everyone, mainly for myself.

It took only one afternoon to prepare and plant the bed. Then I sat on the step to marvel at my very own garden. An elm seed drifted onto the Johnny-jump-ups. I picked the seed off and crushed it as a warning.

The next evening, it hailed. I yelled, "No, oh no!" and ran to protect the bed with burlap. Never mind hailstones like nettles; never mind suddenly freezing air. Done, I stood shivering on the sheltered back step and cursed the sky. My hands smelled the way I imagined India smelled: of wet gunny sacks. After the hail stopped, I rolled the soggy burlap and turned. I saw Amma through my pained reflection in the sliding glass door.

She held a plate on which she was crushing eggshells and mixing them with tea leaves. She had heard the mix would stimulate roses. Not that we had any, but she always looked ahead. She made as if to slide the door open, then turned away and left me with my reflection.

Soon the diary warned, *They'll never look as perfect as they did that first day. Poplar fluff snags on alyssum like lint. Snapdragons fall off and shrivel like moths. The Johnnies bob like idiots. They're all mine, though. Can't ignore them now. If only my father could see them.*

That's when I understood why Amma wanted her garden. It was a
second chance at doing something right.

"But why such a huge garden?" I asked her. We were putting up
hanging baskets. She hadn't wanted thumbergia or fuchsia; I
hadn't wanted ivy geranium. The new baskets held wax begonia.
They swung in the wind like censers of red, pink, and white,
coaxed blooms from the newly planted beds, both hers and mine.

"I shall need room for the vegetables," she said.

"Strawberries don't qualify as vegetables," I told her. Those
strawberries would become one of my few failures. She had let me
choose them for her, and I had chosen June-bearing instead of
ever-bearing.

"Give me time," she said. "I am experimenting. I want the
romance of flowers before I must face the reality of vegetables.
Perhaps it is like the difference between loving a man and marrying
him." I think we both laughed. I'm sure she did. I couldn't
imagine any man loving me the way Joseph loved her. It showed in
little things, in the way he used dowels instead of screws when he
made her bookcases.

"Thank you for beginning my garden, dear," she said at last. "I
shall take good care of yours while you are gone."

I couldn't be a tourist all summer, so I had enrolled in a college
in Strasbourg. Joseph had approved. First I would have a month of
travels. Geneva beckoned, and not only with answers about my
father. In my favourite photo of Uncle Jagadish, he wore a turtle-
necked sweater under a blazer of the merchant marine. He stood
next to his wife, who wore a flowered kimono. How could he be
anything but heroic?

The diary again: *Amma says Jagadish's boss in London pilfered the
office bank account. She claims he fled to Brazil with his fortune and
his secretary, but every family needs its clichés like Frank 'n Stein.
When Bombay ordered Jagadish back for a new posting, he said he'd go
back only if it made him chief engineer. Pity ambition doesn't run in
my father's blood. Bombay said Jagadish couldn't dictate terms, not
after having let such a disgraceful incident happen. He quit. I guess he
had his principles. Bombay froze his assets, even the condo on Malabar
Hill he and Amma inherited from Grandfather. Now the story gets
downright romantic. Aunt Kimiko went back to Japan with Cousin*

Eso. Jagadish vanished. He drifted around the world for years. When Amma married Joseph, Jagadish spent his last few pounds to phone congrats from a cheap hotel in Glasgow. Then, thanks to fate again, he stumbled into what Amma calls his reward. He joined The Bank. It finances ships, and he approves the plans of every ship it finances in Asia.

That included Japan, and Japan built supertankers. By now he was a vice-president. He, Kimiko, and Eso all had ships named for them. Tankers, perhaps, but real ships with proud names like *Jagadish-Maru.*

*   *   *

When Jagadish met me at Geneva Airport, he wore a suit from Saville Row, Italian shoes, and a Rolex. He drove a silver-blue Mercedes coupe. My father wouldn't have been seen in a car like that. For a moment I despised both men, thought of them as boys with their toys, but hating Jagadish wouldn't bring back my father. Amma didn't need him back; neither, I decided, did I.

Jagadish had heard I was big, but he winced when I shook his hand. He drove me slowly through Sunday-morning streets and pointed out the sights. Famous banks hiding numbered accounts lined the quay north of the lake. A chocolate-box fountain spouted from the lagoon. On the south shore, a floral clock ticked.

"The Vandoeuvres in our address?" he said. "It's on the outskirts. I couldn't find a nice old house in the city, so I acquired a chalet at some distance. I hope you find it comfortable."

It certainly looked comfortable. The wrought iron gate faced a pasture bordered by apple trees, and his chalet was larger than our house. Looking for Kimiko and Eso, Jagadish and I wandered first into a study lined with bookcases. I doubted he had made them himself. He tapped the spine of one book proudly, and I tilted my head to read the title. It was Amma's *Lexicon of Indianisms.* I followed him through a second door into a living room. Hand-painted vases covered lacquer step-tables. Foot-high geisha dolls smiled in glass cases. Above a brocaded sofa, a screen spread its four panels along the wall; a coastal landscape changed from left to right, from fall to Fujiyama winter, from summer to cherry-blossom spring.

We found Kimiko behind the house. She stood with her hands on her hips and looked from the dirt bordering three hedges to a pile of flagstones. She had varicose veins. She looked old and tired, not a bit like a banker's wife. She made Amma look like the queen she deserved to be.

"Pleased to welcome you," Kimiko said in her hesitant English. She had to reach up to shake my hand because I didn't bend.

Jagadish and I left her frowning at her unfinished garden and re-entered the house, this time through yet another door that led past the kitchen. We found Eso in a dark room in which a TV set flickered pastel colours across his face. He was puny, and he looked annoyed at my hello. He reminded me of a mole. I hadn't been in the house ten minutes, and I missed the way Laurie bared his braces at me. I missed the twins' building castles in their sandbox. The only person who seemed able to converse, though he chose not to, left an hour later. Jagadish had to be in Paris by lunch. The previous week, he explained, he had flown to Scotland for a meeting. It had been held on a golf course at St. Andrew's-by-the-Sea. "I'm sure we shall have much to discuss," he said from his car, "but it must wait until Tuesday."

I could do little except wait. Lying open on the floor while I lay on my bed in the guest room, my diary said, *Welcome to Geneva, Lou. Now all you have to do is ask the right questions.* After that I stared down at the diary, but it gazed blankly back. It no longer felt like mine, because I no longer needed it to make sense of things. That was when I began suspecting, though I couldn't have articulated it, that some things might never make sense.

Monday afternoon, I wandered through the Old Town. I wanted to see how the real Swiss lived, but everyone I passed seemed to live for work. There were no geraniums on boxcar houses here. The edelweiss in one café was plastic. After I asked people for directions back to Vandoeuvres, I chafed in a crowd for my bus, then saw Eso approach. I knew his school was miles away, but he didn't seem to care what I might think of his avoiding classes. After we caught our bus, I gripped the overhead bar while he clung to a dangling leather strap. No one could have mistaken us for cousins; yet I still hoped we had more in common than our fathers' meeting by chance.

I pointed at a two-wheeled velo weaving through traffic. "Do all the teenagers have those?" I asked.

"Once I get my licence," he said, "my father will buy me a car."

I envied him, but I also felt like the outsider who could do no right. I tried again: "What will you do when you finish school?"

"Study engineering," he said. "Then join The Bank."

Had I still needed it, the diary would have said, *Oh right, kiddo, end of interview.* While we walked from the bus stop to the house, I made one last try. I pointed at a snow-capped peak in the south-east.

"Mont Blanc," he explained, "the highest mountain in the Alps. It's nearly sixty kilometres from here, in France, and you can see it only on clear days. I prefer skiing in Zermatt. The Matterhorn is more—"

After he gave up searching for the appropriate word, it came to me: imposing. So was I.

Once home, he scuttled into his TV room. I washed, then searched for Kimiko.

She stood in her garden with her hands on her hips. It was not a European garden; it was Japanese. She moved her hands into the small of her back. A landscaped hill rose gently on the left. On the level ground to its right stood a stone lantern. I had watched her ritual the evening before, and I watched her now: she began circling her garden. She plodded on the dirt where the flagstones should have been and stopped whenever she found a pleasing view of both lantern and hill. Far beyond the hedges, far beyond rooftops of other so-called chalets, Mont Blanc rose into the sky. She never once looked at it. She stopped her circling and frowned at me before her eyes flicked to the flagstones. They were huge, twenty-four by twenty-four.

I grinned and nodded like an idiot miming in pidgin. Then I picked one off the pile and gingerly lowered it onto the dirt. After the third one, I began to sweat. After the fifth, I changed my jeans for shorts, my cotton sweater for a T-shirt of the CN Tower. The tenth flagstone reached one corner of the garden.

She brought me a glass of instant iced tea and said, "You may stop now to eat." I shook my head. I had decided to leave in the morning, after Jagadish returned from Paris, and I wanted to leave something behind. Something that said, "Lou was here."

I kept working even after sunset. On his way to bed, Eso came out to watch. He left without saying goodnight. Suddenly, I would have given anything to see the twins run through that garden Kimiko could only circle; anything to see them scuff the mani-cured hill with gravelly sneakers, play *Star Wars* around the lan-tern. I knew what the garden needed: a hummingbird feeder. Then something that didn't belong here could flit past like a velvet bee, bring some fleeting excitement into that sadly perfect place. My arm muscles were turning to bran; my fingers felt two inches longer; half my fingernails were chipped. I even caught my hands straying to the small of my back, but I kept on. Finally I jiggled the last flagstone into place.

"Come," Kimiko said. We padded upstairs, past the second floor and into the attic. It was finished with pine. Near the door stood a bar; in the middle crouched low tables and seemingly new chairs. From shelves crammed with miniature liqueur bottles, I picked up a blue and white ceramic house. "KLM," she said. I raised my eyebrow to mean, "Of course." She sat on the edge of a chair but didn't swivel as I did, with my sock feet, damp, planted on the dusty floor. She kept her hands cupped in her lap as though awaiting inspiration. When she spoke again, it sounded like a question: "He never invites his bank."

I was tired. I ached. That's the only reason I thought what I did: "At least he comes back."

"Drink," she said.

I couldn't bring myself to twist the cap off the chimney, so I put the house next to its Dutch neighbours. Bottles of Pinch and Courvoisier beckoned, but none of them were open. I shook my head and said, "I'd never get up."

She knew then I was leaving. She tried to shrug with her hands, uncupped them with her little fingers hooked so her hands looked like the gnarled wings of some grounded bird. "Thank you for completing my garden," she said.

Like a fool I said, "It was nothing."

Next morning, I sat in the study and flipped through Amma's book while I waited for Jagadish to return. I'd always known words like jungle were Indian, but now I discovered more. Both *jangal* from Hindi and the earlier Sanskrit *jangala* meant wilderness. I'd always thought of a wilderness as empty like a desert, not brimming like a tropical forest. Our own house may have reminded visitors of a jungle, but it was no desert.

When I heard the Mercedes, I carried my luggage outside and dropped it at my feet. I could have carried it to the bus and train, but I needed to say goodbye to someone.

Jagadish squinted at the bags.

"There's a storm coming in day after," I said. "Thought I'd take the Jungfraubahn from Interlaken tomorrow, while it's still clear." At least that part was true. Even now, clouds drifted across the sky; shadows vanished into shade, then reappeared with the sun.

"It's best to travel when one is young," he said. Then, almost sheepishly: "We haven't seen you since you were a baby in London. My wife and I would like to arrange your travel by first class. You can stay in hotels instead of *pensions*. Your mother wrote you are eager to see Hanover, something about giving your stepfather's regards to J. S. Bach, but have you considered Vienna or Amsterdam? I know of some nice hotels there." He placed my knapsack and carryall next to his suitbag in the trunk.

I knew what he called nice hotels were likely palatial. I refused, politely.

"Very well," he said. I expected him to add something else; something like, "Your father rarely accepted gifts either, and he never travelled first class." Then we could have discussed why I had come to Geneva, but I no longer needed answers. Not to those questions. Jagadish asked, "Have you said goodbye to your aunt?" He knew I hadn't.

I crossed the study into the living room, passed artwork no one appeared to notice, and stepped outside.

Kimiko sat with her back to the house and her hands cupped in her lap. She looked from the stone lantern to the closely cropped lawn to the gently rolling hill. She sat in her Japanese garden on the outskirts of Geneva, and she never once raised her eyes to Mont Blanc. At last she spoke, without looking at me. She spoke so softly, I had to bend to hear her. "My father was a poor soldier," she said. "He died in the war." She looked at the flagstones and, when she spoke, it again sounded like a question: "In Japan, I could never have had such a garden."

I wanted to touch her shoulder in farewell, but I only brushed it. After I slid the glass door shut, I watched her through my reflection, and the longer I watched, the more she looked like Amma.

Before Joseph had driven me to Regina Airport, I had said goodbye to Amma at home. She couldn't abide seeing people off. With her hands resting on her knees, she sat cross-legged on the back step. She admired my garden while I knelt behind her. She frowned at her still unfinished one as though wondering whether it could ever be a real garden. But she had faith. She never tired of reminding us it would soon be crowded with wood violet, snow-on-the-mountain, lilies-of-the-valley, snow-in-summer. She clutched my hand to her cheek. Then, as though I were the one who could not let go, she pressed my hand to her shoulder, never mind my moist palm wrinkling the cool nylon of her sari. "You write often, dear," she insisted. "You know how much the twins enjoy receiving post cards. But you will remember? A separate one for each." I nodded with my chin on the careful part centred in her greying hair. It smelled of rosewater.

After I re-entered the house and eased the door closed, I watched her through my reflection. A cloud covered the sun, and my reflection grew distinct in the darkening glass. Once the cloud moved on, the glass brightened, and now I saw Kimiko. Gardens apart, the two women might have been sisters, yet Kimiko mourned the past in a garden her father could never have given her; Amma pondered the future, dreamt of snow-in-summer.

No matter what my father hadn't been able to do for Amma, no matter what Jagadish still couldn't to do for Kimiko, nothing would stop me from taking chances — the way Amma had, even a second time. Someday, I knew, I would find a man who might love me as much as I would love him.

*   *   *

I have found such a man in Anand. His name means joy, and he has brought me much. Often I forget that.

My very own garden is larger now. Laurie works in Toronto; the twins are studying at York. Amma and Joseph have retired to Bombay. Anand and I live in Regina. We have carpeted the hardwood floors and so filled the house with furniture that our voices refuse to echo. He has helped me replace the June-bearing strawberries with ever-bearing, but for some time we have known he can never give me children. When I find it difficult to begin my day, to plan experiments or set exams, he says he would understand if I found someone else. I call him a fool, tell him to leave me alone though I mean the opposite.

After he does leave, for work, I sit on the back step to watch our wood violet, our snow-on-the-mountain, our lily-of-the-valley, our snow-in-summer; monkshood, peony, dead nettle, hollyhock; periwinkle, columbine, bergenia, Chinese lantern; shasta daisy, maiden pink, California poppy; our forget-me-not. I try to feel rage over the laughter of children on their way to school through the park along the creek. I try to blame my neighbours for their three and four children when I have none. Where once I planted impatiens along the fence, now I raise pansies, three beds full of Swiss giant mix, Viking mix, imperial blue. They alone are annuals, but they continue reseeding themselves like the pansy-violets, the Johnny-jump-ups I planted the spring I began suspecting some things might never make sense.

Three of the newest pansies raise their heads. This one, purple touched with pink, is Nirmala. That one, indigo on red, is Jayanti. The goldenrod flash on blue is Haymanth. He often lags, keeps his hands closed as if in prayer yet poised to applaud the sudden appearance of hummingbirds. Two girls and a boy, they leave the shelter of lilacs and skip toward me. They stop with the girls in front, their brother tall behind. They look uncertain they are welcome until I raise my hands from my lap. Only then do they greet me with words I have so often rehearsed for them:

"Good morning, Amma."

"Good morning, Amma."

"Good morning, Amma."

The Evil Eye

Sinu lies at the base of a shrine to Goddess Saraswati. His arms are crossed behind his head. He clutches a reed with his toes, paints indigo white clouds up from the river into an ultramarine sky. Searching for prey, a brahminy kite wheels into view, threatens to spoil his composition. With two flicks of his foot, he paints a curved vee, reddish-brown, pierces the wings with sunflower rays, and fixes the kite to the sun. He rolls onto his stomach, digs his elbows into the damp earth, and props his chin on his hands. Distant unseen goatherds call to their flocks, gather them for the journey home.

Townspeople often smile when Sinu passes, but none can guess how he feels. Happy is not the word. He feels bubbly. Not like the bubbles he once blew from soapy water. Those were many-hued like the squares, now long dried, of his watercolour paintbox. He feels like the bubbles in bisleri soda — invisible until someone shakes a bottle the way his parents have shaken him by announcing they have found him a bride. Fields of ripening sugar cane stretch from the river to Nanjangud Town. By the time they are ready to harvest, he will return with a girl named Janaki, a South Indian born and raised in the North.

He looks at the goddess in her shrine, a niche of whitewashed mud opening onto the river. A crescent moon rises from her brow, and her head tilts toward one shoulder. With two of her hands, she clutches a veena. One is poised near the instrument's neck; the fingers of the other hand pluck the strings. She asks, *What shall I play for you next?* He replies, *Whatever you wish.* In the third hand she holds a book. Her fourth hand reaches for the head of a swan rising from the lotus at her feet. Now she asks, *Who will read my poetry or listen to my music while you are gone?* He fingers a petal of the lotus where chipped red paint reveals grey stone. *Janaki will help me restore you,* he promises. *We shall listen on moonlit nights to your songs.*

He rises and bids the goddess farewell, then crosses the lower canal by a footbridge and fans his way through sugar cane to the Nanjangud Road. He always takes the long way home, for he wants no one to know where he hides after school. By the time he reaches the eastern edge of the town, coconut palms cast their shadows toward him. Even as he nears his father's house, Sinu's footsteps slow.

His mother Sharada never tires of telling him his father Iruve had always wanted a son. When Sinu's eldest sister was born, Iruve was too young to worry about having fathered a girl. With the second, third, and fourth girl, he began to feel cheated. He found fault with even his growing prosperity, for he wanted to watch his own son, not some overseer, supervise the harvest. After the birth of the fifth girl, he began fearing for his soul. "Who will bring me a daughter-in-law from the city?" he cried.

"What is one daughter-in-law from a city against five sons-in-law from our district?" Sharada asked.

He spat on the floor, next to her foot, but her toes barely twitched. "My soul shall not go to heaven if my pyre is lit by a son-in-law," he scoffed. "Even you should know that." He left her nursing the baby and trudged through his fields. No one knew where Iruve hid.

The sixth time Sharada gave birth, he remained hidden in his fields until past sunset. He returned to find the latest child asleep in the crook of her arm.

She folded back the towel wrapped around the child and weakly said, "A boy finally. Let us name him Srinivas." She crooned over the baby, "Sinu? Welcome, Sinu."

That very night, squinting by the glow of a kerosene lamp, Iruve painted over "Kempe Gowda House" and painted "Srinivas House." The new name dried unevenly on the whitewashed stone, but Iruve thought it grand. Not everyone owned a house as posh as that belonging to the Kempe Gowda clan; not everyone could name his house after a son. Next, Iruve applied black paste around

Sinu's eyes. It would deceive the evil eye into thinking he was deformed, unworthy of attention.

Iruve delighted in his every discovery about his baby son. "See, he sees his toes," Iruve said; or, "Listen, I tell you he is speaking words." On Sinu's first birthday, Iruve took him to a portrait studio in Mysore City. There they posed in front of a painting of yew trees among the ruins of a Christian church. He had the photo tinted and displayed it, his first coloured photo, in the main room.

This evening, Sinu finds his every move watched. "Eat more slowly," Iruve says. "Do you want your future in-laws to think we are ill-bred?" Sinu forces himself to eat so slowly, he is still eating when the others are finished. "Hurry, you lame bullock," Iruve says. "Do you want your future in-laws to think you expect the world to revolve around you?"

Sinu looks to Sharada, but she looks away. After Iruve leaves, she pulls Sinu to her, cradles his head in her lap. "Never mind, son," she says. "Your father is afraid only that the evil eye will notice if he praises you. It is so full of mischief, there is none so vigilant as the evil eye. Think, though. If he did not love you, would he have secured a bride from Delhi itself?" Sinu looks up to see tears in Sharada's eyes. "My son, my son," she croons. "You will soon be a man." She hugs him so close her fleshy arms feel like the jaws of a velvet vice. He clutches her wrists, but still he feels as though he will drown in her flesh, smother beneath her breasts. One sags onto his brow, the other onto his throat. He has always felt trapped like this, in a house that feels like the womb: his father with a tongue as searing as flame; his mother with breasts like sodden earth.

He wonders whether his sisters would envy him if they knew he dreams his own death. Sometimes he dreams Iruve throws him into a fire made of dung cakes. Other times, he dreams Sharada buries him alive in a field. Soon his days in brahmacharaya, in studentship, will end. He will enter the second stage of his life, that of the householder. Only then can he pursue the three ends of man: pleasure, material gain, and virtue.

Best of all will be pleasure.

With all the sights of Delhi awaiting them, the family has little time to linger over those in Bombay. Sinu spends two days dashing in Iruve's tow to landmarks like Colaba Causeway and Sassoon

Dock, Taraporewella Aquarium and the Hanging Gardens on
Malabar Hill. Sharada spends her days immobile on Chowpatty
Beach. There she snacks on kulfi ice cream while she chuckles at
the antics of contortionists and sandcastle sculptors. At night,
breezes blow off Bombay Harbour. Perhaps it is these breezes;
perhaps it is the hectic pace Iruve sets; whatever the cause, Sinu
reaches Delhi in the first flush of a fever. Everyone mistakes the
light in his eyes for excitement. On the morning of the one day he
and Janaki will spend alone before their marriage, he wakes to find
not dew but a faint white dust on the compound of her uncle's
house. People here call it frost.

Janaki speaks Hindi and English; Sinu speaks Kannada and
little else. Despite their difficulty in understanding one another, he
does not tire of their outing. At home he has only to look up from
his plate, and Sharada calls for sambar and rice. He has only to raise
his tumbler and his youngest sister mixes water with curds. She is
still unmarried, for no one wants a girl with protruding teeth. Yet
Janaki allows him to open doors for her, allows him to pay for
autorickshaws with coins that jingle in his pocket.

There is so much to see in Connaught Place alone, they spend
the entire morning in the white colonnades, the arts and crafts
shops, the airline offices with their coloured photos from Fiji and
New Zealand. After lunch in a hotel restaurant, they linger silently
until Janaki speaks of Jaipur, where her eldest brother lives: of the
Old Town's pink sandstone buildings, which sparkle like jewels in
a desert setting; Jantra Mantra, the observatory with its gigantic
sun dial; the jewellers' market, Johari Bazaar. She frowns when he
says in Kannada, "I will buy every jewel there for you," but he does
not repeat himself in English.

He leads her back to the Rajasthan Emporium and bids her wait
outside with her back to the window. There he examines rows of
Rajput miniatures. They lie on velvet below glass. He has spent
most of the money Iruve gave him but, before Sinu left the house,
Sharada pressed a twenty-rupee note into his hand. She whispered,
"You show the girl what we are worth." The note buys a single
ivory square no larger than a square of paint in his watercolour box.
The miniature depicts a warrior prince in amber robes and a
cinnabar turban. While leaving, Sinu notices a painting of a Rajput

lady, gold and viridian green on a surface lacquered black; painted in the style called nirmala, or perfect. She cradles a lotus in the palm of one hand. After whispered entreaties, the clerk agrees to exchange a second miniature for the wristwatch Sharada bought Sinu in preparation for this journey. The second miniature is of a princess.

He rejoins Janaki on the pavement. The brown-paper packet he holds should make him feel worthy, but he feels ashamed as though he has betrayed someone with his extravagance. He thrusts the packet at her, then hurries away with his hands buried in the pockets of her father's warmest cardigan. He hugs himself, but not tightly enough to suppress a shiver. How cold it is here during Chaligula, the season northerners call Shishira, the one Britishers call simply the cold season. No wonder hawkers rub mustard oil on their bodies to keep warm. No wonder some even stand with braziers suspended under their garments. He turns when Janaki touches his elbow.

Her questioning eyes confound him when he tries to explain. He nearly says, "A sample only of what I can offer." Instead he forces himself to say, "A promise we shall visit Jaipur after we are wed." When she blushes, so does he, and they stand face to face, inches apart. He knows she feels anxious about the first night they must spend together. One does not speak of such things. If only his parents would not insist the second ceremony, the tying of the kankanam that will herald their complete union, await their return to Nanjangud.

"Let us be off," he says. When she reminds him they still have the afternoon, reminds him of the old fort Purana Qila and of Humayun's Tomb, he shakes his head. "We must walk," he says. He confesses he has squandered all his money, even parted with his wristwatch, all for her. He waits for her to scold him, but she does not.

They cover a furlong before she touches his elbow again. "Thank you," she says.

They walk in silence after that, sometimes drifting apart, sometimes drifting so closely their sleeves brush. By the time they reach her father's house, sweat drenches Sinu's hair; yet his throat feels like the moulted skin of a lizard, brittle and cold. After he claims,

"We were robbed," Janaki hurries from the room. He prays she
will keep the miniatures a secret.

It will be their first of many.

On the evening of the fourth day of the wedding, Sinu arrives at
the house of Janaki's father. Music blares from loudspeakers to tell
the district a marriage is still underway. As befits the groom, Sinu
wears his finest clothes, gifts from her uncle; yet no sooner does
Sinu enter the compound than her brothers strip him to his new
dhoti. They lead him to the inner courtyard and seat him near the
fire blazing on a dais. His skin glistens with mustard oil and
turmeric; he begins to perspire. When he wipes his face with his
hands, he secretly wipes away tears. He has eaten nothing since his
sunrise meal of crisped rice and curds. He wants to sleep. This
grand adventure, this journey all the way north to secure a bride
has become a gauntlet of rites.

He and Janaki have observed malai-matral three times. She sat
astride her uncle's shoulders; Sinu sat astride her eldest brother's.
Both Sinu and Janaki wore two garlands of marigold and jasmine
entwined. They tried not to laugh, for the garlands tickled their
necks and ears. After her uncle and her brother stopped face to
face, grinning and grimacing, Sinu took one of his garlands and
placed it around her neck. By this he showed he willingly shared
half his spiritual force with her. She, in turn, did the same.

They have also observed nalangu for three evenings. They sat
facing one another on mats. First he stretched out his legs, and she
rubbed turmeric paste on them. The yellow paste stung and closed
his pores; yet he bit the inside of his mouth to keep from smiling
when she touched the soles of his feet. She allowed herself a smile
when he, in turn, did the same for her. Then she took up two
handfuls of crisp yellow rice, raised them above his head, and
scattered the rice in the air. He, in turn, did the same. Iruve
laughed with Sharada, for only now could anyone see the bride and
groom at play. Once married, Sinu and Janaki would play behind
closed doors as husband and wife. They sat side by side while the
women of her family passed a plate over their heads. On it was a
mixture of turmeric and slaked lime to cast off the evil from the evil
eye. Then, while the women sang accompanied by men playing

pipes, Janaki's mother distributed sandalwood paste, flowers and
fruits: papaya, guava, tender coconut.

Sinu repeats the Sanskrit phrases sung by the priests to induce a
proper frame of mind:

"A man by himself is an imperfect being. Husband and wife are
halves of a spiritual whole, the husband the left, the wife the right."

"Man and wife wed in the presence of Agni, the god of fire, and
because the gods attend the marriage, no human may sever its tie."

"Marriage is a sacrament, not a contract. Though the husband
may die, he will wait for his wife in the heaven world, and both will
return once more to wed."

At last the priests judge him ready. Her mother leads Janaki into
the courtyard. The end of Janaki's gold-embroidered sari covers
her head. She stops at the dais, allows her mother to uncover her
eyes, and Sinu and Janaki gaze at one another. Designs drawn with
sandalwood paste cover her hands, her feet, her face. She, too, has
eaten little since sunrise. She sits thankfully next to him on the
dais, and they pretend to ignore one another while the ceremony
continues. The women of her family create a pass-not by waving a
camphor flame around the dais. The pass-not will confound
invisible beings contemplating malice.

Guests come and go. They eat and drink in the house of Janaki's
father, but Sinu and Janaki must wait. By midnight, he feels so
keen of sense that every act he witnesses appears significant: the
smile of one of her unmarried classmates, the raised eyebrow of her
distant male cousin. Smoke from the fire burns Sinu's eyes, incense
clouds his throat; yet most of all, worst of all, he feels chilled.

The priests make their final blessings, and the ceremony ends.
Janaki's close relations and friends bring jewellery and clothes. In
return they receive fruit or pan supari: betel leaves stuffed with
slaked lime and areca nut. Distant relations and ordinary friends
give small amounts of money. It will buy her a ring. They receive
pinches of yellow rice and, laughing, shower it on Sinu and Janaki.

Sinu wraps a shawl about his shoulders. When he rises to make
his ablutions, he staggers. People around him laugh, and he rubs
his legs as though they have lost their feeling. A few minutes more,
and he can eat. A few hours more, and he can sleep through
sunrise. When he passes his parents, already seated for yet another

feast, Sharada looks up with pride in her moist eyes. Then she looks at Iruve as though pleading with him to admit he is also proud of his son.

Iruve's lips purse. He eyes the plantain leaf on which his meal will soon be served. At last he says, "You look so handsome, son. So much like a man."

Sinu feels cheated, for such words would have meant more had his father spoken them freely. Sinu nods his thanks and leaves his parents to their meal. Even as he finishes washing, his mother screams. Janaki's father, Sinu's father-in-law now, bursts into the room.

"Your father is no more!" he shouts. He gestures as though throwing away his heart like a worthless possession. He pulls Sinu, staggering, into the main room.

Sharada sobs while she cradles Iruve's head in her lap, smothers him with her breasts. Sinu's legs grow numb. He finds himself on the floor.

Making no apology, guests flee the house. Music no longer blares in the compound.

Through daybreak and morning, Sinu and Janaki remain with Iruve's corpse while Sharada wails in a tiny room beyond the kitchen. Like Sinu, Janaki sits cross-legged next to the body, but she remains motionless while he rocks with his hands clasped over his ears. At last he stretches out on a mat. Sharada's screams keep him awake.

At noon, the city corporation van arrives to carry the corpse to the crematorium. Sinu climbs into the back alone, but even here he cannot find solitude. People stare at him through the high glass sides of the black van. He feels so chilled that, later, when an attendant rolls the corpse through the open steel doors of the crematorium, Sinu takes a step toward the flames.

The attendant raises his palm inches from Sinu's chest. "Not you, sir," he insists.

When Sinu returns to the house, his father-in-law says, "You are welcome to remain here until the immersion. We have no heating coil for your bath, but you may not go out now in any event. I see the chill air does not agree with you."

For ten days, Sinu, Sharada, and Janaki never once leave the
house. At night the two women sleep, but each sunrise finds him
looking more haggard. At home he takes a head bath only once a
week; now he must take one every day, and that with cool water.
While the days wear on, he wanders about the house. There is no
place to hide. Often he staggers as though the flesh has been
scooped from his limbs. He no longer feels bubbly. He feels like a
single bubble: sometimes so hollow, he expects his chest to collapse
onto his spine; other times stretched so tightly, he thinks he may
burst. If only Janaki could keep him warm at night, but that
cannot yet be. They exchange many looks, but they exchange few
words beyond, "Rest yourself," or, "Take some food."

On the eleventh day after the cremation, Sinu, Janaki, and
Sharada hire a taxicab to drive them to the outskirts of Delhi.
Sharada fills the front with her bulk, squeezes the driver against his
door. Sinu holds an unglazed pot containing ashes. Once, when
the taxicab jolts and the lid scrapes aside, ash falls on his thigh. He
brushes away the ash, then licks a fingertip and tries to erase the
yellow-grey smear. Janaki stops him by placing her hand on his,
and his cheeks burn. At a small temple on the bank of the Jamuna
River, the taxicab stops. They are downstream from the city,
toward Agra. There, Janaki has told him, North Indian couples
observe a rite called a honeymoon. They view Taj Mahal by
moonlight.

Sharada hires an old priest. After she pays him he walks, clad
only in his breechclout, into the river. Just then, a young woman
fans her way through reeds, clambers up the bank some distance
away. Sinu's eyes linger on the wet sari clinging to her breasts.

"I cannot do this," he tells Janaki. "Appa's ashes belong in the
Kabini River." Before she can say anything, he moans, "Oh, God,
I am so cold." He stumbles down the stone steps into the river. For
a moment, the hollowness leaves him. He feels his heart beat in his
chest if only because a hand seems to clutch it under the water. He
wants to immerse the ashes and be done with them, but the priest
makes him wash himself and stand with his hands clasped during
an endless Sanskrit prayer. When the priest finally nods, Sinu takes
the clay pot from the bottom step. Clasping the lid, he lowers the
pot, turns it upside down, and pushes it through the surface.

Bubbles rise; the clay pot sinks. He emerges trembling to find
Sharada gazing balefully at him.

"You should have scattered the ashes," she says. "Not drowned
them like that, son."

During the long rail journey from Delhi to Bombay, from
Bombay to Miraj Junction, from Miraj to Bangalore and then
Mysore City, from Mysore to Nanjangud Town, Sinu pretends all
is well. He knows he should feel warmer coming home, back to
where the sun traps even brahminy kites with its rays, but the chill
spreads from his hands and feet through his limbs to his heart.
Srinivas House no longer feels like a womb; it feels like a Muslim
or even a Christian tomb. When his lungs begin gurgling with
fluid, he finds little comfort in Janaki's embrace. He knows she
piles shawls on him, chafes his wrists to speed the flow of blood,
and feeds him scalding tea with a spoon, but it all seems wasted
effort, wasted like the years his parents spent in schooling him —
all those years when he longed for praise.

One night he wakes to find Janaki cradling his head in her lap.
He raises a hand to touch her face. He has done nothing wrong. He
has so much still to do. He wants to say, "Promise me you will
restore the statue. The shrine of Goddess Saraswati will be our
secret place."

"What is it?" Janaki asks. When she bends closer, his hand slides
into the hollow of her throat, down onto her blouse. She unbut-
tons it, moulds his hand onto her breast.

He mutters, "Promise me—."

The world turns white, wet and softly white, and a boy floats on
the surface of a river, floats between water and air. Waves rock him,
breezes nudge him, yet he lingers to twirl like a lotus freed from its
roots. He sinks while his reflection in the quicksilvered surface
waves. Warm mud blankets him; reeds embrace him. Many-hued
bubbles glide from his mouth when he smiles. They break the
surface, rise through an ultramarine sky, pass indigo white clouds,
and pluck free a kite drying on the still damp sun.

Honestly, as in the Day

I cannot deny it: I am an old man.

My small house occupies a rear corner of my son's lot. In India, such dwellings are often built behind large houses in order to secure rent. They are called outhouses. My daughter-in-law bridles if I tell people this. I therefore call my dwelling by its proper name here: a granny flat.

My son finds both terms equally humorous. He would rather I lived under his roof, but I prefer staying out of my daughter-in-law's way. If my grandchildren wish to see me, they skip through the garden, mince between the pine trees, and knock at my door.

Every Sunday, I eat lunch with my son's family. My daughter-in-law prepares the meal after they return from church. All other times, I eat alone so I can read. I long ago perfected the art of wielding a book with my left hand while eating with my right. I do use cutlery at my son's table, however, because even he considers eating with one's hand to be quaint.

Some of my habits I can hide, but I am unable to change the few that most irritate my daughter-in-law. For instance, I seldom refer to my relations by name. I do address them by name, but I habitually refer to them as my son, my daughter-in-law, and so on. She does not understand when I say that, for me, my relation to another is more important than his name. She claims I am as detached as my house.

One thing else irritates her: my practice of not spending Christmas with them. Each year, after Thanksgiving Day in October, I leave Regina for Victoria, one queenly city for another. I return on the first day of April. I used to say, when she came to fetch me at the airport, "April Fools, I am still alive!"

I ceased this practice after my son confided that my greeting upset her. He no doubt relayed her words diplomatically. She still smiles, however, when I claim she secretly gives thanks on Thanksgiving Day for my impending departure. She reminds me that if she and my son wish to fulfill their social obligations during my absence, then she must hire a sitter for the children.

She has developed the notion that I have a fortune set aside for my grandchildren to inherit, funds I could better spend on them during my lifetime. The matter has become a serious irritant for her, because the children have begun pleading with my son to take them to Walt Disney World. They do not understand when he explains he is experiencing some difficulty with his practice.

It surprises few people that he is an MD. They expect such things from Indians here. I still find it surprising that the son of a mere college lecturer should have become not only a physician but also a specialist. His practice is not yet so established that he may take his family on exotic holidays, however. The family spends most holidays on the farm owned by the parents of my daughter-in-law.

They are somewhat religious people in the sense that they feel compelled to reaffirm their faith weekly. That is why my daughter-in-law recently mentioned some people in her church were becoming curious about me. They have welcomed my son to their fold, but I appear enigmatic to them. I suppose I should be flattered.

"I was talking to Reverend Miller," she announced. She was clearing the dishes after last Sunday's lunch. "He's dying to meet you. He even said how much he'd love it if you'd come give the lesson next week. He's read some of your stuff."

I had been wondering when such a thing might happen. Most of my works once appeared only in British or Indian periodicals. Now certain college presses have begun distributing collections of my more popular tales in the United States and Canada. I suspect this latter is more by default than by design.

I must admit I hold my work in low regard because, like me, it is from another age. It reminds me too much of moralistic fables with surprising endings: the sort favoured by the Frenchman Guy de Maupassant and the American O. Henry. I trust my admirers will not immortalize my name on a chocolate bar.

After my son nudged my foot under the table, I looked up from stirring my tea. "Is that so?" I inquired.

"Yeah," she said. She never says yes. Neither does my son, although I corrected him often when he was young.

Some habits I have never acquired during the forty years I have lived on this continent. Among them is the practice of comfortably using the vernacular. Even now I speak slowly, not because I am old but because I must first translate everything into my native tongue and then back to English.

"So," she repeated, "Reverend Miller said how much he'd love it if you'd come give the lesson next week. It's not like a sermon or anything. You can even pick your own topic. Today Mrs. Sargent — she's organizing the fowl supper again — gave the lesson about charity."

"Did your Mrs. Sargent speak about the Good Samaritan?" I inquired. Old age has improved my ability to detect subterfuge.

"I didn't know you've read the Bible," my daughter-in-law exclaimed.

"Oh yes," I replied, "three times. But I have read the Koran only twice."

My son grinned. He raised his hand to his mouth and coughed before she noticed he had allowed himself a temporary taking of sides.

"It doesn't have to be from the Bible," she said, "as long as it's a lesson."

"Tell them the one about the Bombay talkie producer, Dad," my son said. He calls me Appa, which means father in my tongue, only when we find ourselves alone. That now seldom occurs. He frowned eagerly at me. "I love that part about Hollywood trying to produce a musical about Gandhi."

"It is too long," I said. "Besides that, it would not do to have your congregation roll in the pews."

"That's aisles, Grandpa," my elder granddaughter said.

When I rose, she quietly pulled my chair back from the table. She thinks I never notice such things. I continue pretending I do not. She and her sibling might otherwise grow to think I expect such kindness, and so not give it freely.

My daughter-in-law seized the opportunity, as always, to speak the final word. "Don't strain yourself," she said.

I returned to my dwelling and searched among dusty boxes for my journals. Then I made minor corrections to an unpublished tale. It has been some years since I wrote anything new, for I find it taxing to put words on paper. They are no longer as malleable as I once thought them. Either that, or my mind is no longer nimble enough to knead and reshape them before they set on the page.

This morning my son assisted me up the steps of my daughter-in-law's church. I clutched a sheaf of yellow papers. On the lawn stood a signboard proclaiming, in white plastic letters, that today's sermon would be about wrath. I permitted myself a smile.

Reverend Miller mistook it for one of greeting. He pressed my hand between both of his. He had telephoned some days before to inquire about the subject of my lesson, so he could plan his sermon. I realized now I had misled him, for I had answered cryptically, "You will find my subject in the Book of Job, chapter five, verse two." He introduced me to various strangers, whose names I immediately forgot.

I did notice he always introduced me as Mr. So-and-So. If I have one complaint about growing old, it is that no one addresses me by my given name. Most of my contemporaries are dead; I shall soon join them. I should like to have my ashes immersed in the Kabini River, which flows past my birthplace. I suspect my son will merely scatter them on Wascana Lake.

After we took our seats, Reverend Miller greeted his congregation, and the choir sang a hymn. Then he announced that the congregation was in for a surprise. The two people about to be most surprised were my daughter-in-law and the Reverend himself. I could do nothing to help him, however, so I took my place at the lectern, adjusted the microphone, and began to read.

I confess I felt nervous. It has been some fifteen years, after all, since I lectured. That is why I never looked up from my papers. I trust everyone was delighted. The only beaming face I recall was that of Mrs. Reverend Miller. She sat hunched over the keyboard of an organ. I hoped she would not pounce on its keys if I myself struck a discordant note. She fortunately sat with her hands in her lap while I read this tale:

Her Sister's Shadow

The rivalry between Sharada and Vasanta began in their mother's womb, yet it went unnoticed in our village of Debur until they reached womanhood. As infants, the twins slept in hammocks joined so their mother could rock both of them by pushing only one. As toddlers, they left a single track in the dust outside their hut, since Vasanta followed Sharada more closely than a shadow. Once, when Sharada stopped to pet one of the village curs, Vasanta bumped into her so that Sharada found herself trapped between her sister and the snarling dog. Sharada clambered over her sister to safety. When Vasanta began to shriek, their mother kicked the dog aside and scooped Vasanta up. Villagers who saw what had happened merely shook their heads and smiled behind the mother's back. For some time, she suspected both girls were idiots, for they rarely exchanged a word. Sometimes, though, when she caught them eyeing one another guardedly, she thought each resented the other's existence.

In truth, each girl grew to envy the other. Except for a nose too sharply hooked, Sharada had perfect features with large, almost sultry eyes and a wide, almost sensuous mouth. Sharada means autumn, and though she was the elder by a mere twenty minutes, she developed a mature beauty that overshadowed Vasanta's innocent looks. Vasanta means spring, but her beauty was like the spring of promise, forever on the verge of bloom. Her face had neither perfect proportions nor a charming imperfection to make it lovely; yet one could have understood a blind man's assuming Vasanta was the beautiful sister and Sharada the plain one. While Sharada rarely smiled or sang, the sight of a common parakeet sent Vasanta clapping with delight or humming an improvised tune. No wonder, then, that when their parents searched for Sharada's future husband, they received offers only for Vasanta. Sometimes Vasanta's despair over having to wait until Sharada married upset the entire family; more often, Vasanta gloated. Sharada betrayed no ill will, for in response to Vasanta's extreme moods, Sharada had cultivated her natural calm into aloofness. They became two faces of the Kabini River: Sharada its rock-strewn bed easily forded in the dry season; Vasanta its waters swelled by the monsoon, shallow in spots, unpredictably deep in others.

After two years of unsuccessful inquiries beyond our district, the parents agreed to match Vasanta to the Kempe Gowdas' eldest son provided his brother married Sharada in a joint ceremony. Such an event had rarely occurred in our village. At first, Mrs. Kempe Gowda opposed the agreement since she, too, wanted her children to marry outside the district, but for all their land, the Kempe Gowdas lacked the status to attract city-bred wives for their sons. On an auspicious day in February, soon after everyone had washed the dyes and coloured water of the Holi festival from their clothes, Sharada wed the younger son, and Vasanta wed the elder. Sharada's husband was nicknamed Iruve, or ant, for his nervous energy. Vasanta's husband was nicknamed Nona, or fly, for his protruding eyes. During the month it took Iruve to build a bungalow north of the Debur-Nanjangud Road, Sharada lived with her parents in our village, but Vasanta immediately moved into the Kempe Gowdas' home south of the road. To distinguish the two houses, local wags called Iruve's smaller one the Lokh Sabha after the Commons and the Kempe Gowdas' larger one the Rajya Sabha after the Senate.

Within the year, Mrs. Kempe Gowda died. Her husband soon followed her — according to many, from grief; according to local wags, from boredom, since he no longer had to defend himself from her tongue. The village council voted as one man to split the Kempe Gowdas' land equally between Iruve and Nona with the Debur-Nanjangud Road as the boundary. To compensate Sharada for living in the smaller house, Vasanta begged Nona to give Sharada all his mother's jewellery. Secure in his position as schoolmaster of Debur, he agreed. Before handing the necklaces and ear rings to Sharada, he stared at them as though with regret, but Vasanta knew him well enough to realize he never merely looked at anything; he stared with his fly-like eyes. On the first anniversary of her father-in-law's death, she invited her parents to leave their hut in Debur and move into the Rajya Sabha. Aside from the grand joke of having finally acquired a seat in the Senate, her father cherished her gesture, for he had not only escaped our village but also moved to within a mile of the town.

One day, the district engineer announced plans to build two irrigation canals parallel to the Debur-Nanjangud Road. Each four miles in length, the canals were completed in what for us seemed a record time of five years. By then, Sharada had borne three daughters while Vasanta had borne three sons, but the canals separated the sisters further than the shame Sharada had brought Iruve and the honour Vasanta had brought Nona. The canals reversed the sisters' fortunes.

Nona lacked the funds to install an irrigation pump to tap the waters of the upper canal, which passed south of his land. Mainly dependent on the monsoons, his land continued producing only tomatoes. He hauled water from the well into his fields before leaving for his school, but the hotter the weather grew, the more slowly he moved. Toward the end of the dry season, he refused to stir from his bedroll to tend his land. Instead, he waved his limbs like a helpless fly and gestured for drinking water while cracks snaked through his fields. The lower canal, however, bounded the northern edge of Iruve's land. It took little urging from Sharada to set him digging a channel into his fields. True to his nickname, he worked as industriously as an ant. Since the land sloped down, past the canal toward the river, he hired a youth from our village to scoop water up from the canal into the channel. Iruve then gave in to Sharada's demand that he use his entire salary as buyer for the Ganesha Rice Mill to replace his tomato crops with sugar cane. At Deepavali, the festival of lights, when he closed his account book for the old year and opened one for the new, he found himself surprisingly well off. He beamed when Sharada bought the first silk sari ever owned by a girl from our village. She rewarded Vasanta's earlier generosity by presenting her with an embroidered sari made of Lancashire cotton. True to form, Vasanta gave the sari to her mother, who never wore it for fear of upsetting Sharada.

The years passed, and power lines appeared on the Debur-Nanjangud Road. A diesel train shuttled between the town and Mysore City. Vasanta gave birth to three more boys; Sharada, cursed by having borne five girls in all, finally presented Iruve with a son. She had grown so broad and heavy-limbed that her bangles settled into furrows on her wrists; yet while the worries of feeding and clothing six sons, a husband, and two aged parents subdued

Vasanta's spirits, Sharada's rose with the birth of her son. She became prone to extremes while her sister lapsed into silence. Even more noticeable, Vasanta's face grew pinched and dry while Sharada's remained curiously unchanged. She spent a small fortune on lightening creams ordered through the post all the way from Delhi. She mounted face mirrors in every room of the new house Iruve had built for her in the town. While supervising the servant who swept the house daily, Sharada admired herself full-faced and in profile.

Unknown to everyone except the postmaster of Debur, whose silence she bought with Iruve's threadbare shirts, she also received illustrated magazines. In one, from Bombay, she read about a star who had paid to have his jowls tucked and about a starlet who had paid for injections of silicone in unmentionable areas of her body. Convinced this new technique, called cosmetic surgery, could correct her nearly perfect face, Sharada discreetly secured the name of a reputable surgeon in Bangalore, the largest city in our state. He had learned his craft in America and returned to establish the MGM Clinic. His fee equalled the value of Mrs. Kempe Gowda's jewellery, but since the novelty of showing off her son had paled, Sharada had sought a new goal. She told Iruve she planned to visit Bangalore for a nature cure and paid Vasanta a farewell visit. It was their first meeting since the wedding of Vasanta's eldest son, which had been celebrated the previous year.

Sharada blocked the light by which Vasanta patched her husband's umbrella, yet Vasanta did not notice the shadow cast upon her. She raised her head only after Sharada greeted her cheerfully. Vasanta's hands fumbled when she put her sewing aside. Shading her eyes, she smiled with embarrassment. She turned from the sunlight and sat with her ear tilted toward her shoulder as though more eager to listen to Sharada than to look at her. They spoke of whose cattle would balk at the flames lit during Sankranti, to separate cows that would be bred from those that would not. The sisters spoke of this in inflated tones until Vasanta's youngest sons ran home from Debur School. They collapsed giggling into her lap. Their affection infuriated Sharada, for lately her own son had begun whining if she petted him. She abruptly stood and made her farewell. She suffered her nephews to kiss her cheek and observed it would be some time before they saw her face again. During the walk back to the town, she consoled herself by imagining the well-bred sons she would find for her daughters. The next morning, she took the diesel train to Mysore City, where she changed to the longer steam train for Bangalore.

She returned two months later with a new compact mirror clutched in one hand and a kerchief in the other. If she noticed fellow passengers' questioning frowns each time she gazed triumphantly into the mirror, she betrayed nothing. She inwardly laughed. Almost as often as she checked the mirror, she dabbed at her nostrils with the kerchief. The surgeon had cautioned her against blowing her nose, however carefully, until the pressure in her sinuses had eased. At Mysore Railway Station, her spirits rose so high that she gave one rupee to an astonished beggar limping down the platform. At Nanjangud Railway Station, she agonized over whether to go home and change into her newest sari, acquired at Shantala Silk House in Bangalore, or whether to leave directly for the Rajya Sabha. Impatience overruled both her vanity and frugality, so she hired a horse-drawn cart. She chafed until Nona's flat brown land appeared on her left and Iruve's green sugar cane fields rose on her right.

After the cart finally stopped, she hurried through Vasanta's garden, planted with groundnuts so as not to waste a patch of soil, and entered the house uninvited. The veranda was empty. When she shouted her sister's name, Vasanta's daughter-in-law appeared from the kitchen to explain she sat behind the house in the sun. In the twenty years since they had left our village, Sharada had never known Vasanta to indulge in anything as frivolous as sunning herself. Puzzled, Sharada followed the girl back through the veranda and around the house to the well.

Seated on its stone edge, Vasanta leaned against the beam supporting the pulley. She faced directly south toward the distant upper canal with her face tilted to the sun. The girl announced Sharada's arrival and left the sisters alone. Sharada drew near and pointedly sidestepped her sister's shadow. Gripping the beam for balance, Vasanta carefully turned. Sharada dabbed at her painful nostrils one last time and tucked the soiled kerchief into the waist of her nylon sari. Her opening words, "Yes, it is really me," so often rehearsed during her convalescence, died on her lips.

Vasanta's right eye had turned the colour of diluted milk. Her left eye had turned even whiter than the blinding sun.

I returned to my place while Mrs. Reverend Miller played the organ.

Reverend Miller proved to be as quick of mind as I am slow of foot. After the congregation was apprised of certain upcoming events, after the brass plates for the offering were circulated and after yet another hymn was sung, he began his sermon. "We read in the Book of Job, chapter five, verse two," he said, "'Wrath killeth the foolish man, and envy slayeth the silly one.' Our guest dealt with envy, so I'll deal with wrath."

I wondered how I should deal with my daughter-in-law's wrath. She could not have supposed, after all, that I might presume to teach her the lesson. She remained unusually quiet during our drive home, and I wondered whether my son would suggest I consider an early retreat to my winter home. He would no doubt relay her words diplomatically.

My elder granddaughter helped me from my son's posh automobile. I turned toward the path which skirts my son's house and leads to my own.

"Aren't you coming in?" he called.

I glanced at my daughter-in-law. He doubtless anticipated a confrontation, so he shepherded the children into the house. I found myself abandoned to her judgement.

"I wasn't trying to put you on the spot by saying you'd give the lesson," she insisted.

"Nor was I trying to embarrass you by choosing to speak of envy," I said. I placed my hand upon her arm. "Come," I declared, "'Let us walk honestly, as in the day; not in rioting and drunkenness, not in chambering and wantonness, not in strife and envying.'"

"More Bible?" she inquired.

"Yes," I admitted. "From the Book of Romans, I believe."

"What happened to the two sisters?" she inquired.

"I do not know," I answered. "I suppose they made a peace of sorts." I squinted at the sun, already lower in the sky than the sun of summer. "I have been thinking a change would do me some good," I said. "If I spent my winters in Florida, do you suppose all of you might visit me there?"

"I'm sure we could swing it," she replied. "Some day."

I turned toward my son's house. "I make only one condition," I said. "I shall purchase the children passes to Walt Disney World as their Christmas gift. However, I shall not be taken, as one might say here, for a ride."

I expected her to raise the no doubt transitory nature of our truce, but she said nothing. She merely chuckled. I trust she appreciated, at last, the prerogative of an old man to speak the final word.

A Promise We Shall Wake in the Pink City After Harvest

Janaki rests under a neem tree and braids her hair. She dabbles her toes in the river. Downstream, women wash clothes. When they arc backward, the rolls of their midriffs vanish into taut convex bellies. Then the women arc forward to slap the clothes, twisted cotton whips, against slabs of rock. Farther out, children splayed across oxen and bullocks spray one another with water. Two boys pull a girl off an ox, and laughter follows the splash. With so many people flocking to the river even as the red glow of the sun softens to orange, then glares to yellow-white, more birds wheel in the sky than perch on the bank. And the higher they rise, the more they look like sea gulls, curved white vees chalked across a blue slate.

Janaki knows Sinu's ashes have floated downstream or settled in the dark mud of the river bottom; yet she likes to pretend they swim with the fish that dart around her feet and stop at times to kiss her toes. "Come with us," the fish say. "Why do you watch others enjoy themselves when you cannot join them?" Often the fish wake her at night. When she nods into sleep, they whisper, "Janaki," call, "Jaa-na-ki," and always they ask the same question. "I want to dream," she calls back. "Can I do that if I am no more?" But to dream the dreams that make her smile, she must remain awake, and so she does until she falls asleep exhausted. Then the other dreams come unbidden, those about running or flying or searching.

There must be a way home. True, it lies north, farther than the far bank of the river, but she can cross it only by ferry or by train, and she can buy passage on neither. She could sell the ivory miniatures, but they would take her no farther than Mysore City, and what should she do there? She has heard of what befalls girls in unfamiliar cities. She would sooner be reborn as a reptile or an insect.

How simple it would be to join the fish, to slip beneath the cool water, feel her braids ripple on the surface until the current wove them into the reeds. But she could not bear the pain of her heart pounding while the water filled her lungs. She would struggle to free her hair and die thrashing. Would these women and children notice the bubbles breaking the surface? Would the fish hover nearby to calm her? "Just a few more dreams," she assures them. "Wait for the harvest to begin." She picks apart the knot in a corner of her sari, the only one Sinu's mother Sharada has left to her, and removes the ivory miniatures. She raises one to her lips, kisses the face of the pale bearded prince adorning it. With one miniature in the palm of each hand, with fingers shading them like cobras dancing under a tree, she dreams.

*   *   *

"It appears we have found you a husband at last," Janaki's father told her. "It has taken months of correspondence, but we did not want to raise your hopes."

"The boy is named Sinu," Janaki's mother said. "He is your age, a little older perhaps, but he is Mr. and Mrs. Kempe Gowda's youngest child. The only boy, and they are old. His mother Sharada has written she wants nothing more from life than to acquire a city-bred girl for him. Think of it! You will be the only daughter-in-law under their roof. Why, you can simply count the days until you become mistress of their lands!"

The prospect of escaping a house in which she was the only girl intrigued Janaki. Yet she felt betrayed, for the Kempe Gowdas lived in Nanjangud Town, somewhere south of Mysore City and a town so small she failed to find it on the map in her school. She knew why her father wanted this match. His village elders had once mocked him for claiming the future lay in the valley of the Kabini River, so he had turned his back on the south and moved all the way north to New Delhi. She had grown up Hindi-speaking, and she heard her father use Kannada for the first time at the meeting with the Kempe Gowdas. They reached New Delhi in the midst of Shishira, the cold season.

With his dark pocked face and wide credulous eyes, Sinu was neither as handsome nor as self-assured as the boys in her class. He sat through the meeting with his eyes fixed on the calendar picture of Jatayu, King of Vultures, battling Ravana, the many-headed King of Lanka. True, she balked at the Kempe Gowdas' insistence that she accompany them home after the wedding, even before completing her education, but now she faced a boy who offered more than a Secondary School Leaving Certificate. He would be her companion for life, and she would bear his sons; many sons.

"Can I be alone with him for one day?" she asked her parents.

Sinu's eyes shifted from the calendar picture to her face. Mixed with his ill-concealed hope, she sensed a hint of fear that she might reject him. When her father translated her request, Sinu's tensed shoulders relaxed. He returned his gaze to the calendar picture, to the anguished Sita praying for Lord Rama to rescue her while the vulture and the black king fought. After a whispered debate, one dominated by his mother, Sharada, the elder Kempe Gowdas agreed. Her father slapped his thighs and said something in Kannada that sounded belittling.

"He says he will allow these youngsters their freedom if it will speed matters," her mother explained. "You may soon tire of the outing, however. The boy speaks little English and not a word of Hindi. Except perhaps wallah or chai."

Without thinking, Janaki leaned forward to take Sinu's tumbler and call to the ayah for more tea. When all four parents smiled, she regretted the act.

* * *

Janaki glances from the ivory miniatures to the river. She looks up at the rustling twigs of the neem tree. She likes to pretend that on moonlit nights the tree rains jasmine on lovers, who then saunter home with darkness concealing joined hands. She folds her hands so the portraits touch, clicking softly while the prince and princess kiss. But when they lie face to face, she cannot see them except with her mind's eye. No, in such a place romance thrives

only in villagers' tales, tales that change with each telling until the
gossip of generations past becomes the legends of those awaiting
rebirth. And even if anyone here would speak to her, she could
only guess the meaning of his words from the movement of his
hands, the play of light in his eyes, the boldness or hesitation in his
voice.

*   *   *

Despite their difficulty in understanding one another, Janaki
did not tire of the outing. Any boy who could treat her with the
respect Sinu displayed, opening doors and fending off impatient
fares when she dismounted from the autorickshaw — such a boy
would make an ideal husband. There was so much to see in
Connaught Place alone that they spent the entire morning in the
white colonnades, the arts and crafts shops, the airline offices with
their coloured photos from Paris and Rome. After lunch in a hotel
restaurant, they lingered silently until she finally spoke, enunciat-
ing the English words while he frowned in concentration. "Some
North Indians observe a custom called 'honeymoon,'" she said.
"They journey to Agra and view Taj Mahal by moonlight."

Nodding at the traffic swirling around the circle, he said, "I
should like that." Most of the private cars were Hindustan Ambas-
sadors or Morris Minors. He delighted in pointing out the rare
Chevrolet of a high civil servant or general officer. "First we return
south for the harvest." He sighed. "That is the rush here to be
wed."

"But I would rather observe this honeymoon in Jaipur!" she
exclaimed. When he frowned, she repeated herself. "We could
travel on the Pink City Express." Willing herself not to say,
"romantic," she cried, "How wonderful that would be!" Then she
told him about Jaipur, where her eldest brother now lived: about
the honeycombed windows in the pink sandstone Palace of the
Winds; the seven-storied moon palace, Chandra Mahal; Central
Museum with its ivories of kings and queens. She spoke for so long
and so longingly that, when he abruptly rose, she feared she had
bored him. But, no, he led her back to the Rajasthan Emporium
and bade her wait outside with her back to the entrance. A full ten

minutes later, he emerged to thrust a brown-paper packet at her, then walked away with his hands in the pockets of her father's warmest cardigan. She opened the packet to find a pair of Rajput miniatures, portraits of a jewelled princess and a warrior-prince on ivory squares no larger than postage stamps.

"Why?" she demanded, running after him.

He hugged himself, but not tightly enough to suppress a shiver. She knew he found New Delhi cold, and she had to smile each time he wrinkled his nose in distaste at people who rubbed mustard oil on their bodies to keep warm. He had never seen frost until this morning, when she had pointed at the white dusting on the lawn of her father's compound. Unable to face her, Sinu stumbled over words he must have been practising while in the shop: "A promise we shall wake in the Pink City, after harvest." When he blushed, so did she, and they stood face to face, inches apart. She knew he wanted to ask whether she too felt anxious about the first night they must spend together. She secretly welcomed his parents' insistence that the second ceremony, the tying of the thread that would herald their complete union, wait until after the harvest. She wanted to thank him for his uncertainty but did not know how. She looked at the miniatures, then at him.

"Let us be off," he said.

"We still have the afternoon," she reminded him.

He shook his head. "We must walk. Everything our parents gave me for this day, I spent. Also I gave the shop wallah my wristwatch." Rubbing the impression left on his wrist by the strap, Sinu turned away.

Janaki wondered how she could scold him for his extravagance without hurting his feelings. She wanted to touch the pale band, encircle his narrow wrist with her fingers, but he set off. They covered a furlong, he with his hands in his pockets and eyes downcast, before she summoned the courage to touch his elbow lightly. "Thank you," she said. They walked in silence after that, sometimes drifting apart, sometimes drifting so closely their sleeves brushed. When they finally reached her father's house, two hours later, they found the adults gathered for afternoon tea.

Her father took in her dusty clothes and demanded, "What has happened?"

Sinu needed no translation to understand the question. After glancing at her, Sinu mumbled, "We were robbed."

Amid exclamations of horror and demands for detail, she left the room clutching the miniatures. She could not bear to watch his guilty face while he fabricated an unlikely tale about a Sikh autorickshaw driver, then improvised answers to further questions.

When her mother entered Janaki's room to ask, "Have you decided, Modern Miss?" she shrugged. But she knew her smile, dreamy despite her attempt at worldliness, explained her decision. "You will be so happy with him, I know it!" her mother cried.

*   *   *

Janaki shakes her head while she hides the miniatures in the wrinkled corner of her sari. The women leave the river bank to take their washing home to dry spread under the hot sun; the children lead the oxen and bullocks into the fields; the birds return to swoop over the water. The fish, who flick among the reeds, have no interest in her now. She rises and slaps red dust from the back of her white sari, then turns from the river to walk south. When she reaches Debur Village, the dogs growl at her. The people, even the children naked below the waist, avoid looking her in the eye. She ignores the two young goatherds laughing over her, for if she scowled they would merely let their eyes, slitted against the dusty wind, rove down from her face.

When she tries to enter the tiny post office, the postmaster blocks her way. "*Naleba,*" he says, as he does every day. Perhaps tomorrow her parents will reply to the telegram she begged him to send, but she fears he agreed only to stem her tears, to stop her kneeling and pressing her brow to his feet. At times, she suspects he did not send it. On the feast day of Holi, she saw his wife clad in one of the nylon saris Sharada took. No doubt Janaki's silk saris, her gold anklets and earrings, even her glass bangles adorn Sinu's married sisters now. The only unmarried sister, a girl with protruding teeth, brings Janaki's meal every day in the middle of the morning, but she does not think of the girl as a sister-in-law. On the few occasions Janaki addressed the girl, she hurried away biting her lip.

Janaki turns east and walks along the Debur-Nanjangud Road. When she reaches the two houses halfway to the town, she pauses to glance at the larger one, which belongs to Sinu's uncle. It is a whitewashed bungalow roofed with fine orange Mangalore tiles. She knows that behind it Sinu's blind aunt sits on the edge of the well, but she speaks no English or Hindi, so Janaki can do nothing but watch her staring at the sun.

Janaki turns to look at her own small house, set back from the road. She skirts the compound, heads north and stops at the lower canal. Perhaps she will notice something new today. She has learned so much already. Only tomatoes grow in the fields around the large house because the land slopes down to the river from the road; watered by the lower canal, sugar cane grows tall in the fields around the small house. She hears Bestha's song, the only one he knows, one he must repeat a hundred times in a day. Protecting her face from the long sharp leaves of the sugar cane, leaves already edged with brown, she follows his voice until she reaches the junction of the canal and an irrigation ditch.

Bestha stands waist-deep in the canal. Singing without break from sunrise until noon, he scoops water into the ditch with a bucket. Then he stops to eat without leaving the water. She thinks she knows why: his legs would cramp if he did. He continues working, singing until sunset, when he emerges wrinkled like a fig. She can see from his lined face and greying hair that he is older than her father, yet Bestha's body looks as young as Sinu's did before the fire on the ghat reduced his corpse to ashes. A break in the flow of Bestha's work, scooping water upward, ever upward, tells her he feels her presence. She knows he wears only a breech-clout, but below the waist his body wavers indigo in the murky canal. What she can see of him constantly moves. His spine arcs like a dancing snake, straightens like a knotted whip; his shoulders and back ripple like corrugated tin. She wants to drape herself over him, press herself against those hard ridges while he carries her like a child, but she does not want him to touch her.

*　*　*

The day Janaki and Sinu reached Nanjangud Town, his chills worsened. She piled shawl after shawl on him, chafed his wrists to speed the flow of blood, fed him scalding tea with a spoon. Still he gasped for air, and the little he forced into his lungs gurgled in the fluid that filled them. One night, she realized she had fallen asleep while seated with his head in her lap. She blushed when she recalled her dream. Not details; the sense of abandon. She felt his hand touch her face. "What is it?" she asked, bending closer, but she made little sense of his words beyond, "Promise me—." When his hand slid into the hollow of her throat, then down onto her blouse, she felt her pulse quicken under his fingers. Slowly, she unbuttoned her blouse. When she finally squeezed his hand under hers, tried to mold his hand onto her breast, he did not respond.

*   *   *

Janaki turns her back on Bestha. Instead of growing faint while she walks away, his song remains loud as though he must urge himself to work harder, to put her from his mind. She wonders how a widow could affect him, then remembers she is still a girl, a young woman. Perhaps he is the only man in the district who realizes that. No, the goatherds realize it, and soon other men will tramp through the fields to cut down the sugar cane and refresh themselves at the well behind her house.

She enters through the back door. The shutters sag on their hinges, and the roof has fallen through in every room except the kitchen. She sleeps here on the bare floor. In the middle of the kitchen, she keeps an empty soda bottle in a pan of water. Every morning she returns to find her food, wrapped in banana leaf tied with string, perched atop the bottle. A half seer of milk, in an earthenware bowl, balances on the packet. She allows ants to troop across the floor and clamber into the pan. The kerosene for the single lamp is too precious to waste; otherwise she would splash them with kerosene, feel no pity while they died squirming. The food is hers, not theirs. Once a day she scoops their slowly turning bodies off the water. Now, though, she sees neither food nor milk. The bottle lies on its side, and already the water from the over-turned pan has dried in a stain on the packed earth. Someone moves heavily in the front room, and she enters to find Sharada muttering while she fans herself with a fleshy hand.

Sharada is so broad and heavy-limbed that her bangles have settled into furrows on her wrists. She wheezes with the effort of walking here, over two miles from her house in the town.

"Namaste," Janaki says and bows over clasped hands.

Sharada's lips curl at the Hindi expression. "*Namaskaara,*" she responds and continues to mutter. She slaps a green-brown packet against her thigh. She carries no bowl of milk.

Janaki feels suddenly hungry, but the muttering frightens her, and she refuses to reach out her hand for the food. No, she will not beg. She returns to the kitchen and rights the bottle and pan. A packet drops, feet scuff behind her, and she shrieks when hands grasp her hair. She sinks to the floor, and the ants scurry from her. "What do you want now?" she cries.

Sharada kicks the bottle aside, then shouts at the cobwebbed ceiling, "*Idu nanna mane. Illi irabeda! Nimage eshtu halu beku?*"

"You have my dowry and my clothes!" Janaki cries. "I could be a servant in your house, but you imprison me here!" While she weeps, cowering on the floor, Sharada harangues her, then spits on her. The spittle, red from betel juice, runs down her forehead. She wipes it off with the back of her wrist when it soaks into her eyebrow. "What are you saying?" she cries. "What more do you want from me?"

Sharada snatches up the lamp, and the glass chimney shatters on the floor next to Janaki. Sharada shakes the lamp until kerosene splashes on Janaki's sari in round oily drops. Now she understands: Sharada also offers a means of escape. But when she picks up the matchbox and strikes a wooden match, Janaki waves the sulphureous smell away. "No!" she shrieks. "I shall decide. It is the only thing you have left me to decide!" Sharada looms over her and drops the match. Janaki brushes it away. Sharada strikes another match and offers the hissing flame. It flickers down the stem; the charred end droops. When the flame reaches her fingers, Sharada flings the match at Janaki. It singes her hair before she can pluck the match out. She sucks on her prickling fingers, then spits out the burnt-rubber taste of shrivelled hair. Sharada tosses the matchbox onto the broken glass. Waving at the flies and mosquitoes, she waddles into the front room to kick the packet of food across the floor. Then she leaves.

Janaki huddles against the wall while ants troop from the kitchen into the front room. She does not want the food. She has heard of a plant whose juice, when mixed with sandalwood paste, renders the body insensible to burns. Perhaps it is only a tale, but widows smeared this salve on their bodies so they felt no pain when they flung themselves onto their husbands' pyres. Yet where can she find this plant even if it exists? The kitchen grows so hot she can no longer breathe, no longer bear the stench of kerosene and dust, the sight of ants linked end to end. She stumbles out the back door past a pale dead lizard, runs through the fields toward the river. Roots and twigs stab her feet. The long leaves of the sugar cane scratch her face. From far away she hears Bestha's song, one he must repeat a hundred times in a day while he scoops water upward, ever upward. And while she runs, she feels herself taking flight.

And a girl in a white unravelling sari flails at groping sugar cane. Her hair shines with coconut oil, waves in braids, eighteen of them, each on fire. The wind lifts her above the fields until she can hear the fish call from the river, smell the trees rain jasmine, watch the sun rise in the north while the pink city glows.

Sand Dollars

When the children saw their first palm tree at Tampa Airport, they squealed like the three little pigs and made me take a picture of them reaching for its fronds. Vikas looked at it, stood there a long time soaking in the humidity, and shook his head. Later, after the children fell asleep without the usual, "Aw, Mom, just this once?" he told me what bothered him. Not so much bothered. Niggled. He's been back to India a few times with his folks, but this is the first tropical place he's seen that's so developed, so refined. The second day he still kept an eye out for beggars and for cows grazing in the street and said even the palm trees look refined. When the girl at the condo, the recreation director, said the City manicured the trees, he laughed and said to me, "Welcome to Florida," but I'd already guessed he would say that.

It happens a lot now, guessing what the other person thinks. Janine calls it a symptom of easy love. She envies me so much, sometimes I feel like telling her everything, like that affair Vikas had when I was pregnant with Alma. Now when our anniversary rolls around, I look at him and wonder how we ever managed six or seven years, never mind thirteen, fourteen, but I wish someone could tell me why we've started guessing what the other person thinks. We haven't done that since before we got married. And it's because we're doing it again that I had to come down here, never mind how tacky you said it would be.

You were right about one thing, people are ready to sell you anything down here. Alma just had to buy a Florida Snowman. Know what that is? A plastic jar full of water with a top hat and two little eyes and a carrot-like nose, all floating on the bottom. I think there's even a red plastic scarf. I thought of you when I saw it, thought how you'd melt under the sun here. You belong back home — sorry — you're getting so cold and distant. If I ever did give in, I'd keep you as my winter lover, but that's not enough. I'd start wishing you were softer, hoping you'd melt the way he does. I used to hate it when he fell asleep afterwards, but now I guess I'd think something was wrong if he didn't. Janine's right, it is easy love, not like ours would be, the one we'd share like tramps huddled under a bridge.

There's a bridge called the Skyway here, which swoops up into the sky and down again, kept up by bright yellow cables. Next to it's the old bridge with two separate spans, one for traffic going each way. Problem is, the one going south ends halfway because a ship rammed it. That's you, I'm afraid, my bridge to nowhere. If you tried, you could be the other span, the one that keeps going, skims the water on low wooden pilings, but even that's too scary for me. You see why I leave the driving to him? It's all these bridges. There's even one called the Gandy Bridge from St. Petersburg to Tampa. There's a sign before it:

LONG BRIDGE AHEAD
DO NOT STOP FOR FLAT

I watch the water and try to ignore his knuckles turning pale while people pass without signalling. I used to hate it when I saw how unsure he could be about some things. Now I guess I'd think something was wrong if he never had any doubts. At least as long as I can pretend he's in control, I feel safe. It's true with you I don't have to pretend, but sometimes I wish I did have to. Sometimes I wish you weren't so damned sure of yourself. That's why I wish you'd fly down here. Not to save me from the gilded cage you pretend I'm in, but to see the real Florida. It's not at all like you imagined, you just have to know how to look for things.

Take the bird sanctuary. It's called the Suncoast Seabird Sanctuary, started by a man named Ralph Heath, Jr., after he found a cormorant he called Maynard staggering down Gulf Boulevard with a broken wing. We drove up and down Indian Shores looking for the place till we nearly gave up. Then we got out and walked and found it hidden among the condos. It's mainly full of pelicans, permanently crippled, living out their lives in huge pens covered with chicken wire. There's a sign near the office:

EMERGENCY BIRD ADMISSIONS
RING BELL
WILD BIRDS ONLY
WE DO NOT TREAT PETS

If Janine were here, she'd say, "Guess that leaves you out." Meaning me, of course — they would take you. The children's favourite was the pen with a turkey vulture and a black vulture, because they were eating off plates of dead chicks. The girls kept going, "Eyuck!" but I had to drag them away to look at the scarlet ibis and the sandhill crane.

Or take the light. Vikas has a theory people paint their houses according to the colours around them. Or in reaction to them. All the buildings here are vibrant. Pink and green, even shimmery grey. Know where it comes from? The light in the sky and the water. You've never seen light like this — you have to keep your sunglasses on even when it's cloudy. And it's true what they say about the sun in the tropics — it really does just drop out of sight like that. Why everyone has to say it's really true, I don't know, as if it's just a trick.

The other evening we went shopping on the boardwalk at John's Pass and I heard a woman squeal, "Sand dollars!" All behind her stood shelves of real ones, but she stood there mooning over placemats and reading the legend of the sand dollar to her husband. There's a star for the manger and a bell to ring, and the five holes stand for the five wounds of Christ — a little one for each of the nails and one above the centre for the spear. I'm as religious as the next person, but ask me what people see in sand dollars. I like pinks, those mirror-perfect shells we see back home only at gas stations. Thanks to her, I found myself fingering a pair of earrings for Alma, gold-plated sand dollars the size of little golden suns.

The girls both claim they saw him first: the man who danced farewell to the sun. There he was on the end of a pier in his white shorts and T-shirt just dancing away. He kept his feet rooted to one spot, so he wouldn't get slivers I guess, but from the ankles up he moved like a gyroscope, a little to the right, a little to the left, like a cobra following the hole in the chanter. Did you know they don't really follow the music? Just the hole. He flapped his arms slowly, held them out and swivelled his wrists till I was sure they were double, even triple jointed. Snapped his fingers and danced for the sun. Poor Janine would've drooled on her manicured toenails. He reminded me of you, maybe a few years older; then I saw him up close and he must've been fifty. If you look like that twenty years from now, I'll gladly walk away from it all even if that would remind me how much older I looked. Who am I kidding, though? You won't. A person can't age gracefully back home. They wither and wrinkle from the wind and the cold, and their eyes turn blue. Not a warm inviting blue like the gulf at sunset where it's deep. An icy blue, a blue you won't see down here except in ads.

I saw a great one the other day, on a billboard with a huge handgun pointing at these words:

MORE LOCAL NEWS
WLFN RADIO

Sickening, maybe, but it was also Florida, like the tollbooth signs on the Bee Line Expressway to Cape Canaveral:

WARNING — ROBBERY CHALLENGE AREA
WHEN CHALLENGED BY AN OFFICER
DROP YOUR WEAPON
RAISE YOUR HANDS
DO NOT MOVE

Kennedy Space Centre's in a wildlife sanctuary of all things. It was Vikas who mentioned it, of course — it wasn't me. There we have the military hovering like vultures over the shuttle program because it'll help them with Star Wars, and here we have an armadillo scurrying away from traffic. Rockets and armadillos, that's Florida.

More than just flamingos and oranges, though there are lots of those. The first three days I made Vikas stop at every orange stand I saw, bought so many bags I could start my own grove. I even took pictures of houses with orange trees in their yards till this blimp in a muumuu yelled across the street, "Never seen an orange tree before? That's how they grow, dearie!" Then her husband came out wearing a Blue Jays cap. As for flamingos, the only real ones we saw were at Disneyworld.

Oh yes we did that too. First the Magic Kingdom. They should put a statue of Happy the Dwarf in front, because that's how everybody feels. Happy the Dwarf. It must be the music everywhere you go, always zippity-do-dah. No blues here, no melancholy baby. These Disney people know their stuff. Once I even sat next to a flower bed and music exploded from the begonias like pollen.

Alma just loved 20,000 Leagues Under the Sea, that ride through the lagoon. She's read the book and seen the movie, but I never knew she had a thing for Captain Nemo, all that stuff about the visionary hunted by the armies of the world because he wouldn't share his inventions with them. Hildy's favourite was the Haunted Mansion. She loved the part where you look in the mirror and see this ghost leering next to you. Will's was the Country Bear Jamboree. He clapped along and hooted when they did John Denver's song "Country Boy," except this one ends, "Thank God, I'm a country bear!" Vikas went for the Jungle Cruise of all things. Even bought a Styrofoam pith helmet at a kiosk called Bwana Bob's. It's almost as if he's forgotten he's Indian, something he can't do back home where people ask him things like, "So how do you manage winter?" and he says, "The first five years were tough. The last thirty have been a breeze."

Then we did Epcot Centre, starting at the far end in the World Showcase, ten gorgeous pavilions around a manmade lake. Like Expo in Vancouver only better because these are permanent. The Canadian one looks like a scaled-down Bessborough Hotel or Chateau Laurier. Vikas pretended he was American and said loudly with a straight face, "Caynayda, thayt wheyre they geyt all thayt snow in suhmer?" and I slapped his elbow, but it kept me from laughing at the poor hostess. Turned out she was from Winnipeg. She must hear such dumb lines everyday, but how could she say anything with him grinning like an Oakie from Muskogee?

The children saved Future World for last. Mickey Mouse may rule the Magic Kingdom, Donald Duck may keep trying harder because he's number two, but the darling of Future World is a pink lizard called Figment, short for Figment of the Imagination. Will just had to have a Figment hat because the girls both got Mickey Mouse caps. The hat has orange horns growing from the top and two huge yellow eyes in front, even nostrils on the pink peak or beak. When he lowers his chin, you can't see him, only this pink lizard face. He can't see where he's going, of course — people just laugh when he bumps into them. Vikas and I bought matching Spaceship Earth sweatshirts. He hasn't worn his yet, but he said he might under his lab coat.

It's almost as if he's a different man, as if I'm having an affair with my own husband down here. It's exactly what you keep offering, the novelty of waking up with someone new. He's left the old him back in Regina, the one who starts work at seven every morning, comes home at seven every night. I never told you this because I didn't want to sound as if I was looking for an excuse to give in, but I eat with the children, then sit with him while he eats and goes on about the day's appointments. It's his way of unwinding, talking about his patients. He calls the latest Madam X after the Lana Turner movie, one of his favourites.

Poor Madam X. I know more about her insides than she does. The week before we left, Vikas did a diagnostic D and C on her and a laproscopy and a retrograde dye transit. He never pushes, but I can tell he wants her to go ahead with an operation to free her right ovary. He won't guarantee success past fifty/fifty, but he loves a challenge. It scares him sometimes how good he is, and he thinks he'll get even better. His favourite quote's become, "Chance benefits the prepared mind," but if his patients knew what I know, they'd never go under his knife. He says when he's clicking, when everything goes perfectly, his instruments talk to him. His hands are there just to hold the tiny lasers. They help him pretend he's in control more than when he had to nick and snip and slice.

Can you see it now? How could I ever turn my back on a man who believes in himself so much? A man who helps God bring babies into the world. Oh I know you don't think the world is fit to bring babies into, but face it, you like playing things safe. No pun intended. I nearly did throw you out of the house because you were sure I'd give in. You'll never believe how close you came — it wasn't just a line when I said it was me I didn't trust.

That Janine. I can't remember how many times she asked me after you'd been over, "So how's the leaky faucet?" or, "How's the burned-out thermocouple?" and I said it was just business like I really meant it, and she knew it still was. She must've known what could happen though, because you replaced her thermocouple too, didn't you? Except I'm not going to use you as an excuse the way she did when she left what's-his-name. Besides, you said it yourself. You're getting too good at playing the halfway house. If I leave Vikas, I'll leave for myself, not for another man.

I guess I've finally said it. I don't know what would hurt me more, if you shrugged and said, "Have it your way," or if you begged me to cross that line just once, so I wouldn't spend the rest of my life wondering how it would've been. Don't you see? That's my problem. I'm never sure with you. At least with him I know where we stand, even if it's far apart sometimes. Sure it's easy love, but so what? I deserve something easy at long last.

Damn it, damn it, damn it. Yesterday I kept hoping you'd turn up.

Once I even thought you did, disguised as a security guard. When I said, "Excuse me," and he turned around, I had to say, "I'm sorry, I thought you were someone else." He said, "Ah'm sorra ah'm noat," and swaggered off as if he'd made my day. We were in Sarasota. Vikas and the children spent hours in the circus gallery with its old wagons and posters of clowns. I never realized he always dreamed of running away to join the circus, or his favourite movie when he was little was *Toby Tyler*, a Disney movie, of course.

The Ringling House was great. More than rockets and armadillos, more than flamingos and oranges, that house is Florida in a nutshell. It's a hodgepodge, a mishmash of east and west built by a man with more money than taste. The windows are shaped like oriental doorways, with that fluted arch Vikas says he's only seen on Indian palaces, or sets for quaint French operas. The music room has paintings on the ceiling with dancers from different countries, and the women from India and somewhere else exotic

have bare breasts. I guess that's the closest you could come to porn
in the twenties or thirties. You couldn't show a European woman
naked, but it was okay for an Indian or an African. That's Vikas
again. Not that he said as much, but he smirked, and I knew
exactly what he was thinking. It's the only time since we got here
he's gone back to playing Dr. A, that brilliant young surgeon with
opinions on everything.

My favourite part wasn't the circus gallery or the house. It was
the statues. There's a "Perseus and Medusa" just outside and even
"The Dying Gaul" in a sunken garden full of bougainvillea and
hibiscus. The best was the life-sized "David" in front of a row of
palm trees. I couldn't take my eyes off those hands. They must be
the most beautiful hands in the world, especially the one curled
against his right thigh. If I ever met a man with hands like that I
don't know what I'd do. Janine would say, "Trust Mrs. A to love
hands made of bronze," but a bronze hand can't ignore you, can it?
It's always there, never pulling away like yours did that last time. It
is the last time, and don't bother trotting out something snide like,
"Methinks the lady doth protest too much." No, snide isn't fair,
but then you haven't always been fair to me, have you?

Please, please be happy for me. I really am on a second honeymoon, cruises and all.

This afternoon, we left the children with the recreation director
and booked ourselves on a yacht called the *Innovation*. Vikas said
as soon as we stepped aboard he knew Captain Mike had fought in
Vietnam, by the webbing belt wrapped around the compass in
front of the wheel. Captain Mike had his wife to help out. They
had speakers up on deck and listened to a station that played
chestnuts like "Ma Cherie Amour" and "Close to You." Non-
stop, so it couldn't have been WLFN RADIO: MORE LOCAL
NEWS.

Captain Mike turned out to be the only native Floridian we've
met. All the rest are from somewhere else. That's what they call
themselves here, sums up their complexions too. Florida may
mean land of flowers, but it might just as well have been named for
the people, florid from the sun. Vikas says it's unhealthy.

Captain Mike also works as a fishing guide, and he told us things
like why people shouldn't fish in shallow water in winter, standing

out there in hip waders. It's because in summer the rain dilutes the salt in the intercoastal waterway, and that keeps the sharks out, but in winter the sharks come farther in, so these people are asking for it. We never once left sight of land or an old pink hotel called the Don Cesar, where Captain Mike said F. Scott and Zelda Fitzgerald once stayed. We even went under a drawbridge. The cars make a humming noise when they go over the metal grate, and the faster they go, the higher pitched the hum is from the tires. It was Will, the family musician, who noticed on the first day. He calls them musical bridges.

After an hour's sail, we got into a rubber raft with a motor and got dropped on a barrier island to hunt for shells. It was fairly windy the night before, but we couldn't find many interesting ones. For the children's sake, I gathered a lot of pinkish orange ones called pectin; Vikas found a couple of broken ones called pelican foot. After a while, we realized we were looking in the wrong place. The water's edge is the wrong place to look for shells, because any there are fairly beat up. The best are about thirty feet in, where high tide leaves them to dry in the sun. It's strange walking on sand made of millions of seashells crushed into powder so fine it's like soya flour. I'd nearly given up when I started finding them. Sand dollars.

First one, then another one, then two so tiny they would've made great earrings. I could tell the ones you see in stores are hardened somehow. These were so brittle, if you even waved them in the wind they snapped in two. One of them did, and five V-shaped pieces fell out. They're doves that sing the praises of Christ, like the dove that perched on His shoulder after John baptized Him. That's the woman in the store gushing, not me. Off in the distance rose the pink hotel, and way off, our condo. By the time we turned back, Vikas had a plastic bag filled with pectin and olive and whelk. He'd even found a huge pink Florida roller with its tips broken off. I'd collected a dozen white sand dollars, but I wouldn't put them with the others. I carried them like newborn kittens back to the boat. When we went to climb the short rope ladder, Vikas put them in the zippered pocket of his windbreaker. After we set off, he unzipped his pocket and looked inside.

He hadn't done anything. Hadn't banged against the side of the boat, nothing, but when I reached in the pocket, I pulled out a handful of broken shell as brittle as potato chips. He looked so apologetic, I had to say, "It wasn't your fault," but I kept wishing I'd hung onto them even if it would've made climbing the rope ladder hard. At least I could've taken the blame for them turning back to sand. Then, at the bottom of his pocket, I found five whole ones buried under the chips. I took them out and held them all the way back to the condo. There I took a chance. Don't laugh. I sprayed all five with hair spray. The two I wanted to make earrings from aren't among the five, but that's all right. One day we'll go back, and I'll find more, and I'll know to hang onto them myself. For now I guess I can afford to feel good about things, because I've learned the secret of sand dollars. Know what that is? Once you know where to look, there's no trick to finding your own. The real trick is preserving them.

Speaking of which, we finally got a picture of the five of us together. Till now it's been Vikas with the children, me with the children, the two of us with two of them. They kept saying we should ask somebody to take one with my camera, but I couldn't trust just anyone to get it right. Alma found the answer, made the other two pitch in on a lightweight tripod. Picture me on the beach fussing with the camera, tilting it this way and that, digging the legs first one way, then another into the sand while the children yell, "Hurry, the sun's going down," and Vikas calls, "It doesn't have to be perfect!" Yes it does, and now I've got it on film, safe in my camera, the last picture for the album of this trip.

No, that's Alma showing off her new gold earrings. Hildy's the one in the Mickey Mouse cap. The pink lizard, all orange horns and huge yellow eyes, is Will. That's my Spaceship Earth sweatshirt already needing a wash, and Vikas is finally wearing his. The white dot on the pier? It wasn't supposed to be in the picture but, no, it's not a pelican. He's the man who moved like a gyroscope from the ankles up, flapped his arms and swivelled his wrists and snapped his fingers. The man who loved dancing for the sun.

Understanding Maya

His most serene holiness Guru Baba Vivekananda Swamiji—called Baba only by those who observed his five precepts and obeyed his seven injunctions—felt a quiver in the cosmos: a ripple spread by matter passing from one dimension to the next. "Someone approaches," he announced.

"Darn right," Adrian Burnett said. "The bagman approacheth."

The grating voice made Baba drop until his robes brushed the floor. He lowered himself completely and opened his eyes.

"How do you do that?" Adrian asked. "It's an illusion, right? That's why you keep the lights down. Even a simple trick like that would've satisfied Revenue Canada. It's not as if they wanted you to walk across the swimming pool at 24 Sussex, you know, or change the chlorine into wine."

"I am neither a fakir nor a faker," Baba calmly insisted. "Have I not said it before? The entire universe is ultimately a lie, an illusion created by God, an illusion called maya. Only God is real. He creates; he preserves; he destroys. Salvation lies in knowledge, in selfless actions, and in devotion to God."

Adrian snorted. "You still sound like a Bible thumper."

"Perhaps," Baba said, "but your Bible-thumpers offer only a choice between the fires of hell and the frippery of heaven. I offer release from eternal rebirth, a release called moksha."

"Whatever," Adrian said. "I'll do the talking when he gets here, okay? I know people."

"And I do not?" Baba rose to his feet and stepped out onto the balcony. The breeze smelled faintly of diesel fumes and kelp, a seaway smell visitors called refreshing. The setting sun tinged his homespun robes pink. He spread his hands to indicate his guests on the lawn below. They lay as peacefully as infants in baths of warm oil. Guests, perhaps, but wealthy enough to afford his week-long island retreats. He called this one, "Physician, Heal Thyself."

"If you ask me," Adrian said, "some of them aren't all here. In body, maybe. Definitely not in mind."

"Dear boy," Baba said, "that is precisely what I offer your fellow Canadians: what I now offer millions of my fellow Americans: to leave their bodies among the concrete and glass, to send their minds past Andromeda to the edges of the silky Milky Way."

Adrian spaced his words for effect: "Give, me, a, break."

Baba smiled mischievously as though he had been parodying a parody of himself. He enjoyed nettling men like Adrian: function-aries, who wore cynicism like suits of armour while they duelled in boardrooms.

"Let's go over the strategy again," Adrian said. "I know, we've done it lots, but I can't afford to screw up my first case." He looked about before continuing. "Tonight we hand over the donation. The bagman holds it till your exemption gets through cabinet. Gives you a month or so to make good on the cheque." He blurted, "I still say you should make it a million US like they asked. The exchange rate's dropping, you know."

"Dear boy," Baba said, "I am not running a charity here."

Adrian responded with, "Haw, haw." When Baba dismissed him, Adrian left with a parting shot: "Don't forget, your unflappa-ble holiness. The visitors' dock, ten sharp."

After Adrian's footsteps faded, Baba re-entered his dimly-lit study. He sighed and began climbing a spiral staircase. As much as they tried his patience, he needed people like Adrian to handle temporal details while he concentrated on spiritual ones. If that meant compromising his principles for his followers' sake, so be it. God would understand. Adrian's had been the only firm in Ottawa willing to guarantee success, clearly because it switched with ease from the legitimate to the nefarious. His followers would thank him for it one day. But not these guests, who now trooped indoors for their supper of yoghurt and fruit. True followers would soon embrace him across Canada. Even more than the professionals and dowagers suffering from angst, the true have-nots needed him to make sense of their lives. He knew he was genuine even if the revenue department did not, and his followers would know it, too. He was also pragmatic. He could never admit, for instance, to having rediscovered his Hindu roots by visiting a somnipath, a disbarred physician who languished behind an erotic massage parlour in Times Square. Such things were best kept secret. Was it Baba's fault he had been born to a Catholic father and Moravian mother? At heart, Baba was Hindu, as he had been in his previous life.

The stones unexpectedly trembled beneath his feet. Again he felt someone was coming: someone other than the revenue minister's campaign manager.

Baba stepped into open air and savoured the view from the turret. Up here, the air smelled truly refreshing. The eastern horizon grew dark. A freighter sounded its horn to ward off smaller craft in the channel. The merchants of Alexandria Bay, New York, still resented him for refusing to allow boats to bring tourists here, but Heart Island was his now. "Of course, Mr. Swamiji," the town historian had told him, "these Thousand Islands have seen their share of eccentrics, but you have to realize people around here like their eccentrics to be historic. Take Mr. George Boldt, who started out as a bellhop and ended up owning the Waldorf Astoria. First he reshaped your island so it looked like a heart; then he built your castle. What some men do for their wives!" After a throaty chuckle, Baba gazed at the north shore of the St. Lawrence River, past the imaginary boundary snaking across local marine charts. He shook his head with dismay. How could he possibly raise a million dollars in one month? Had he been a Christian, he could have worked a miracle, but he wasn't one, certainly not the sort who marketed lawn sprinklers shaped like the Star of Bethlehem.

The wind rippled through feathers. He turned to watch an orange-brown kestrel hover in search of prey. Suddenly, the falcon — easily mistaken for a sparrow hawk — dove among the shadows lengthening below the turret.

The blueing wisps of cloud whirled as if in a cosmic wind. He felt faint. He also felt confused. There was no such thing as a cosmic wind. The cosmos represented order; yet this wind did not stem from its antithesis, chaos. There was some peculiar sense of order in this wind, even if it did swirl about him to upset both his

physical and spiritual balance. The grating squeal of machinery
grew behind him, and he turned. The cooling breeze no longer
smelled refreshing; it smelled of plastic. The air shimmered as
though a hundred tiny mirrors refracted the setting sun. They
aligned themselves into the form of a young woman. Startled by a
sudden flash, he closed his eyes, then opened them to find, yes, a
young woman who looked vaguely astonished. After her eyes
focused, she squeezed her limbs as though assuring herself that
none had broken.

"Hello?" he asked.

She wore a violet jumpsuit that shimmered like amethyst — a
single piece of cloth so snug that, in his younger days, he might
have imagined her spraying the fabric onto herself. Had it been like
buff sandstone, a light brownish yellow, she could have passed for a
magically animated statue from the temples of Khajuraho. But
those maidens looked demure in spite of their poses; this one
appeared self-conscious, as if she bore her beauty like a curse. A
silvery belt encircled her narrow waist. On one cocked hip, she
clasped a video camera. When she released it, it dangled from a
strap fastened to her epaulette. She pressed her hands in front of
her chin and bowed while saying, "Namaste, Swamiji."

He returned the bow over clasped hands. "You may call me
Baba if you wish," he said, "and you are—?"

"Miss Maya Kumar," she announced. "ICS."

How an officer of the Indian Civil Service had materialized on
his turret intrigued Baba. "I suppose you are from the future?" he
asked.

"Actually, I'm from the present," she said. She spoke like an
Indian raised on American movies, with an accent even more
pronounced than the clipped Bostonian phrases that still crept
into his speech. She beamed now like a child with an unbearable
secret. She glanced at a wristwatch, a miniature computer of sorts.
"I've just returned from the past," she said, "where I've done some
filming."

His calm "Oh?" nettled her.

"You were quite the philanthropist in your previous life," she
said. Her baiting manner reminded him of Adrian's. "Extremely
successful, yet you squandered a king's ransom and died impov-

erished in a Bombay gutter. I assume you know all this?" He inclined his head modestly. "I'm part of an experiment Rajiv Gandhi ordered," she announced. "Part of a top-secret task force that travels back and forth in time. Forgive me, Swamiji, but you're my first assignment. I don't know how to prepare you for this, so I'll just say it." Perhaps he still did not act as flabbergasted as she had expected him to. Perhaps he looked too bemused. Whatever the reason, her next words tumbled loudly from her lips; tumbled much as the Ganges River did from heaven onto Shiva's locks; thundered much as its waters did into the nether world, where they cleansed the tainted souls of the sixty thousand Sons of Sagara. "I'm here," said Maya Kumar, "to collect the taxes you owe. From your previous life."

* * *

Baba's two worlds, the spiritual and the temporal, swam before his eyes. Only decades of discipline saved him from doing any more than tugging at his beard and sputtering, "What!"

Maya appeared proud of herself for having discomfited him. Her defiant tone changed to one more matter-of-fact as though, by playing the functionary, she could retain the upper hand. "My calculations place the figure at roughly two million dollars," she announced. "A certified cheque will do."

"Who does this Rajiv Gandhi think he is?" Baba demanded. He resisted the urge to wave his hands like a marooned sailor. "A mere technocrat! A domestic airline pilot steering an overloaded barge of state on high seas!"

She pursed her lips. She no longer stood with one hip cocked. Her breasts rose and fell with the mounting excitement of a huntress poised to lance her prey. "It's not easy running a country like India," she declared. "We need every rupee we can find. By the end of the century, we'll overtake China as the largest nation on earth. We're already a generation ahead of them in science. I'm living proof of that. To develop such an idea takes foresight. To implement it takes courage."

During these and other fervent words, images flashed before his eyes. She changed from a concierge storming the Bastille to a farm wife loading muskets for the Continental Army to a peasant waving her flail at Czarist troops. He heard the "Marseillaise," the "Star Spangled Banner" and the "Red Flag," all as discordant as the rehearsal of a school band. "You may stop," he said. He had regained his composure with a long, shallow breath. "When must I pay?"

"During this lifetime," she replied. "The interest has been accruing for some ninety years, but you'll receive a discount for prompt payment." She tried to regain her breath but failed. "If it'll make you feel any better, the funds are earmarked for education and health. You can appeal to the PM, but—"

"An apple has a peel," he said. When she frowned, he explained, "That was a jest."

"Oh." She forced a crooked smile. The smoothness of her skin, especially the absence of lines around her eyes, told him she rarely laughed.

"May I copy your tape for my records?" he asked.

"I've already transmitted one copy to my supervisor," she warned, "so don't bother erasing it."

After she handed it to him, he secreted the black cassette in a butterfly sleeve of his robes. His few powers paled in comparison to those of a woman who could travel through time. His estimation of Rajiv Gandhi — even now embroiled in a scandal surrounding his minister of defence — rose. Baba knew he could do little at present, so he invited Maya to tea.

She accepted with a glib, "Why not?"

Once downstairs, he served her tea and biscuits. He barely noticed her beauty now; only that she appeared intent on masking a kindly disposition with the stony one of a civil servant burdened with the destiny of millions. "You look weary," he noted. "Will you rest after your mission?"

"We get as much time off as we spend in the past," she said. "It took me a month spread over ten years to film your activities. You were very careless with money, you know. I assume you've learned your lesson?"

"Let us not speak of it," he said. "How do you keep your project secret from the rest of the ICS?" He did not consider himself a devious man, but he had a motive for changing the topic. As long as he discussed his dilemma, he could never solve it, so he focused his conscious on her while his subconscious roamed the cosmos in search of solutions. He focused so intently, he heard the explanations before they left her lips. Her amethyst clothing suited her, for the gem symbolized sincerity.

"It's the easiest thing to keep secret," she was saying. "We're either travelling or on holiday. We report to the PM while he pretends to golf. He recruited me himself when I was an air hostess. He really is a great man, you know."

To stop her subsequent rambling about nonalignment and dual-use technology, Baba asked, "What does your family think of your career?" He regretted the question, for her eyes flashed like polished jet.

"They don't know," she said, scowling. "And if they knew, they wouldn't care. It was my mother's idea I become an air hostess. She even wanted me to enter the Miss India Pageant, but I was too old or too something for the local judges. Too difficult, probably. Soon she'll want me to marry some gazetted civil servant. I'm not about to give her the satisfaction of bragging about her son-in-law. All my life she's treated me like nothing more than a brainless doll. Now she wants to watch me play house for real. If she really wanted me to play the dutiful Indian girl, she should have made less free with her tongue! And her hand." Maya's face burned so brightly, he saw a white hand imprinted on her left cheek. Even so, the fury in her voice disturbed him when she vowed, "I'll marry when I'm ready, and I'll marry whomever I please. I'll show her how children should be raised!"

For the first time since having rediscovered his spiritual roots, Baba felt sad, sad not for himself, since he had long ago relinquished the desires of the heart — desires which led to self-pity when unfulfilled. He felt sad for her. She appeared poised on the edge of a chasm. She looked so desirable that in centuries past she could have made fools of kings; yet who would marry a woman so embittered she would use her children for revenge? His sigh ended the sudden rise of temperature in the room. He leaned across the tray to clasp her hand and slowly peel back her fingers. He feigned surprise when he found her hand empty. "You see," he said. "Your anger is like the centre of a clenched fist. Open, and there is

nothing, but keep the fist closed, and you can always imagine
something hidden there: something brooding, gnawing at your
soul like a plague-infested rat."

"I didn't come here for enlightenment," she scoffed. She drew
her hand back.

"I do not offer it," he said. "All I offer is to help people make
sense of their lives. In that way I am no different from an astronomer—an ancient philosopher, really—searching for the music of
the spheres. If you happen to leave with your hands open, what
harm is there?"

She nodded pensively at the lattice screen behind him. It hid the
only television set in the castle. It also hid a video recorder and a
collection of western films about India: everything from chestnuts
like *Elephant Boy* to less condescending fare like *Heat and Dust.* He
liked to watch them alone while feasting on Indian sweets and
savouries. Even a guru was entitled to pamper himself. A smile
played across his lips. When he judged the time right, he slapped
his knees and rose. She willingly took his hand and rose. "Since
you need a holiday," he said, "why not remain here for a while?"

"I have no time," she said. She walked away with her shoulders
squared as though she had just remembered who she was: a
commando in Rajiv Gandhi's microchip army. She was not the
child of her own mother but of Mother India herself.

"Dear girl," Baba said, "you have all the time in the world."

She turned, laughing.

Adrian burst into the room.

Baba felt as though he had spent the past hour in the eye of a
hurricane.

"It's quarter after!" Adrian scolded. "Your visitor's been cooling
his heels on the dock for nearly—!" His eyes widened when he saw
Maya.

"I have been entertaining a more important visitor," Baba said.
"I shall join you soon. I will need a moment to copy the tape," he
told her.

He gestured toward the stairs, but she addressed Adrian as she
might a clerk: "Would you direct me to the ladies' room?"

"Down the hall," he stammered. "Second door to the right."

After she slipped out, he said in a low voice, "Now I know what cantilevered means!" His eyes gleamed with a lust Baba had thought impossible in one who had likely spent his previous life as a courtly eunuch. Perhaps Adrian and Maya would make a good match. "What was that!" Adrian demanded.

Baba turned away to hide his annoyance. "A child's soul trapped in a woman's body," he replied. "I fear I may be unable to save her from herself—"

"Ask me if I care," Adrian said. "The guy's not waiting around all night. This is really bad form, you know. He's starting to pressure me for US dollars. Hard currency—"

"Then your commission will increase," Baba said.

"I'm on salary," Adrian declared.

"I meant your firm's commission, of course," Baba said.

"It's just business," Adrian snapped. "You get your exemption, the minister's campaign fund gets a boost, and I get—"

"Let us cease with these word games," Baba said wearily. "The evening has been much too taxing." He scowled at Adrian's haw, haw. "Tell your visitor I am considering his request," Baba commanded. "Show him the grounds. He may like the swan pond. And do stop braying like an ass."

"For your information," Adrian said, "I'm still on your side. I've figured out how you can raise the million." He bided his time until Baba nodded apologetically. "I got the idea when I saw this sparrow hawk carry off a shrew just now. All you have to do is tell your guests here that God appeared while you were levitating. It's not really a lie. Call it an illusion." He smirked at Baba's mild scowl. Adrian raised his hands and tried to imitate a preacher: "Alas, my children, if I do not raise this money, God will pluck me from my earthly form, this one you so adore. He will return me to earth as a gila monster. Perhaps even a brutish komodo dragon. Can you let such a thing befall your beloved—?"

Baba turned on his heel and headed for the spiral stairs. He allowed the word "leeches" to cross his mind. Adrian was no hypocrite, but he could be as mercenary as the rest: all the accountants, publicists, lawyers, and even the elected officials who acted less civil than their servants. Too annoyed by this new demand for payment in hard currency, too disturbed by the demand for unpaid taxes even in soft currency, but mainly distracted by Maya's future, he barely felt the stairs tremble once more. He also forgot to copy her tape. He realized it only when he felt its weight in his sleeve after he reached the open air. He once again savoured the view from the turret. It often soothed his mind.

A great blue heron approached the southern end of the island — in the left auricle of the heart shape. It glided past the Alster Tower, which still reminded him of the painted lids of shortbread tins. The heron was gangly like him. On his first visit to these islands, he had watched a great blue at the edge of a marsh. It stared intently while waiting to thrust its beak at a pumpkinseed sunfish. Each time the heron missed, it sulked, but when it finally caught one, it strutted. After its meal, it alternated satisfied grunts with a trumpeted, "Kwark, kwark!" That first heron now reminded him of Maya, but he did not want to be the sunfish. After rounding the granite turret of the tower, tonight's great blue landed in the waters beyond. It tried to float among a raft of black-headed greater scaup, but it looked awkward and conspicuous. It had been born a heron; it could never imitate a duck. He gazed past the Alster Tower, dark against the lights of Alexandria Bay. Perhaps he was not the sunfish. After all, he was a predator of sorts. Yes, he was the great blue heron, and Maya was the kestrel, often mistaken for a sparrow hawk.

The greying wisps of clouds whirled as if in a cosmic wind, one still too orderly to be chaotic. This time he did not feel faint. He felt overwhelmed by *déjà vu.* The pleasant whine of well-oiled machinery grew behind him, and he turned. Once again the smell of plastic filled the air. It shimmered as though a thousand tiny mirrors refracted the rising moon. They aligned themselves into the form of a woman. Ready for the flash this time, he closed his eyes, then opened them to find, yes, yet another woman before him. Her eyes focused and she squeezed her limbs, but she did it quickly as though it were second nature to her.

She too wore a jumpsuit, but it revealed less of her form than Maya's did. This one shimmered sapphire instead of amethyst, and it had been cut loosely, with padded shoulders and flared legs. A gold belt encircled her waist. The obvious contrasts with Maya reminded him of her. If the woman also worked for Rajiv Gandhi, both she and Maya must know one another. The woman, well into middle age, might even be Maya's supervisor. Sapphire symbolized clear-thinking, after all; yet she reminded him of Maya's mother, she of the sharp tongue and quick hand. The newcomer held no camera. She clearly left the field work to her subordinates. She pressed her hands in front of her chin and bowed while saying, "Namaste, Swamiji."

He returned the bow over clasped hands. After saying, "Baba will do," he cleared the last traces of *déjà vu* from his mind.

Instead of introducing herself, the woman said, "You don't seem surprised to see me."

"Should I be?" he asked.

"It can't be every day a time traveller materializes on your roof," she noted. She too spoke with the accent of an Indian raised on American films. "You'll be meeting another one soon," she said, "in about three weeks, but you can tell her to ignore her mission. Mine over-rules hers. I'm from the future. Part of an experiment Rajiv Gandhi ordered twenty years ago."

"The tax force," Baba quipped.

"How could you know that?" she asked.

"Because," he said, "the traveller who will supposedly arrive in three weeks did so earlier this evening."

"That can't be!" she cried. She squinted at her wristwatch computer.

"Perhaps it is a bureaucratic foul-up," he suggested. "Perhaps one of your time traffic controllers fell asleep."

She laughed, first with unease, then with self-deprecation. "Nothing that unlikely," she said. "I travelled east to get here. I must have crossed the international date line twenty-some times, but if that's so—?" Her voice trailed off.

"At any rate," he said, "your over-ruling her mission raises an interesting legal question. Does the future take precedence over the past, or does the past set a precedent for the future?"

Maya would have taken him seriously, but this woman did not. She even chuckled. "We have a new program to boost India's revenues," she said. "You can ignore the demand you received for taxes from your previous life."

"Thank you," he said, relieved.

"Instead," she announced, "you'll have to place roughly four million dollars in trust. It should triple by my time. You could say that for fiscal purposes, the future takes precedence over the past. There's no case law on the subject, but —" Her eyes shifted from his, which showed signs of exasperation. "My god," the woman gasped, "she's still here!"

"I did not say she had left," he said, but the newcomer was not listening.

She backed to the castellated edge of the turret. "Keep your distance," she ordered.

From the head of the stairs, Maya asked, "And just who are you?"

He stepped aside to watch both women, the junior one with her belt silvery and the senior one with hers gold. He could not decide whether to feel amused or perturbed, for he already suspected the answer. "Dear girl," he asked Maya, "do you not recognize her? This is how you will look in twenty years. No, Rajiv Gandhi has not recruited your mother as well. Allow me to introduce you. To yourself."

Baba watched the younger Maya, whom he now thought of as Maya One, approach her elder self. This latest tax notice from the future; the nullified one from the present; Adrian and the minister's campaign manager biding their time on the dock — all these problems had become mere side-shows to the main event.

"Stay back!" Maya Two ordered again. "You know we can't touch."

"How so?" Baba asked.

"It could be fatal," Maya One said. "It would be like matter touching anti-matter: the end of the universe. Or so the boffins claim." She examined her elder self critically as if searching for signs of aging: of sagging flesh or wrinkled skin.

Baba saw few such signs. Maya had aged — would age — gracefully.

"I'm not willing to take the chance," Maya Two said. "I must go." She tapped commands into her wristwatch computer, but her fingers moved slowly.

"Wait!" Maya One said. She retreated a step to reassure her elder self. "Are you really me?"

Maya Two tilted her head as if to say, can you doubt it?

"Tell me something then," her younger self pleaded.

When Maya Two frowned, Baba asked, "Can you deny your own self a few answers?" He sensed the same determination in Maya Two as he did in Maya One, but the elder also appeared more weary — whether from her travels or from a change in outlook, he could not guess. He did not really want to know. He found himself as fascinated with the two Mayas as a child might be by the spiralling climb of a bird, especially the gyre of a falcon: so precise and yet so resonant. What if a Maya from every year of her life met on his roof? It would be like sitting in a barbershop with a mirror in front and another behind; like seeing an endless reflection of one's self, yet each version would age slightly in one direction and grow more youthful in the other.

When Maya Two finally sighed, her younger self asked, "Will I have children? I mean, did I have children?"

Maya Two shook her head. "I never married," she replied, "not in this century at any rate. The PM himself tried to match me with one of his bright young men, but he was a member of the task force like me. The tax force," she said and smiled faintly at Baba. It pleased him that Maya had developed — would develop — a sense of humour with time. "We all laughed in private over that," she said. "The PM offered to give me away as father of the bride and to be the groom's best man. I actually considered it if only to see the look on my mother's face when I took my new husband home. Why, we could even have spent our honeymoon in the past, camped on the shore of the Agra River while Taj Mahal was being built. But it was all just fantasy, something to chuckle over while the PM gave us those periodic pep talks."

"You mean his inspirational speeches," Maya One said.

Baba smiled to himself. Even more than the sense of humour, it pleased him that Maya had developed — would develop — a healthy skepticism with time.

"I forgot how idealistic I was at her age," Maya Two told him. "Shall I tell you what happened to the taxes I collected?" she asked her younger self. "The taxes you will collect? They pass from the PM's control once he deposits them in the treasury. Some go to line the pockets of his ministers. Some even go to buy arms. Maybe half

go to education and health, but half isn't good enough. It is for him
of course, but he's a pragmatist even now. How else could he have
survived so long in public life?"

The growing indignation on Maya One's face prompted Baba
to suggest, "I believe your younger self is more interested in
personal matters." Why deny it? So was he.

The younger Maya's eyes glistened with tears. "You mean I
never married?" she asked.

"Oh yes," her elder self replied. "Amma — my mother and
yours — tried to force me into a match with a widower fifteen years
my senior, but I merely hid in the past. That's where I married, and
that's where I nearly did myself in, because I found myself impersonating Sultana Razia. I assume you're familiar with Indian
history?" she asked Baba.

"Not as much as I could be," he said.

"She was the daughter of Iltutmish," Maya One told him. "A
slave king who ruled North India during the thirteenth century.
He named his daughter to succeed him, because his sons were
incompetent. That's all I remember from school."

Maya Two smiled fondly at her younger self. "He may have
named his daughter," the elder Maya said, "but I was the only
woman to occupy the throne of Delhi."

Maya One cried, "What!"

Baba merely sat down, cross-legged, to listen while the elder
Maya roamed the past in her memory.

Maya One leaned against the head of the stairs and also listened
— first skeptically, with her arms crossed, then in a more receptive
attitude.

"I spent four years in the court," the elder Maya said. "All but
six months impersonating Razia. She refused to accept the throne
because she knew the Forty Amirs, the powerful Turkish nobles,
would never accept her as queen. I was under the roof of Jamal-
Ud-Din Yaqut, the keeper of the royal stables, and he convinced
Razia to change her mind." Maya Two smiled as though embarrassed at her own deviousness.

"Whatever happened to the rule about not interfering with
history?" the younger Maya demanded.

"I forgot what a stickler you were for propriety," the elder Maya said. "You should learn to trust your judgement more. You will learn to trust it more."

When the younger Maya's lips pursed, Baba prompted the elder with, "About Sultana Razia?"

"No one had ever seen her in public because she wore a veil," Maya Two said, "so I became her, and she became my lady-in-waiting. Good thing, too, since I wasn't familiar with all the Muslim customs. Some of them I got away with violating, though, like not wearing the veil and even dressing like a king." She shook her head as though with disbelief. "What a life that was. I brought peace and order to the kingdom. I built roads, dug wells, encouraged trade, dispensed justice; best of all, I established schools and libraries, patronized poets, painters, and musicians . . ." Her voice rose with pride until it trailed off. "Of course it couldn't last."

"Of course?" Baba asked.

Maya One tilted her head at him. "Of course not," she said. "Anyone can see it was too perfect."

"With hindsight, yes," Maya Two agreed, "but even I was blind to what might happen. Not until after I abolished the jaziah, the head tax on Hindus, did I see clearly. I rid the tax to stop my people from being humiliated; after all, there I was, a Hindu impersonating a Muslim. By then I had another supporter, Amir Altunia. He had developed a passion for Razia though he had never seen her face. He saw only mine and declared his everlasting love for me. After he helped me stop a coup by the other Amirs, I named him Governor of Bhatinda. He wanted to marry me, but I couldn't allow that. Supposedly because I had to concentrate on affairs of state. Really because I didn't want to get too attached to him. And yet I was, because I could see he was too good for his time. He refused to treat me as superior merely because I was a ruler. He refused to treat me as inferior merely because I was a woman. Then I made my second mistake. I named Jamal Yaqut the Amirul Umra, chief of nobles. The other Amirs weren't pleased, and they were clever, oh so clever with their poison. They poisoned Altunia's mind. He sent a message saying that since I'd betrayed him by courting another, he no longer felt himself loyal to Delhi. He meant loyal to me. I had no choice but to lead an army to

Bhatinda. What a mistake that was. All I'd wanted was to escape
the expectations Amma had for me, and I found myself even more
powerless. It was the month of Ramadan, when all good Muslims
fast from dawn till dusk. By the time we reached Bhatinda, the
army began questioning my authority. It was all so ludicrous.
There I was leading an army when all I wanted to do was talk to
Altunia, but I never had the chance. His men attacked, and Yaqut
was killed. Who says the past is so romantic? Altunia jailed me in
his palace. With me off the throne, the Amirs proclaimed Razia's
half-brother — supposedly mine — as sultan. For a while at least, I
went back to being just an ordinary woman."

"Hardly that," Baba protested kindly.

"Not ordinary at all," Maya One declared.

"Altunia visited me every day," Maya Two said, "and I found
myself unable to resist him." She stared at her feet and shook her
head while she said, "To think I'd have to go back six centuries to
find a man I could marry. After the wedding, he and I set out for
Delhi, but the new sultan met us with all the forces he could
muster. I'll never understand what drives men to war. It can't be
courage; it has to be fear, a fear of looking like cowards."

Baba nodded.

"I stood on the hill with my entourage," she said, "and watched
the enemy surround my husband. All they wanted him to do was
declare his allegiance to the new sultan, but he wouldn't. 'I'd rather
die for Razia,' he said, so they obliged him. They knocked him off
his horse and pinned him to the ground with their spears — first
one shoulder, then a thigh, then another shoulder, then —." She
raised a hand as though to wipe away tears, but she shook her head
angrily and continued. "I never reached him. The last thing I
heard was the rush of air before the arrow struck." She rubbed her
left side. "Oh, I know they say the arrow struck Razia in the heart,
but sometimes historians exercise too much poetic licence. The
next thing I knew, I was lying on a golf course with the blood
ruining my embroidered robes."

"What happened to the real Razia?" Maya One asked.

Her elder self shrugged. "I suppose she spent the rest of her life
impersonating someone's lady-in-waiting and dreaming of the
place I gave her in history — the place she could have earned for

herself had she been more than a mere woman among mere men. That's what I left behind, and what I brought back was the realization that I didn't want children after all."

"I wouldn't marry simply to have children," Maya One protested.

"But you'll feel that way soon," her elder self said. "No man could offer everything I wanted. Not even Altunia, who was only too human for my liking — too ready to believe lies, too proud to save himself. I decided all I wanted was someone to father my children —"

"Excuse me," Baba interrupted. "I thought you said . . ." He rose and frowned at both Mayas before addressing the elder: "Yes, it was you who just said she didn't want children after all."

"I knew I only wanted children to take revenge on our mother," Maya Two told her younger self.

"Not so," Baba said. He wagged a fatherly finger at Maya Two. "Your younger self already knows that. She has already admitted as much to me. You, my dear, have come to understand it."

"Who says I know that?" Maya One demanded.

"Your words betray your thoughts," he said, "and you have not thought everything through. I saw this often in my younger, more scientific days. People who have allowed the entire process to occur — to savour it, even — they understand a thing however unpleasant it sounds, because it feels true. They say, 'I understand,' not simply, 'I know.'"

"And what I came to understand," Maya Two told her younger self, "was that if I wanted children for revenge, then I would be as poor a mother to them as Amma was to me. And to you. I should say, I would be no better than her." She sounded less sure of herself now, as though she wondered whether her younger self believed her. "What I really wanted," Maya Two said, "and all the time travelling helped me to understand this, was to be the mother to myself that Amma never was to me and to be the daughter to myself that I never was to her. Don't you see? What you and I really want from life is to be our own mother and our own daughter."

Baba felt a surge of delight. "Then you are on the brink of achieving moksha," he said. "Is that not why you did not leave

immediately or, for that matter, why you did not take every
precaution against meeting your self in the past?"

Maya Two nodded silently, but Maya One looked skeptical.
She frowned at her elder self and at him as though they conspired
against her.

"Come, my child," he said, offering his hand to her. She took it
hesitantly, then squeezed it in agreement after he said, "You will
never find a man who will love you as much as you can love
yourself."

"The warning!" she suddenly cried. "Matter and anti-matter!"

"Groundless," he said. "True, you are matter to the anti-matter
of your elder self, but perhaps your boffins merely wanted to ensure
you would never meet your selves. The universe will not end. That
is scientific fiction. At the worst, your touching will subject those
around you to intense radiation. But you must touch. Oh, I have
often said it is only by achieving communion with God that a soul
can find release from the endless cycle of death and rebirth, but I
understand that I only 'knew' it until now. The two of you — the
one of you — may be the only person I shall ever help to achieve
moksha in this present life of mine. Here is the truth as I now
understand it," he said while drawing them together. "It is only by
achieving communion with yourself that you can achieve moksha.
God himself is maya. God himself is an illusion."

Even as he brought Maya One to her elder self, Baba stepped
back. Maya Two held out her arms and cried, "My daughter!"
Maya One held out her arms and cried, "Amma!" She placed her
head on her elder self's shoulder and wept. Maya Two blinked
through her tears at Baba. He raised his hand in farewell. She
moved her lips, perhaps to comfort her younger self, but he could
hear nothing except the wind sweeping those words away. Not the
changeable wind blowing from the lake onto his island. That was a
mere breeze. An orderly cosmic wind surrounded both Mayas,
entwined them until the amethyst of one fused with the sapphire
of the other into a blinding ruby light. He peered over his arm,
raised to protect his eyes. The wind swept him back toward the
spiral stairs, a wind as searing as a solar wind. The ruby light grew
so intense he could no longer distinguish Maya from her self. The
ruby light swirled about her, bathed her in the colour of content-

ment. She glowed like a red giant, a sun which consumes itself, and raised her arms to the night sky. She began to grow younger. When she called, "Thank you, Swamiji," her voice echoed like a chorus of her own countless selves. Finally, she looked as tiny as the day she had been reborn. She glowed faintly like a white dwarf star. Even as he blinked back tears, even as he laughed at the startled sky, her every being scattered throughout the cosmos. Maya had achieved moksha.

*   *   *

He fell exhausted at the head of the stairs. Feet pounded up and hands helped him rise. Voices — no, one voice — shouted, "You all right? What was that!"

The incredulous voice was Adrian's, but the rough hands belonged to a stranger, the visitor from Ottawa. Baba staggered, regained his balance, and waved them off.

"I believe we had an appointment, *M'sieu*," the visitor said indignantly.

"If you're through with your magic show," Adrian said, "we can get on with business."

"We have no business with one another," Baba said calmly. "There will be no donation."

"Now wait a minute!" Adrian protested. "You're in no position to get high and mighty all of a—"

"We shall see," Baba replied. He took the video tape from his sleeve and toyed with it. "Tomorrow I shall send a copy of this to your minister's department," he told the visitor. "It will prove I qualify for your precious exemption. I need not stoop to bribery after all, and I have no further use for your services," he told Adrian. "Even you treat me as a pretender, but it is you—and your so-called bagman here—who are the charlatans."

The visitor shrugged, said, "As you wish, *M'sieu*," and descended the spiral stairs.

"If you need a good lawyer," Adrian said, "you know where to find me. If you need a shrink, check the Yellow Pages."

Baba pointed at the stairs, and Adrian left.

The night air remained absolutely still. The sound and light had chased away the raft of greater scaup and the great blue heron, but they would return. Baba wondered what the residents of nearby islands would make of the pyrotechnics atop his castle. No doubt it would pass into local legend. When his eyes caught the lights of Alexandria Bay, he decided to visit his acquaintance, the town historian. He lived in a brick house attached to the library. A half-hour's leisurely walk brought Baba to the south shore of the St. Lawrence. When he stepped off the water onto a dock crowded with sailboats, he found two lovers staring at him while they clasped one another in fright. He reached down to wring water from the hem of his robes. Then he raised his wet hands in greeting, smiled reassuringly, and strolled past the lovers. "All is maya," he insisted. "All is illusion."

Mosaic

(I) ELLEN WHITMORE

Who? Oh, you mean Mr. Ramesh. Of course I remember him. He was the sweetest little man. If he'd been taller, he would have been quite the ladies' man, too. I don't see what that particular incident had to do with anything, but, yes, I saw it all. He walked in just after twelve, not the best time on a payday. Especially not before Labour Day weekend. He took one look at the line-up and turned to leave. Then he changed his mind and started making out his deposit slips. What did he call them now? Chits. He did the same thing every month. He deposited half his cheque and bought a rupee draft with the rest.

I don't know if I should say, but he cleared about fifteen hundred a month. He sent the draft home, to India, for about five thousand rupees depending on the exchange rate. I teased him once about having a wife hidden away back home, and he came right back with, "A Muslim can have as many wives as he pleases. I send the money to a different one each month." I thought he was serious until I remembered his telling me once he was an orthodox Hindu. When I asked if he ate meat. That's why I liked serving him. I learned something every time.

He was concentrating so hard, he didn't even hear the man. They made such a strange pair: the man with his pot belly hanging out over his cowboy belt buckle, and Mr. Ramesh in his charcoal grey suit. That's one thing I could never get over. He had such fine clothes, but he never had that extra bit of sense about how to dress. He always wore cufflinks and a tie clip, though they went out of style years ago. At any rate, he didn't even hear the man say, "Buddy, can you help me out?" Those were his exact words. The second time, the man spoke louder: "I said, can you help me out here?" This time Mr. Ramesh looked up and did something so totally out of character I thought, "This can't be the sweet little man I know!" He picked up his things and turned his back on the man. Normally he was so polite he even held doors open for other men. It was all a misunderstanding. Still, there was no reason for the man to shout what he did.

Something like . . . no, I can't repeat what he said. It makes you wonder when you hear language like that in public. Half the people in line turned to look, and some of them had the gall to smirk. Now, it's one thing to laugh at ethnic jokes. I like Irish ones myself, my maiden name being O'Reilly. But racist slurs are a different matter. Mr. Ramesh pretended he hadn't heard, but he had. He was facing me, and I saw his mouth go hard, and the tips of his ears turned red. It's strange, isn't it? You'd never think coloured people blush, but they do. You just have to know where to look. Let me tell you something about observing people. We take the train every Christmas to see our grandchildren in Vancouver, and I always insist on sitting near the washroom. Everyone has to go to the washroom, so that way I see everyone in the car at least once. I get to know a lot of people by the end of the trip. Elwood, my husband, says I'm just a snoop, but that's not snooping. That's taking an interest in your fellow man.

Anyway, I felt so sorry for Mr. Ramesh, I called him over. Some of the people in line grumbled, but if anyone deserved a good deed just then, it was him. The slip was made out exactly the same as every month, but this time he wanted a hundred dollars in cash. Almost immediately, he said, "Imagine that fellow begging in a bank! No one begs indoors in India, and certainly not in a bank." He had such a cute accent, it always made me want to laugh, as if he were imitating Peter Sellers imitating an Indian. "Oh, Mr. Ramesh," I said, "'help me out' doesn't mean 'give me money.' It means exactly what it says. Look, that lady is showing the gentleman how to make out his slip. He must be new with us." Mr. Ramesh's face fell after he looked, so I simply had to reassure him. "I think you did the right thing, though," I said. I handed him his cash and his passbook and started making out his draft. "We have people like that in India," he said. "They are called scheduled

castes. They used to be called outcastes, but one cannot call them
that any more." He raised his eyebrows, like this, only they joined
in the middle. "It would be discrimination," he said. "So now the
government discriminates against good students by lowering pass
marks in college so these people will get degrees. It results in
mediocrity only, not equality." I asked him did he mean they still
have castes in India. "What caste are you then?" I asked. "Is it not
obvious?" he said, almost proudly. "We are brahmins. We are
lighter skinned than most South Indians because, centuries ago,
our ancestors intermarried with the Aryans, who came into India
over the Hindu Kush. That fellow had no business calling me a
black man!"

No, those weren't the man's exact words, but they were close
enough. "Don't you worry about him," I said. "He couldn't know
a thing about East Indians. But just a second now. I thought
brahmins were priests. I read that somewhere." I simply had to
keep him talking, he was so interesting. "We used to be priests and
teachers only," he said. "That is why most modern brahmins are
well-educated. But now anyone can become a teacher. There is no
future in India for brahmin boys, so I came away here." I said,
"Well, you certainly are making a fine contribution to Canadian
society." I meant it. "All your people do," I said. He laughed then
and said something I still don't understand: "That is because the
government lets only well-educated Indians into Canada." Do you
think he meant we keep the uneducated ones out? "Well," he said,
putting his draft away, "I must be getting back to my office. I am
expecting good news this afternoon." I asked him oh, what's that,
but he simply grinned and waved as he walked away.

(II) KAREL LUCHINSKI

Gimme a break. I don't ask people their names. Ya can't reserve a
table 'cause there aren't any, not for sittin', an' there's lotsa guys in
suits come in. Used to be lot more 'fore that Corn-hole Centre
open' up.

Oh him. I read papers too. You sure you're not a reporter,
Sweetheart?

Okay, he came in three, maybe four times a week. Always
bought a veggie sub. Come to think of it, he does stick out in my

mind. First time he came in must've been, Christ, I don't know.
Asked for ground chilli peppers on his sub. I told him, "You want
ground chillies, go find a pizza joint." Yeah, he was in that day all
right. I remember those two girls were in here. Do you believe it?
Twelve-thirty on a Friday and I could swing a cat in here. Hey,
know how to make a cat go woof? Use a bit of starter fluid, light a
match and it goes, "Whhooof!"

The girls that were in here same time as him. Came in just
before and ate in. Didn't ask their names either. Made a real mess
and didn't throw their garbage in the can. But they were whores, I
know that much. You can smell them a mile away. This neigh-
bourhood always smelled of whores and it's getting worse. Used to
be they hung out at the hotel other side of Broad. Then people
around there got all pious. Cops shut it down, made it respectable.
So where do they hang out now? Half a block that way, past the
bank. Maybe not such a bad idea. Deposits, withdrawals.

It's coming back to me now. What they looked like, I mean. I
only noticed because the guy kept staring at them. One of them
was about your, ah, his height. Couldn't've been more than
fourteen. I don't care if it was hot that day, I'd blister my daughter's ass if she dressed like that. Problem is, she does. Now this first
whore, she was dressed like she was open for business. Haw, haw!
Get it? Used to be the government's motto. Had a yellow halter top
on. Hell, her old man could've strained Sterno through it, that top
was so skimpy. Plus she was wearing these shiny blue gym shorts
and sandals. I've seen more cotton on a Barbie Doll. No wonder
the little guy's eyes were popping out of his head. He pretended he
was trying to make his mind up what to order. As if he ordered
anything but a veggie and a milk, day in, day out. Now the other
girl, she was older. More sensible, too. Didn't have a sign saying,
"Rape me," across her chest. Wore a red tube top and real tight
jeans. Bet nothing got between her and her Calvin Kleins! Only
she wasn't the Brooke Shields type. Sort of dumpy, with boobs like
sacks of flour. Bit on the dog side. Hey, know how to make a dog
go meow? You freeze it, lay it on a table saw and it goes,
"Nnneeow!"

Funny thing but she was white, so I thought maybe she wasn't a
whore after all till she starts coming on to him. Right here, in front

of the cash. Smiles real nice and says, "Hi, want to go somewhere?"
That pisses me right off. I yell, "Hey, I'm selling subs in here, I
ain't selling ass!" She just shrugs and goes back to her friend, but
the guy actually a takes step over. "Go somewhere for what
purpose?" he asks. Is he kidding or what? Thinks they're tour
guides or something? The younger one, the native Barbie Doll
looks him straight in the eye and says, "To fuck." They start
laughing and so do I. Who wouldn't've? The guy had it coming.
He was practically slobbering over Miss August there, checking her
navel for staples maybe. But when he turned around, he didn't
look pissed off at all. Sort of squared his shoulders and said, "One
vegetarian submarine and a white milk, please." In that Poonjab
voice of his. I had everything ready so I handed it over. He must've
been pissed off, though, because he paid with a five and and walked
out before I could make change. Maybe he was just embarrassed.
Just the type who would be, all clean hands and genteel. Don't get
me wrong. I keep these hands clean because they handle food, but
these nails have seen their share of dirt.

No, I didn't go after him. Gimme a break. Christ, he must've
had money to burn. Me, I have to work for a living, on my feet.
Look, you want a coffee or what? It's on the house, but you don't
have to drink it on the roof. Haw, haw! Get it?

(III) JONI LEWVAN

You know what gets me? Ramesh was the only guy I ever worked
with who never made a pass at me. When he talked to me, he
looked at my face, not my body. He had class. I'm not crying the
blues about how tough it is to have looks, but the way some guys
look at you sometimes, it's like you're a banana they're itching to
peel. I can see if it happened to a guy like Joe Tschepurny (he's one
of the other consultants), but why a nice guy like Ramesh? Getting
fired, I mean, not. . . . You know what Joe does if I'm wearing a
low-cut dress? He makes sure he's got a handful of paper clips, and
when he walks past the word processor, he tries to toss one in here
—two points if it slips down. Honestly. Ramesh told him off once,
just after starting here, so Joe stopped. I was so proud of him.
Ramesh, I mean.

That's when we had the going-away lunch for Mel Smith, at the
Chelton. He's our old business manager. Ramesh said he couldn't
make it on account of having a doctor's appointment, but I knew
he was just making excuses. He came to a barbecue we had on
Willow Island in June a couple of months after he started. A meet-
the-clients do. You get good at saying, "Now, now!" when they get
you alone and hum, "You Light Up My Life." He was so tongue-
tied, he just stared at the lake all afternoon. He was the only one
who showed up without a date. Poor guy. He just didn't fit in.
After four months he still called Mel, Melvin, and Joe, Joseph. Al
and Yvan he always called Mr. McKendrick and Mr. Larouche.
They're the ones the outfit's named after? McKendrick-Larouche
Consulting. Mel said once Ramesh was too....
    Not just distant. Aloof. But that's what I liked about him. It's
like being introduced to a guy at a cabaret, and every time he
catches your eye, he sort of bows. You know if you even dance with
him, you'll end up not liking him as much. That's what being
married is like, I guess. If I had to do it all over again, I'd still marry
Steve — it's just that before we got married I never thought I'd be
hiding his hockey equipment. So he wouldn't sneak out of the
house for a game with the boys. Honestly. I put my foot down last
winter when he broke his nose again.
    I left the lunch a couple of minutes early to drop by the
hardware store and get Steve's cheque. Ramesh was in his office
when I got in, just after one I guess. He was kind of down, but after
I told him Al and Yvan asked about him at lunch, he brightened up
for a sec. He'd been waiting to hear about this survey he was
designing for one of our clients. Then he went sort of dull-eyed, so
I figured I'd sit right down and try and cheer him up. When I asked
what the matter was, he said, "Oh, it is nothing." He always talked
like that — like he learned his English from a book coming over on
the boat. Then he told me how he'd made a fool of himself at the
bank. "Oh Ramesh," I said, "that guy probably didn't even need
the help. I remember this Indian pulled the same stunt at the credit
union last week. Expected everyone to help him and tried to butt
in ahead of me. The main problem with guys like that — I meant
the guy at the bank, not the Indian; everyone knows they've got it
rough — is they don't have enough pride." Ramesh thought about

MOSAIC   115

that for a while and said, "It is probably true what you say about pride. I suppose that is why I am still angry at the fellow. Why could he not have tried to fill a chit and taken it to a teller? She would have helped him." Then he bursts out with, "No one helps landed immigrants here! We have to work harder than white men, because we have no constitutional right to be mediocre!" I laughed at that part. "Oh Ramesh," I said, "you don't have to work harder. You're smarter than us. All the Indians I've heard of are doctors or lawyers or big-shot professors." That's true, you know. The doctor who operated on my mom's spine is East Indian. You won't find many of them running grocery stores like the Chinese people do. Though I hear there's one just opened up near the General. Ramesh used to buy pickles and stuff there. Not dill pickles, mango and lime. He liked his food hot, and I don't mean temperature-wise. He kept a jar of ground chillies in his filing cabinet to eat with his subs. He always had subs for lunch, or cheese sandwiches. That's where he kept those newspapers he read during lunch, flimsy ones that came rolled up in brown paper. First time I opened one, I thought it was an Indian skin mag or something. I wouldn't blame him for reading them, though. I don't know how anyone could live alone like that, but then he has this girl waiting for him back home. I still don't see why he didn't just bring her over here.

He told me once, but I'm lousy with long names. Can you imagine having someone arrange a marriage for you? No way for me, boy. Ramesh said when he finished his degree, he wrote home to his mom and asked her to find him a wife. She sent back a list of six girls with — would you believe it — their pictures. He picked out the three he liked best and went back to India to meet them. He got along really well with one of them, and they decided to get married after he saved up some from working here. Isn't that the craziest thing you ever heard? I wouldn't kiss a guy my mom picked out for me, never mind . . . let him touch me. Ramesh never talked about her much, but he said once her name was really poetic and she could play the violin. Not that I know anything about classical music. I could listen to Waylon and Willie till kingdom come. Plus Anne Murray. It really gets me when they talk about that farmer who's always chasing her. They always say he's from

Saskatchewan. They drag out "Sas-katch-e-wan" like it's the boonies. Honestly.

The only thing you could call unusual was after Ramesh went into Al's office. After I got back to the word processor. The door was closed but you could hear them yelling. I even heard Al call Ramesh a wimp. Ramesh opened the door and said something foreign-sounding to Al. Then he slammed the door and walked into his office. He didn't look mad. He just looked . . . defeated if you know what I mean. Didn't even look at me when I asked, "You okay?" Ten minutes later he left with a cardboard box. I went in his office and saw his degree wasn't on the wall, and the garbage can was full of those flimsy newspapers. He — Oh, shoot, there I go again. I'm sorry. I can't help it. It's just so unfair. I mean, why him of all people?

(IV) AL MCKENDRICK

Sorry about the mess. These are just temporary quarters till we move to the new location. Business is booming. So, let's kick this thing off. Now there's one thing I want to set straight from the start, so there's no misunderstanding. I didn't put Ramesh on waivers because he was Indian. Or because he was short or had an accent. The people we play ball with don't care about such things. They want results. Of course I knew what a blow losing the job would be to him, but it's happened to all of us. Ramesh was out of his league, and he fumbled it. We had good defence in the form of Joe Tschepurny, though. He's the one who suggested, when I first handed Ramesh the ball, we send a draft of the model to our client. To see if it was what they wanted. The answer came back pretty damn quick: n-o. Like a rebound. By the way, are you interested in sports?

Rowing, eh? I took one look at you when you walked in here and thought, "Now there's a young woman who knows how to look after herself."

Basically the contract was to study the fiscal health of volunteer organizations. Ramesh had to design a model to survey them and analyze the results. It wasn't a huge job, so I thought he could go it alone. Besides, he'd been treasurer of the international students' club at York. He had an MBA from there and a BSc in math from some Indian university. His qualifications in the statistical area were first class, and he did two years as a stat clerk in Queen's Park before coming to us. He wanted a private-sector challenge, he said, so we gave him one. Unfortunately, he knew as much about our provincial scene as I do about . . . gourmet cooking. I'm a meat and potatoes man myself. Are you hungry? There's a new steak house around the corner.

That's all right, and it's Al, remember? I won't pull any punches, even at myself. I used to shadow box until my knuckles got too bruised. Hah! Certainly I overestimated his ability to learn about the province, but there was more to it than that. We were up to our eyeballs in alligators. Joe never had time to go over Ramesh's model in detail before we sent it off.

I don't concern myself with details. Now Joe's in extra innings revising the model. Something about nominal variables being used instead of ordinal ones, and too many open-ended questions on the survey. You likely know more about those things than I do. I'll be the first to admit I wasn't easy on Ramesh, but he didn't exactly make it easy on me. If he'd been at Mel's lunch it might have been a different ballgame, but damn it all, he wasn't a team player. Never went for a drink with us after work. Didn't even enter Corporate Challenge. Yvan — Mr. Larouche, my partner — wanted me to fire him to set an example, but I convinced him to let the rookie opt for free-agent status. It was the decent thing to do. After lunch, I went to his office, the one next to the word processing station. Great girl, that Joni. You should talk to her too. Ramesh was reading his *India-Canada Times*, as usual, waiting for Joe to assign him more work. He'd always drag out a copy at coffee break and lecture us about why the Tamils were massacred in Assam or the Moslems were massacred in Sri Lanka. Sorry, it's the other way around. Last Friday, I remember he was circling an article about Sikhs rioting over that Golden Temple business, something about Mrs. Gandhi getting herself in too deep. He grinned and said, "Good afternoon," as he showed the paper to me. "These Sikhs are such violent people, you know. They would make good ice hockey players." I wasn't too amused, but I wasn't about to break the news with Joni listening. I asked him to step in here and close the door. When he saw me take the letter from our client out, he leaned

forward and said, "So, how do they like our model?" He grinned,
he was so excited. "They don't like your model," I said calmly. I
never raise my voice. The grin stayed on his face, but a twitch
started pulling at his right eye. "That's not possible," he said. "You
are making a joke." I told him to see for himself and held the letter
up for him to read. Then we had an exchange about how everyone
had approved the model before it went out. "You've embarrassed
both Yvan and myself," I said. "It practically says in here
McKendrick-Larouche doesn't know anything about the volunteer sector. If I hadn't smoothed things over, we'd be out a twenty-
thousand-dollar contract. I was late for lunch, but you wouldn't
have noticed. How did your appointment go by the way?" He
fumbled for an answer, and we both knew why. If he hadn't been
so big on playing games, if he'd only admitted he wasn't God's gift
to mankind—Womankind? Personkind. Under different circum-
stances, I might have gone to bat for him more. He said, "Sir, there
is no need for all this worry. I will revise the model." You had to
give him credit, he was cool. Even picked a piece of lint off his suit
and put it in this ashtray. Nice, eh? It was a going-away present
when I left Manitoba. Know what *Nil Illegitimi Carborundum*
means? "Don't let the bastards grind you down."

Cute? I suppose so. At any rate, I told him, "You won't revise
anything except your CV. You don't know a thing about this
province. We knew that when we hired you, but you're obviously
not too quick on the uptake. I'm sorry but you'll have to submit
your resignation." I told him to make it effective the end of
September, but not to bother coming in next month. Meaning this
month. No one can say I'm not generous, but he read my signals all
wrong and said something that riled me: "You simply want to
replace me with a Canadian. I shall report you to the Human
Rights Commission. I shall even take you to the Supreme Court!" I
didn't know whether to laugh or pick him up by the scruff of the
neck and throw him out. If there's one thing I hate, it's minorities
trading on their so-called disadvantages. It's all the rage now. Of
course, it's different with women. "You don't have a hope in
Hades," I told him. Then I remembered the day I received my
notice in Winnipeg, after the last election, and put myself in his
shoes. First comes the disbelief, then the shock, then the anger.

You need someone to show you the bright side of things. "Look," I said, "can't you see I'm trying to do you a favour? I convinced Yvan to let you resign even though UIC will penalize you for quitting. It'll look better on your CV." He stood up with his fists clenched and his eyes simply wild. I didn't know what to expect. He looked as if he'd either throw a punch or break down in tears. Punches I can handle. Tears, no. Except from women. "My people do not collect unemployment insurance," he said. That's a laugh and a half. Then he opened the door without looking behind him and said, *"Nil Illegitimi Carborundum,* Mr. McKendrick. At least I'm not being fired for being a well-known party hack as you were."

If he hadn't slammed the door I would have gone for him right there, even with Joni in the outer office. So help me, I was furious. That was truly a low blow. I was a political appointee in Winnipeg, not a hack. I'll tell you the difference. A political appointee is competent. A hack isn't. I guess that would make Ramesh a hack, eh?

I do say so. And what happened to him after he left had nothing to do with our letting him go.

(V) MYSORE, 18TH AUGUST, 1984

My Dear Son,

I received your aerogramme dated the fourth this instant. I am glad to note your duties are proceeding satisfactorily and you expect a good reception of your study. Do not work too hard. You will strain your health, especially during the coming winter, which I have heard can be very cold in the west of Canada.

Your Putu Uncle says he does not know where we have failed. Instead of coming home directly when you became bored with your duties in Toronto, why then did you move to such a God-forsaken place as Saskatchewan? He is still concerned you should secure an appointment here well before your marriage, and he has finally found one for you as purchasing officer at the ISRO factory in Bangalore. It does satellite research and assembly, and your appointment could begin 1st January. He thinks you will be very happy there, and you will be very close to Mysore, so you can visit us often.

I know your late father would be extremely proud of you. The factory is not at all like his foundry. You will have a clerk to take dictation and another to type your letters. I very much hope you will give this opportunity serious consideration.

Shakuntala's parents are anxious you should accept this appointment and be married on an auspicious day convenient to the both of you. She is very dark, it is true, but she is very good-natured, and she has taken a first class in her MSc. Also your horoscopes match perfectly. Please do not think I am insisting. I simply want to see you happily settled before I move to the ashram at Pondicherry. There I can renounce the world, but I can do so more happily if I am assured you also are happy.

Your loving Amma

Postscript. I hesitate to write this, but I feel you are postponing your return to India without intimating the reason. Do you not remember how Shakuntala's namesake, the heroine of Kalidasa's play, pleaded with her husband after he returned to court and forgot her? I realize you are not King Dushyant and this Shakuntala is not a heroine living in a forest, but please consider these words for your future peace of mind. No matter how much you earn there, you will always be a stranger in Canada.

(VI) PRAKASH DAVID

You copied the letter?

You're welcome. Nothing but the odd bill since. His mother phoned again last night. I still don't see what good flying all the way here will do. She can't even leave for another week, what with all the red tape over there. Still, I suppose she could do some good. They became really close after his father died. Now that was bizarre.

It doesn't really have anything to do with what you're after. Not directly, anyway. Ramesh's father worked his way up to foreman in a foundry. Seems one day the overhead crane got stuck, and his father decided to climb up to the catwalk to take a look. A mechanic could have done it, but Ramesh said he thought his father was trying to prove something — maybe that he hadn't gone soft as foreman. He must have, though, because he had a stroke up on that catwalk. Not that they could prove anything afterwards. He clutched his right arm and doubled over. Fell right off the catwalk, but instead of landing on the ground and breaking his back, he fell into a vat of molten lead.

You can say that again. What really hurt Ramesh was there wasn't even a body left to cremate, never mind ashes to immerse. I didn't find out about this till after he moved here. We were at an Indian film night at a prof's house in March. He was showing a classic, *Three Daughters* by Satyajit Ray. Ramesh came right up to us and introduced himself. I didn't care for him at first — he shook hands like overdone broccoli — but he knew a lot about Satyajit Ray films. Told us things like why the fellow in the beginning had to be a postmaster and not, say, a teacher. It turned out Ramesh was in town for his interview with McKendrick-Larouche, so we gave him a standing invitation to stay here till he found a place. If he got the job. Turned out he did, and a month or so later he was back for good. That's when I regretted the invitation.

It's hard to explain without going into the story of my life. He had this habit of crying, "Rama! Rama!" if he spilled something or the baby started crying when he made a funny face. My sister used to do that when she got depressed, and I still can't stand people like that, who call on God for every little thing. It's as though, well, as though I'll be contaminated by their weakness. Huh, I'm no saint. I'm no crusader, either. I'd be the last one to say that attack was racially motivated, the way they're claiming in the news. Neither was his being fired. Sure, he was brilliant, but he was out of it even after four years in Canada, and it wasn't his being an immigrant either. Guys like Ramesh would be meek and mild even if they were white. But they survive. That's what I liked about him. Like, I should say. We finally found him the place near the tracks. I'd never live in a place like that — not now, anyway — but I've lived in worse during my BFA days.

I guess he'd gone home to check the mail first, when he showed up last Friday. This was his second home. He even listed us as next of kin. That's why the police called here. He showed up around three. I remember I'd just put the baby down and plugged in the kettle. I could tell something was wrong, he looked so dejected. I unplugged the kettle and got him a beer. He could have used a good stiff Scotch, but he never drank, so a beer was a lot for him. I sat here, and he sat where you are. He liked that chair because he could see the Fafard better. Melissa's parents gave it to us last Christmas. We both think boxing is stupid, but he's sort of grown on us. We call him "George" because he was apparently modelled on George Chuvalo.

Sure, I'm good at giving advice even if I'm not asked. "The Good Doctor," Melissa calls me, after the Chekhov play I think. I told him to accept the new job. It was a gift from heaven. His mother couldn't have timed the letter better, but after we talked for an hour or so, he dug in his heels. I don't know if it was the beer — he was on his third by then and proud he could hold it — or if it was staring at "George," or if it was pride. A bit of each, I'll bet. "Prakash," he said slowly, "I cannot go back. People would laugh if they knew why." I asked so who would know. "Is that what you would do?" he asked, and I said we weren't talking about me. He let his feet fall off the coffee table. I remember the thump. It must have hurt, but he didn't seem to notice. "Oh," he said, "you are somehow better than me? You would not be in this predicament?" He was talking slowly, compensating for the alcohol. I poured some more Scotch and said, "I'm not better, just different." He snorted at that and I got annoyed. "I came over when I was five," I told him. "I grew up here but you, you grew up in India. You belong there with your family. Besides, do you think I could have got a marriage arranged like you? What would I do? Bring the woman over halfway around the world from her folks? You know damn well she'd want to go back for a visit every couple of years. What would I say? 'Sorry, Sweetie, but I'm just another struggling photographer, so find yourself a doctor'? I never thought I'd meet someone like Melissa." Then, right out of the blue, he said, "Do you recall that fellow from Guyana? Sammy someone-or-other?"

Nobody we knew. Sammy Narayan, I think. Ramesh was talking about an incident he'd told me about once. I think it happened the year he started at York. "Strange," he said. "All the bad things happen in Toronto. Those goondas pushed Sammy down on the subway train tracks, and he broke both his legs. He came to Canada to succeed and he ended up being a cripple only.

Why were all those liberal-minded people so shocked when he hanged himself? Everything was in his note: 'I cannot go back like this.'" I asked if that was him talking or you, Sammy or Ramesh. "What is the difference?" he said. "For one thing, you're a professional," I reminded him. "You told me he was a worker. You'll be better off in India than he could ever have been in Guyana. Besides, you were going to go back and marry Shakuntala after you saved some money. You've been working for more than two years." Then it occurred to me. I can be a bit slow at times. "You don't want to go back, do you?" I said. "As long as you stay here, you're a big shot to the folks back home. And what about that poor girl?" That's when he lost his temper. "Go home and leave Canada to people like you?" he said. "People who turn their backs on their ancestry? I will not go home!" I was sure he'd wake the baby. "Look at your boxer," he said. "Sometimes I think he is wondering, 'What am I doing here?' but sometimes I think he is wondering, 'I will show them!' That is what he is thinking now, and I will show them also. If I go back, people will ask me how much I am making as a foreign-returned officer. You know how they talk. They are crazy for coming to Canada or the US, any place to get away from the corruption. But I will know I did not return to earn a higher salary than my classmates. I will know I fled this place. That is exactly what people like Mr. McKendrick and you expect me to do. Such people think I am a coward. I will remain in Canada. I will remain in Saskatchewan. I will remain in Regina. But I will never walk on the same pavement as goondas like Joseph Tschepurny. He is at fault for losing my position!" Ramesh was just livid, but the baby started crying, so I got up. He started following me upstairs. When I reached the landing, I heard a thump. He'd passed out at the foot of the stairs and spilled his beer. I checked to see if he was all right. After I brought the baby downstairs, I carried Ramesh in here and laid him on the sofa. He was still sleeping when Melissa got home from work. The three of us ate out so we wouldn't wake him up. And, I guess, so he wouldn't feel embarrassed at waking up with Melissa around. He had his rules about what men did or didn't do around women. I left him a note saying he could stay the night if he wanted, but by the time we got back—after seven—he was gone.

Not so much uncomfortable around women as ... Too chivalrous would be a better way to describe it.

There's no contradiction. A man doesn't always go to a hooker because he's, um, desperate for sex. Sometimes all you really want is companionship. He didn't know any women except Melissa. As far as he's concerned, we're married, and some Indians won't even talk to a married woman unless her husband's in the room. I remember once the three of us went to see *Gandhi* when it came back. After we found our seats, I went to get popcorn. The minute I turned to go, he got up and offered to help, because he couldn't even stay one seat over from Melissa without fidgeting. The only other woman he knew was his secretary, Joni Lewvan. He couldn't very well visit her, so he sat through two showings of some movie and had a drink — a Scotch, he told me — before he went looking for Irma la Douce. Fifty dollars isn't much, you know. You can spend more than that on an evening out. I don't think losing his virginity had anything to do with it either, though he probably was one. The farthest he'd got was kissing a girl once — in Toronto, after they'd gone out for coffee or something — and he thought that was daring. He was like a kid when it came to women. He'd tell me about the great articles he read in *Playboy* or *Penthouse* and say, "Of course, I only buy them for the articles."

Look, let's leave the magazines out of it. I shouldn't have mentioned it. As for the hooker, you're confusing exploitation with the real issue. Besides, a man who goes to a hooker isn't necessarily exploiting her any more than she's exploiting him. Companionship, that's the issue. Just being able to touch someone. For a guy like Ramesh, fifty dollars is a small price to pay if he can actually hold a woman in his arms for fifteen minutes. It would be the high point of his life. Something he could romanticize till the day he died. Obviously it didn't turn out to be such a bargain.

Tell me what you find out from her if the cops do let you in. Oh, there's one other thing I liked about Ramesh besides his knack for survival. Even if his idea of survival was keeping a low profile. He had a real sense of humour. One day he brought over a song he wrote, or at least the beginning of one. How did it go? He had a thing about Sikhs. Thought they gave Indians a bad name. In

India they tell Sikh jokes the same way we tell Ukrainian jokes
here. The verse he wrote went something like, um:

> Most Sikhs you see have turbans and masculine physiques.
> Carry knives and bangles, don't shave for weeks and weeks.
> But don't forget this simple rule or they can get quite piqued:
> Every Sikh's a Singh, but not all Singhs are Sikhs!

That last line is sort of a litany in India. You know how we
remember how many days in a month, "Thirty days hath September"? The song had a lot of potential. Has, I should say. I don't
know why I think about him in the past tense. Knowing him,
though, he'll wish he were. He's the sort of person who could die of
shame. Promise me something.
    Don't try to see him after he gets better. He couldn't tell you
anything. He wouldn't. He won't need crutches, not like Sammy
Narayan did, but he'll need whatever is left of his pride.

(VII) CHARMAINE DES RIVIÈRES

I never laid a hand on th' guy. You b'lieve me, don'tcha? I tol' the
cops an' the jerk from Legal Aid an' they keep hasslin' me, 'fess up!
'fess up! like broken records, an' that son-'f-a-bitch Wayne's got
somethin' comin' if he thinks I'm takin' a rap for excess'ry. Th'
little oinkers're talkin' outa their assholes if they think they can
keep me here till they find him, an' when I get out I'll find him first
an' break his arms, th' son-'f-a-bitch!
    Talk about a weird scene. This guy you're so keen on showed up
around midnight, walking real slow with his hands in his pockets
and his shoulders all hunched up like a tough guy. I'm just leaning
against a sign, minding my own business, and he sort of slows
down as he goes past. I know the type. Too scared to ask you out,
but they keep licking their lips like you're a double fudge hold the
cherry. So I ask him instead, "Want to go out?" He sort of looks
me over real slow, like he's checking out the ingredients. Instead of
saying okay, he says, "Why not?" in this prissy voice and I think,
"Shit, another refugee." Place is crawling with them. Only he isn't
dressed like one. Has this white shirt on, nice pants, and shoes with
silver buckles. Fancy watch, too. So I tell him to follow me around

back, then I'll go in, open the door for him. Ask what his name is,
and he doesn't answer, so I ask him again, and he says, "Um,
Prakash. What's your name?" Real polite, so I laugh and tell him to
call me anything he wants. Except smoked meat; I'm not. He says,
"Very well," like he's teaching school, "I will call you Joni."
     You heard me right: Joni, like in Mitchell. I stop and look at him
then because, I don't know, the way he says it makes me feel cold
all of a sudden, like he's playing games. Turns out he was, too.
Wayne's in the bar and I get my key from him, and you know
what? The guy's still waiting in the alley near the big red garbage
can, still licking his lips. I was sure he'd chicken out. He's moving
his hands in his pockets like he's checking it's still there or
something, but he just stands there staring at my tits and I think,
"Shit, he needs an invitation." Next thing I know, he comes
running up the stairs like he's afraid he'll lose whatever he's got.
Turns out he must have. After we get in the room, I go to the can
and when I come out he's staring at the bed like he's never seen a
double before. I sit down and say, "Sixty dollars," and he says, "Of
course," so I shrug and undo my jeans. Pull everything down to the
floor, but he's still staring at my tits. Gives me the creeps, the way
he stares at everything. Then he says, "You have such lovely
breasts," and I think, "Shit, this guy's a loser or what?" You want
to see tits, you go to Victoria Park and look at the office girls at
lunchtime. Suntan in those bikinis they wear under their working
clothes like they're not really for sale, just us. I should have told
him that, but he's looking real spaced and says, "Your breasts are
like those of the ap-sa-ras." Something like that. "They are the
daughters of pleasure carved from the unyielding stone of temples." That's when I get scared for real and think, "Shit, the guy's a
psycho. Gets off just looking." But he puts his hand on my
shoulder and it's real soft, kind of nice, so I let him move it down.
But when he slides it under my top — I'm wearing my new red
tube top — I tell him, "The money first. Then you can touch." He
just squeezes my tit, and I look up to see him staring at me like I've
hit him in the balls. He practically whines, "It is so soft. It should
be firm." So I tell him, "You want melons, there's a Safeway other
side of Broad," but he doesn't crack a smile. Yanks his hand out
and takes a step back. Bangs into the dresser and doesn't even feel

it. Says, "This is all so wrong, so unfeeling. No, never mind. I have
shamed you enough." Talk about straight or what? I just sit there
and think, "Shit, the guy's a fucking social worker." That's when I
recognize him. He was in the Mr. Submarine at lunch when I went
with Pearl and she scared him off.

What do you mean so I'm the one? I never did anything to him.
Not there, not later on.

What happens is, he looks like he's going to have a fit, foaming
at the mouth or something, but he turns around and walks out
with his head high like he doesn't like the smell. I do just what
Wayne told me long time ago. I holler for one of the girls to get
him, and before I've got my jeans done up, I hear Wayne flying
down the hall and out the back. I tell him the guy grabbed my tit
and didn't pay, and he says to the guy, "You trying to get a freebie?
Fucking Pakis make more than us and try to get freebies!" The guy
looks real insulted and says, "I am not a Pakistani." Looks down
for a sec and says, "It was a mistake. I changed my mind." Wayne
just laughs and says, "After wasting her time like that? Sixty bucks,
asshole. Let's see your wallet!" The guy looks around, but Wayne's
got him backed up against the wall real good, so he takes his wallet
out, and Wayne grabs it. There's a bunch of bills, so he takes them
all and hands it back to the guy. It's all real civilized up till now, but
Wayne says, "Eighty-five bucks?" The guy starts to say, "It is for a
new battery for my car," as if we care and Wayne says, "A lousy
eighty-five bucks for all our time you're wasting? You're going to
pay. Take that watch off." But the guy says, "I cannot. My mother
exchanged a thousand rupees for hard currency, and I bought this
very wristwatch in the duty-free shop at Heathrow Airport." Then
it all happens so fast. I should have known something was up
because the guy's flattening himself against the wall like he's going
to climb it. I don't know who he thinks he is, Spiderman maybe.
Wayne goes for the watch. The guy screams and kicks him in the
balls. Wayne doubles over, starts swearing, but before the guy can
make his break, he gets one in the stomach. Not hard, but he
probably never took a punch in his life. Talk about soft. Starts
whimpering like a kid, something about, "Ra-ma, Ra-ma," and
Wayne gets a couple in to the face. That's when the guy goes down.
I just stand there, but when Wayne starts kicking the guy, I try to

pull him back. I tried. You believe me, don't you? I yell, "Let it go!"
and the whimpering stops. He must be out cold now, but Wayne
just keeps kicking, kicking, and the guy's jerking like he's being
shot. The way they do on TV? When some guy puts a couple extra
shots in to make sure. In the end Wayne's so tired out he lets up,
and we go back in. That's when I freak out. What would you do,
huh? For all I know, the guy's dead. Wayne brings me down with
some real good stuff, what he saves for when one of the freshies
wants out. They always fall for it. Next thing I know, somebody's
waking me up and the place is crawling with cops. They get the
cuffs on before I can even get my jeans up and march me out the
front with all these people staring. Saturday shoppers. The pigs
throw a blanket on top and we're off, sirens going and the whole
bit, like it was some celebrity Wayne dumped in that big red
garbage can out back. The jerk from Legal Aid says he's going to
get those motherfuckers for police brutality and some other stuff I
can't remember.

Rights? Girls like us don't have rights. Only the customer's
right. Say, do you know if the guy's okay? He won't die or
anything?

Naw, nobody told me shit about him. Just his name. Nar-ay-an-
dra Ku-mar Ram-esh. I can even spell it now, paper's having a field
day. Poor Pakis come over here looking for a better life and see
what they get. What about us? If they've got it so rough here, why
don't they just go back where they're from!

Samsara

1

Mornings I walk to the river. Greet my bodhi tree, my nagas, my ferryman, my bridge.

These are the intimacies of our dance.

Like most Indians, Sam and I take morning coffee. That is, he drinks the coffee I make and munches four Gluco biscuits. I sip water, nibble a rusk. But even as he shaves and I cook his breakfast, I can feel something has changed. I still smell the eggs before I crack their shells, but the nausea I've begun to expect — almost welcome so I can surrender, then salvage my day — refuses to arrive. The morning is different, for me if not for him.

Even as he eats, he prepares himself for his workday journey. He must pedal into Nanjangud, evade questions about me from the soda vendor who guards his bicycle, find a place on the train to Mysore, hire an autorickshaw for the bumpy ride to his college, and wash the soot and dust from his face. It's an ordeal for him, one he endures for my sake six times a week. He opens the gate, glides away while standing on the left pedal before mounting the seat. I padlock the veranda doors before closing the gate. He doesn't return my wave, and I don't expect him to. He has covered so much distance, I must imagine the whirring of the chain. His single-mindedness draws him to work. Mine draws me to the river.

Asphalt patches gleam on the road like gritty oil. The monsoons have arrived, but we've merely traded the heat and dryness and dust for heat and humidity and mud. It's still welcome. I thought it would rain all day, but the downpour lasts an hour at most. Then the sun returns. That happens in the afternoon, when the air becomes so humid it weeps.

I walk barefoot along a bund. To my left, below the path,
women thin seedlings from a paddy. The women have pulled up
the hems of their cotton saris, dark green or the colour of rust, to
form culottes of a kind. This allows them freedom to move, as bent
as they are. They have no use for petticoats; mine, under my
turquoise nylon sari, forces me to glide. The oldest woman doesn't
even wear a blouse. Her breasts dangle like the narrow, black pods
of a sword tree. My breasts, sore for twelve weeks now, will never
look like that, sucked dry by all the children her husband has
forced into her. My body is mine.

Last night Sam said, as he had before, "What about this procedure the doctors recommend? This amniocentesis." We were
listening to classical music, beamed to us by Radio Moscow on
short-wave. I allowed myself to glare in the growing darkness of the
veranda. When I still said nothing, he raised his head so the sun,
setting beyond him, formed a halo. But then saints rarely marry.
"It's harmless," he said. "There are clinics. Darling?"

"I'm listening," I said. I meant the music, Lizst's "Todentantz."
"Wait till it's over." At last I said, "I'm not worried about birth
defects."

When the Russian announcer described the next piece, I understood only Mendelssohn and "A Midsummer Night's Dream."

Softly, so my voice wouldn't disturb the still air, I recited as well
as I could remember it:

> The queen for her attendant has
> a lovely boy stolen from an Indian king.
> And jealous Oberon would have the child
> something-or-other his train to trace the forests wild.

Sam didn't laugh, didn't so much as chuckle. When he muttered, "It's you I worry about," I reached across the low wicker
table between us to squeeze his hand. He drew his back first. "They
misuse the procedure here," he said. "If the foetus is a girl, the
husband forces the woman to undergo an abortion. Many do it
willingly. They know what it's like to be unwanted by their
parents."

Over my, "That's not what I'm afraid of," he said:

"I'm not one of those men."

"I wouldn't have said yes on Valentine's if I thought you were,"
I told him.

"I don't remember you saying yes on Valentine's Day," he said.
"Seems to me you were the one who proposed."

The routine began: "I never did."

"Did too."

"Didn't."

"Did."

"Didn't."

"Did."

When I reached for his hand again, I found it reaching for mine.
The routine ended as it so often does, with our making love on the
veranda floor, cushioned with our spare bedroll. We save it for
guests we never receive. I still receive him gladly. After we learned
of my pregnancy, he changed from a gentle lover into a tentative
one, unwilling to press himself down. When he does, he lies on me
as though lying on eggs.

A woman clambers up the bund, then down to my right. A man
urges two bullocks to drag a wooden plough through mud, fetlock
deep. It dries brown on the white bullocks, grey on the sunbaked
man. The twisted end of his loincloth, pulled tight, separates his
buttocks. With her mind on her work, the woman plants seedlings
in the plough's wake. She moves crablike, bent again, while she
coaxes roots into soil under water. Paddy birds, long-legged and
grey, bide their time.

I cross the lower canal by a footbridge, and my feet thud on
loosely butted planks. I've learned not to clutch at railings which
don't exist. Here the land yields sugar cane, which needs a touch
less delicate than rice. Two boys idly weed the far end of the field.
Two girls play cat's cradle while their family's goats graze on a
distant knoll. Unseen, I cross the dirt road. It joins the town, east
beyond the bend in the river, with the ferry landing, still out of
sight to the west.

Here is my tree, called an asvatta in some of my textbooks, a
bodhi or pipal tree in others, and *Ficus religiosa* in still others. Its
leaves are dried, then painted with animals and birds or pastoral
scenes of elephants hauling teak. When I left my collection of

painted leaves behind, Sam teased me for not trusting India to be hospitable. I countered with a remark about carrying coals to Newcastle. Under another bodhi, Siddhartha sat in search of enlightenment. During those twenty-eight days, he became Bodhisattva. When he finally rose as master of the three worlds, he was Buddha. This is also in my textbooks, which I also left behind.

I continued to leave things when we reached Bombay, two months ago now. After supper in the hotel dining room, Sam insisted we dance. We did, laughed over nothing. Then I told him I planned to change my name. I'd decided that upstairs while we'd changed. I packed Sara Davies with her permapress shirt and slacks, wrinkled from the flight and damp from the heat, in the bottom of my suitcase. With my electric blue sari, a gold lamé blouse and a dark blue petticoat, I unpacked Saraswati Devi. We'd known I was pregnant since two weeks before the wedding, but to Indianize my name — that sealed our bond even more than exchanging vows could. The band played "Lost in Love," a tune by Air Supply. The Hindi words made it unrecognizable at first. He drew me close, but not enough so our bodies touched. He asked if I were sure.

"That's what Madeleine Slade did when she came to work for Gandhi," I reminded him. "Called herself Meerabehn."

"I'm no Mahatma," he insisted. "No great soul. Great, perhaps."

"No argument there," I said. After he drew me even closer, we swayed until the singer stopped in mid-croon.

"None of that, please!" a voice boomed over the speakers. "No intimacies in the dance!" We parted, and the voice said, "Thank you, Madam."

I felt myself turn redder than my hair. The few other couples held only hands, not one another. The women stared at me; the men watched Sam, envied him his foreign wife. I caught one man's appraising eye, and he looked suddenly disapproving.

"Let's get out of here," Sam muttered. The maitre d', standing with his back to the door, kept one hand in his pocket. The other remained free to accept a tip. "It wasn't her fault," Sam insisted. Then he snarled, "Jerks!"

The maitre d' ignored my apologetic glance.

Later, Sam and I made love on the sheltered veranda of our suite. Suddenly he barked, "No intimacies in the dance!"

We laughed so hard, he slipped out of me and rolled, kept rolling like a circus clown across the tiled floor. Stopped by a fern, curled around its unglazed pot like a foetus glistening with sweat, he laughed until he cried, "Ow, ow."

"Shh," I warned.

He shrugged when I glanced at neighbouring verandas.

I turned him onto his back, held his arms flat on the floor and kissed his quivering chest. "I love you, Shiamsundar," I said. He insists his relatives call him Sam, but sometimes he lets me call him Shiamsundar. It means dark, and he is.

When he said, "I love you, Saraswati," he sounded unsure. But he was also using my new name for the first time. His hands slid down from my breasts, which he'd learned to touch lightly. He nestled a fingertip in my navel. "And I love you, too," he said, sounding sure this time. "Whatever your name is."

I kissed him while I guided that fingertip lower. A salty sheen glazed the floor while I made him writhe.

A young woman circles my bodhi tree with her eyes closed. She could keep them open but seems to have no need, for she never once stumbles against the slabs ringing the tree. They bear images of nagas and naginis, some with human faces. Cobra kings and cobra queens, they live in the nether world and haunt rivers; yet they promise fertility to those who observe ritual. At last she stops, bends to touch the largest slab, rises and turns.

Startled, she cries, "Ayoh!" One hand covers her mouth. When I reach out to reassure her, she flees toward the temple beyond the tree. Sam would laugh if I told him of this, would remind me mortal men are known to fall in love with naginis when they take the form of nymphs. Rather, I would remind him of it. He's the Indian; I'm the one who should have been born Indian. I can't blame her: I must be a sight. The end of my sari protects my head yet can't hide the true colour of my hair. My eyes are as blue as lapis lazuli. My skin is pale like the dawn.

Chirping. It's louder than a cricket's. A small dark lizard suns on a slab on which a naga rears its hooded head. The lizard has dropped its skin, a split wrap incised with the impressions of scales.

While the sun warms its new skin, the lizard quivers and basks in the presence of nagas, of naginis.

On our first night in the house, after Sam and I climbed into our one rickety bed, we tucked the mosquito net carefully under the edge of the mattress to cocoon ourselves. I settled sideways with my head on his outstretched arm while he brushed my ear with a fingertip, feathered it the way I imagined he would the tiny ear of our child.

Something clacked.

"Oh, shit." That was Sam. He slid his bare arm out from under my rising head. "Lizards." The bed shook while he tugged the netting out from under his side of the mattress. "They'll keep us up all night." He tucked the netting back in place, left me lying puzzled. I followed and found him in the spare bedroom, the one we use for storage, the one in which he shaves while the rising sun brightens his mirror. Unwilling to enter, I watched him, then saw a shadow flick out an open window. He stood in the glaring cone of the bare light bulb. He was trying to scoop something out of the corner with the bristles of my short broom, a broom invented to break the back of sweepers. I turned, but he called me back with, "Look at this." He grinned like a child aching to display something morbid. I simply had to look. In the corner lay the lizard's tail. It was as long as my baby finger. The wider end looked ruby tipped, left pinpricks of blackish red where the tail flopped.

"They drop their tails if they think they're going to be caught," he said. "It lets them escape." Barely hiding his amusement at my disbelief, he shrugged. "They simply grow another one." At last the tail lay still. He eased it onto the soft bristles, slowly lifted the broom, and slapped it against the window bars. After we climbed into bed again, we tucked the netting under the mattress. We held our breaths to listen for mosquitoes that may have joined us in our cocoon. He said, "Sweet dreams, darling," and he meant it.

While we slept, the lizard's tail slid up into my womb, flopped wetly each time I turned. It became a gartersnake caught by a child swimming out between my thighs blood slicked.

In the morning, while I retched, Sam held me for the first time since the sickness began. "This is turning into a nightmare," he said.

I returned, clutching the walls, back to bed. I shook my head on the pillow, shook it insistently like a child. "India's just so insidious," I said. "It's creeping into my blood as if it belongs there, in through my eyes and ears and mouth and hands. Even my nose, but that's from being pregnant; it started before we left. Can't you feel it?" I spoke to the mosquito net, rolled back now, sagging like a furled sail. "The brightness of it, the smell of kerosene, even the rope at the well prickling my palms. It's just, so, insidious."

"From tomorrow on," he said, "I'll draw the water."

This is the day, the end of the sickness. I'm an Indian mother bearing an Indian child, one who was never meant to be born in a sterile room, far from the chirping clack of lizards. I take my place near the tree, lean back against a slab, and wait for the ferry. It's in midstream.

The ferry is made of old doors. The latches are rusting but intact, latches to which one villager has tethered a goat, another a calf. The ferryman watches me watching him, but he never smiles a greeting. Years of ferrying have bent his neck until his left ear lies flat on his shoulder. It rises and falls while he poles. The smile he saves for children is tilted like the pole. He has little use for me, for I'm content to remain here, south of the river, while he spends entire days poling from south to north, north to south. Sometimes the current drifts him east.

He reaches the dirt landing, packed by hooves and bare feet. Here he waves passengers off, waves others on. The goat butts the calf, and it moos in fright, then kicks spindly legs before finding purchase on the bank. Two young women, balancing bundles on their heads, board the ferry. So does a lone man bearing firewood. Once paid, the ferryman turns, positions himself on the left edge of his raft of doors, and pushes off. I wonder whether the river has ever flowed level with the line of his eyes; which of his sons will grow to see the world tilted so far; how and whether his wife lies beside him still.

Two nights ago, Sam and I slept apart for the first time since we were married. He was late that night. The news had almost finished on Voice of America when our gate clanged. I opened both veranda doors for him so he could lift his bicycle in. He threw it against mine, and both bells dinged. He slammed the doors shut.

He snatched the metal tumbler I keep ready for him and gulped the water. I knew that he would explain his anger, that he had been repeating the words all the way from Nanjangud; perhaps even from Mysore while he brooded on his train; perhaps even from his college gate, where the guard would have hailed an autorickshaw with, "It is for the dean himself!"

"Srinivas," he snorted. "That bloody fool Srinivas. Do you know that he did?" Sam threw himself into my chair, the one closest to the main room so I can slip easily into the kitchen. He propped his feet, made light by road dust, onto the table, then kicked off his Birkenstock sandals. "Three weeks ago I told that bloody fool to make up the lab schedules for the new term."

The news ended, and a program broadcast in Vietnamese began. Instead of turning the dial to Radio Moscow, I sat in the only other chair, the corner one.

"He doesn't tell me he's going away," Sam groaned. "A wedding at Ooty. But does he delegate the schedule to someone else?" Sam's voice rose above the commentator's.

I recognized only Ho Chi Minh City.

"I send for Professor Doctor Srinivas first thing in the morning," Sam began. "I ask for the schedule and he whines, 'I shall have it done by next week, Mister Gurudev.' He loves calling the rest of us Mister." Sam glared at his empty tumbler, clutched it as though wishing it were Dr. Srinivas's neck.

"Do you want more?" I offered.

"Know why I'm late?" he asked the tumbler. "I had to do the schedule myself. Took me all day. Not only does he go away, but he doesn't tell me he's going away so I can at least assign it to someone else. Not only that, it never occurs to him to turn around and delegate. He looks at me as if delegation is a bunch of village louts going cap in hand to some district officer. Shit!"

The tumbler flew into his bicycle, bounced up off a handlebar to clang against the trellised window. When the tumbler clattered onto the concrete floor, I clasped my hands over my ears.

"Can't you change the dial?" he snapped. "You don't speak Vietnamese. You can't even speak Kannada yet."

I hung my head, but only to hide the starting tears. The tumbler rocked on the dusty floor.

Later, we ate supper without speaking. Even the radio could provide no excuse for our silence. Radio Moscow's classical music had ended, and Sam refuses to listen to All-India Radio. Even later, after I finished washing our few dishes, I crept back to the veranda. That's where we eat, talk and love. Even from the kitchen, I could smell a sandalwood cone burning away mosquitos. From the main room, empty except for the table with its radio, I smelled a second smoke. At the far end of the room, as though Sam expected a restless night, he'd laid out the spare bedroll and hung the spare mosquito net. I stopped in the doorway to the veranda and watched an ember glow. He held a cigarette while he sat hunched. With his bare foot, he ground sandalwood ash into the floor. I'd never seen him smoke, but I said nothing beyond, "Come to bed."

"How much can one man do in such a country?" he asked, then inhaled deeply. He exhaled and shook his head. "These Indians," he said. "They're irresponsible people."

Will the ferryman reply if I ask, "Can't you see what you're becoming?" No, he will simply gaze at me with his head forever tilted, watch me as though wondering whether I can ever trust myself to his raft of doors. I too turn away, look past the ferry. Women washing clothes ignore me. Boys who scrub bullocks wish they could ignore me. Girls wave but never approach. I'm still too exotic for them. My sari is too new; my hair, though bleaching to a carroty blond, is still too red. I'm still too much a woman who delights in rivers she crosses only once.

Downstream from the ferry is my bridge, the closest of three. It has been left unfinished. Four pylons rise, one from each bank, two more from the river bed itself. Slapped by clothes, chiselled by water, the concrete bases will one day erode. Beyond rise two more bridges, close to one another. The road bridge connects Nanjangud with the trunk road north to Mysore. The rail bridge carries Sam to work in the mornings, brings him back to me long before the sun itself leaves.

To him the half bridge is an eyesore. He says it was promised to Nanjangud before the last election. Says workmen built the forms and poured the concrete so quickly the pylons must be weak, likely would not hold the spans. That doesn't matter, he claims, for the spans may never be built. This is our problem: he sees only missing

spans; I see the promise of a bridge. I haven't decided on a name for
our child but I have one for the bridge: Kabini, after the river.

Soon the women and children will have to wash farther up the
bank; the ferryman will have a longer distance to pole, for the
monsoons will swell the river upward and out. By then I will have
begun to show even under my sari. The women will stop to grin,
for I will have become one of them. The girls will chant, "Baby,
Canada baby." They will pronounce Canada "Kannada." The
boys will wink behind Sam's back. The men already envy him,
treat him like a prince not simply because he is foreign-returned
but because he returned with a treasure. One weary of their
attentions, of being on display. If only they knew: I found the
treasure, and I found it in my own home. By Christmas, I will
deliver another treasure. In my new home.

This is the beauty of an unfinished bridge, the beauty he can't
see: an opportunity to span rivers. Our child already sees this, and
his pulse quickens. He will finish bridges left unfinished. He will
build new ones. I must tell Sam. Today. Now.

These are the intimacies of our dance.

I rise and slap red dust from the turquoise of my sari. I leave my
bridge and my ferryman, my nagas and my bodhi. I approach the
footbridge across the lower canal.

Mr. Kempe Gowda strides toward me along the bund. Unlike
Sam's father, whom I call Appa as does Sam, Mr. Kempe Gowda
looks ridiculous carrying an umbrella open in the sun. He wears
his dhoti folded up over his knees. The white cotton flutters in his
haste. I hurry to reach the footbridge before he does. I have no time
for the Kannada I glean from him in passing, no time for his well-
meant laughter when I forget to accent first syllables. He crosses
the footbridge first, and we meet on the edge of his sugar cane field.
"Namaskaara," he says. Good morning. He seems delighted to see
me, perhaps because I'm out earlier than I am on most days.
"Cennagiddiiraa?" he asks. How do you do? He stands before a
rounded stone marker on the edge of the canal, then tilts his
umbrella as though offering shade. "Banni," he says. Come.
"Kuutukoli," he insists. Be seated.

I sit on the edge of the marker, but he snaps his umbrella closed and robs me of the promised shade. He scratches lines in the dust between us.

"Cennagiddiini," I reply at last. Fine. "Niivu cennagiddiiraa?" Instead of answering, he puffs his cheeks, blows disgusted soundless whistles at the lines on the ground. "The sugar cane has begun growing only," he explains, "but do you suppose I shall discover enough villagers to help with the harvest when the time is ripe?"

"Alla," I say. No.

He exclaims, "One hundred and ten per cent correct, as your esteemed husband would say! I shall be requiring their services for six days per week. Do you suppose they will be coming all six days?"

"Why shouldn't they?" I ask.

Parakeets chitter in a coconut palm. He mistakes my smile, meant for them, as encouragement. I'm sure I can convince Sam we were right to leave Kingston, right to find the home I longed for all those years — years I grew among red maples that should have offered enlightenment, gartersnakes that should have brought fertility, parakeets that languished in cages. First, though, I must let Mr. Kempe Gowda run his course.

"That is my very point," he cries, stabbing the earth between his feet. "In three and one-half days, they will be earning enough to live for seven. Consequently they will not be coming for the subsequent two and one-half. If they were intelligent like your husband, if they were educated like you, they would be working the entire time and accumulating wealth. But no, it is a foreign notion to them. I say, 'One paisa saved is a rupee earned,' and they stare at me as though I am the idiot. Do they think my family built all this by working three days per week only?" His arm curves from the north through the east, past Nanjangud, south past Debur Road and stops in the southwest, between our house and the village.

The Kempe Gowda house is the only one on Debur Road roofed with Mangalore tiles. Except for our house, with its flat concrete roof, the few others are roofed with half cylinders, clay thrown like pots, then sliced lengthwise into curved tiles. They are

brown, not orange-red like his. Villagers refer to his house as the
Rajya Sabha after the Indian Senate. Once there stood a smaller
house across the road from his, but only its foundations remain. I
rest on the stones of one corner when I walk to Debur in the
afternoons. Today I will not be walking to the village.

"Tumba sundaravaada mane," I agree. It is a very beautiful
house. After he modestly shrugs, I say, "I really must go," and rise
once more.

That surprises him, because I seldom hurry. And I never wear
my watch. It was made for the west, where time moves more
quickly than it does here. "You are expecting visitors?" he asks.

I would rather not answer, but I must share my plan with
someone. "I'm going into Mysore to surprise Mr. Gurudev," I say.
I step onto the footbridge.

"That will indeed be a pleasant surprise." Mr. Kempe Gowda's
eyes flick across my still-flat belly. "Have you more news?"

"I have an idea for a bridge," I call over my shoulder. I laugh
when he shouts: "But your husband is no civil engineer. He is a
systems engin —." I laugh, to myself this time, when Mr. Kempe
Gowda calls out his version of the farewell he learned from Sam:
"Please have a nice day!"

On the bund I quicken my step. "Namaskaara," I call to the
women. "Namaskaara," I call even to the man.

He doesn't look up from his plough. He's too busy whipping
the bullocks, but the women straighten. I see their lips, red with
betel juice. Even from the bund, I can smell the sweet peppery
cloves tucked into their cheeks. The youngest woman waves a
handful of seedlings. A paddy bird takes flight.

As if to egg me on, a flock of parakeets lands in the coconut palm
inside our gate. They have followed me from the footbridge.
Perhaps they will follow me to Sam. "Just don't you spoil my
surprise," I tell them, and they titter. Even the gathering clouds,
when they finally weep, will break into a laughing sunny smile.
Butterfly mates flit among the tamarind. They are red, black and
white: two crimson roses coupled in the intimacies of their flight.

I unlock the veranda doors, newer than the ones forming the
raft. Above the radio hangs our only decoration, a single pipal leaf
painted with the image of Goddess Saraswati. I kiss my finger, then

press it to the leaf. Sam gave it to me, a consolation for the painted leaves I left behind. The travel alarm on the radio warns me to hurry. The next train leaves Nanjangud for Mysore in less than half an hour. My favourite program on Radio Kuwait will soon begin, but Tracy Chapman and George Michael will have to sing without me today, sing of fast cars and faith. There's something I must do, though.

Of all the things about our house, Sam was sure I would like the toilet least. It's Indian-style, a ceramic-lined hole flanked by ceramic footpads. I can laugh now, but my heart sank when I first saw the toilet. He seemed almost delighted by my reaction. It was his way of saying, "I told you so," but no hole in a floor would defeat me. I used it the very afternoon we moved here. First, though, I sent him to Debur in search of milk. I needed the house to myself.

The first challenge was keeping my balance while I squatted on the white ceramic footpads, never mind the incised pattern of diamonds to grip the soles. I managed by pressing one hand against the nearest wall even if that did feel un-Indian. Then came an even greater challenge: pouring the water from a brass vessel with my right hand while I washed myself with my left. Squatting over that toilet, I felt less like Saraswati Devi than like Sara Davies; I wondered what I hoped to prove by living in a farmhouse halfway between a village and a railway junction, over an hour from the nearest city, almost halfway around the world from what Sam calls civilization.

I catch myself smiling while I quickly wash my hands. My child will also smile when I one day relate my trials as an Indian housewife. Hardly that, hardly trials. After I mastered that hole in the floor and the brass vessel, nothing proved too challenging. Not even taking my bath by pouring water from a bucket with yet another brass vessel. Not even balancing the bread and eggs on three soda bottles set in a pan of water to keep our food from the ants. When they become too numerous, I sprinkle the window sill with kerosene. My child won't have to learn such things. He will know them at birth. He will be born with the wisdom of his father, with his mother's gift for feeling at home, even here. My child may feel confined now while he swims in my womb, but he dreams of rivers and oceans. He dreams of a bridge.

2

Indian summer is two weeks away, but even now, before noon, metal burns fingers. The air presses me to the dark blue seat, threatens to rain in the carriage. Men in dhotis smoke coarse brown beedis; men in trousers smoke white tailor-mades. I worry for my child. Even the wind, tainted with diesel fumes, offers little relief. I sit next to the open window on the side away from the sun.

Saris dry on the river bank; bullocks trudge through fields. My bridge seems less like the promise of one than like the four fingers of four separate hands. My bodhi is lost among the banyans near the temple. From this distance, from this height, it looks like a mound of blotchy rock. The nagas, the naginis have vanished. They've taken the ferryman with them. Mr. Kempe Gowda's paddies, light brown and still, his sugar cane fields of dark green scrub — all stretch toward Debur Road. He admires Sam's attention to detail, prides himself on ordering repairs to our house before Sam notices anything awry. "The mark of a civilized man," Mr. Kempe Gowda tells me, "is a love of efficiency."

Jenny was not so easily impressed. Friends called her Jenny, but it came from Rajini. She was Indian, and no Indian man could impress her. The first night I invited Sam for dinner, I insisted she stay. After he left, she reminded me of his longest anecdote. I listened faithfully though I could have repeated it for her, because I could still hear the rhythm of his voice:

"A farmer from the prairies went to Punjab with a combine courtesy of CIDA. It took him three harvests to convince the Indian farmers to use it properly. First they gathered the grain and tossed it into the front. Then they watched it spout onto the ground and winnowed it. Imagine! The following harvest, they let him drive it through the fields. Even then, they wanted the grain to spout onto the ground. They would follow, bending, breaking their backs, and winnow it once more. Only during the third harvest would they allow a truck to accompany the combine to collect the grain directly from its spout. Even then, they winnowed it again for good measure!"

Jenny shook her dark head over the stumps of candlesticks, the dregs of our wine. "He's just another Gucci Gandhi technocrat," she said. "A Rajiv clone. I felt like telling him there's more than one way to be efficient. Especially in a country with so many people. I could've screamed." At my shower she gave me a button that said MARRIED, NOT DEAD. That was Jenny. Later, she cried more than Mother did at the wedding. That, too, was Jenny. When she saw us off at Pearson International, she whispered, "Good catch."

I whispered back, "Bards will sing his praise."

Sam is Yudhi-shthira, renowned as a ruler, son of the god of justice; Arjuna the warrior, high-minded, generous, handsome; Nakula, master of the horse; Saha-deva, learned in astronomy; even Bhima, the unrepentant slayer of foes. Above all, Sam is Rama, rightful King of Ayodhya. "Remember Rama's bridge," I will say when I see him. "The one he built across the Gulf of Mannar to reclaim Sita, his beloved wife."

Sam teases me about my knowledge. Book India, he calls it; India experienced through books. The thesis I wanted to write was called *Ayodhya as Camelot: Rama as the Once and Future King.* Ayodhya, that mythical capital of the Solar race; Ayodhya, which remains as elusive as Camelot. I never did write that thesis, because the parallels became forced. Even if Rama were Arthur and Sita were Guinevere, who were Lancelot and Merlin? What was the Holy Grail if not Sita herself, hidden from the eyes of good men? The thesis I did write was more scholarly, but it was calculated to please the men who grant degrees. It did just that: *The Mythic Bridge: The Influence of Hasidic Tales on the Indology of Heinrich Zimmer.* And in those tales of the Hasidim, those mediators of east and west, I found mythic treasures. I laid the foundations of a doctorate I may never finish, but I have no regrets.

Only a month before that first supper, Jenny dragged me to a reception for foreign students, then abandoned me while she waded through the men, stiff in their suits and ties. No one approached me. Jenny said I always looked so statuesque even when seated, like a maharani in that electric blue sari and gold lamé blouse. I knew it too. At undergrad pubs, I'd looked for any excuse to glide onto the dance floor, then leap like a mannequin come to life under strobe lights while my hair, gathered in a long ponytail, rose like a cobra, froze and fell. I'd collected men's eyes, pasted them on my jeans and top like the shining squares from the mirror ball. But that had been after the man she called "your Kashmiri Casanova" had left me for the marriage he'd known his parents would arrange. So, I'd learned to dance alone, dared anyone to dance with me. Now I swirled memories in my Pink Lady; I smiled over how naive I'd been to think my Kashmiri Casanova would have married me simply because we'd played at keeping house. That was when I heard the voice and found a man smiling down at me.

"I said," he repeated, "I must be quite the wit if you're smiling before I tell a joke! I'd prefer you laughed, though." That was Sam. He wore a plain white kurtha, starched, with its tunic collar refusing to close at the throat. He held a snifter and swirled brandy like a man who would be king.

"You could try," I said, so he did:

"A servant came to her mistress and said, 'Here is the money I have saved while working for you. Tomorrow I shall marry the man you so generously found for me, and I would like you also to keep my money safe.'" He paused to ask, "You've heard this one?" After I shook my head, he continued: "The mistress said, 'Why would you not keep it in your husband's house?' To which the girl replied, 'Oh no, Mistress, I could never trust my life savings to a perfect stranger!'"

I did laugh, and he kept me laughing all evening. When he insisted on walking me back to the rooms Jenny and I shared on King Street, I wondered how to invite him for a nightcap without scaring him off. He shook my hand and said, "I hope we meet again."

He left me with my lame response: "So do I."

Seven months later, at our reception, he could still make me laugh. The guests kept clinking their glasses so often, he finally stood up and said in that cultivated voice, "Ladies and gentlemen, as much as I enjoy kissing the bride, I also like to eat."

The rhythm of the train is changing. Its roll has become more pronounced. Already halfway on its journey to Mysore, the train seems to gather speed.

The rough nap of a towel tickles my bare elbow. I turn from the window, from the treed yet rocky landscape. The man hunched next to me has grazed my elbow with his shoulder, over which he keeps a towel draped. He rearranges it. Towels are so useful here: for wiping sweat from brows, for wrapping around heads, for sleeping on the hard wooden seats of second class carriages, even for drying hands. I've forgotten to pack one in my cloth bag.

The man's shirt is as grey white as the stubble on his chin. No younger man would have dared sit next to me. His buttons, long ago broken from repeated beatings against rock, have been replaced by safety pins. His dhoti is pure white, and he rearranges it across his knees.

"Time?" he asks.

"I'm sorry," I tell him, "I don't wear a watch."

He raises his hand, swivels it next to his ear to tell me he can't follow such rapid English.

When I show him my left wrist, he frowns at the three glass bangles, violet with silver squares. He squints up at me, then at my wrist without its watch. The freckles fascinate him. Slowly, as though he might violate me by doing it, he pretends to close his index finger and thumb around my wrist. His skin, as brown as dried coconut fronds, never touches mine. After he draws away, he points beyond me. I turn to find a herd of cattle in the distance. "Aakalu," he says. Cow.

"Danakaru," I tell him. Cattle.

His eyes widen until the lines around them vanish. He points again and says, "Chikka kudure." Small horse.

It's a donkey, sad and grey, tethered to the back of a bullock cart. When I correct him again with, "Kaththe," he throws back his head to laugh and slaps his knees. I've used it as one might rudely address a vendor.

He twists in his seat to say, "Houdu," and, "Kannada mathu madhura." Yes; Kannada words are sweet. He means this as a compliment.

"Ninna vayassu eshtu?" I ask. How old are you?

"Nanage aruvaththondu vayassu," he replies. He straightens his back, but the top of his head barely clears my shoulder.

Sixty-one, yet he looks older than Sam's father. But then Appa spent his working years at the engineering college. This man likely spent his bent over some desk as a clerk, subjected to as much abuse as a vendor but without the thrill of cheating buyers unwilling to haggle.

It seems strange to think of privilege, but that's how I feel in Appa's company. He's almost courtly, the way Jenny said her father began acting once she left home. During the few weeks Sam and I lived with Appa in Mysore, he and I spent most mornings together while Sam settled into the college. Though seventy-five, Appa strode with his head high, so he seemed taller than me. When I teased him about that, he pretended it was my doing, claimed he felt proud being seen with me. He calls me his red-haired goddess daughter. I expected him to visit us often in our new house, but he allows us our privacy, the intimacy of our dance.

He acts so self-possessed, so aristocratic; he's one of the few men I've seen who doesn't look ridiculous using his umbrella to stave off the sun. The shopkeepers live in awe of him. They never whine for more money, and he never haggles. I followed him from stall to stall in Devaraja Market and carried his purchases: thick slices of yellow-brown bread, or a week's worth of sugar wrapped in a paper cone tied with coarse brown twine. He chuckled if it caught under my fingernails when I picked the knot loose. I wouldn't have had it any other way. Before long, I found it easier to talk about Sam's future with Appa than with Sam.

"If he proves an able administrator," Appa told me, "your husband could become principal by thirty-five. But why does he not want to practise engineering? Will he not contribute more as an engineer than as a dean?"

"Sam says what we really need," I explained, "are people who can run things."

"These youngsters are always so quick to decide how best to run matters," Appa said. "Once they grow older, they discover matters run themselves."

"He might appreciate you telling him that," I said.

"He will learn soon enough," Appa said. "I secured him this position. The rest is his doing, however it affects your future. If he asks for advice —" Appa shrugged as if to say he doubted Sam ever would.

I wonder what Appa will say when I tell him Sam has already learned things run themselves. Thanks to Dr. Srinivas. If I tell Appa. I'm Sam's wife, not Appa's. As for my future, I couldn't ask then and I can't ask now for more than this: to be with Sam where he feels most at home.

The old man next to me asks, "Ninna uru yavadu?" He repeats himself after I turn from the window. Which is your native place? "Debur Road," I reply.

He laughs again, clucks his tongue so he sounds like a lizard chuckling. "Ninna hesaru enu?" What is your name? He looks disbelieving when I tell him Mrs. Saraswati Devi. "Thandeya hesa renu?" Your father's name?

"Arnold Davies," I tell him.

He repeats the name slowly, frowns as though he should recognize it. I'm confounding him, for in a country with so many people, it becomes crucial to place a person according to who he is, where he's from, what he does, and who his father is. Rather, in my case, who my husband is, but the old man hasn't asked that. I would gladly answer, tell him as I told Mr. Kempe Gowda about my plan to surprise Sam.

To ease the old man's confusion, I tell him about my father-in-law, from Mysore: "Nanna mava hesaru Professor Gurudev. Maisurininda."

"Houdu!" the man exclaims. Oh yes? Then he lapses into silence. I can guess what he thinks: how lucky these professors are to find foreign wives for their sons.

The carriage jolts, and the train begins to sprint for Mysore Station. Through the window on the right side, across the aisle, I can see a high, rocky hill. I glimpse the gopuram, the gateway tower, of a temple on its summit.

One morning, Appa hired an autorickshaw to take us out Harishchandra Road to Chamundi Hill. He pointed at the steps climbing the rocky slope and said, "There are one thousand steps to the temple, though we shall not go so far."

Even as I said, "Go on!" he set off.

Seventy-five, and he climbed hills. He closed his umbrella so it wouldn't catch on the overhanging branches of neem trees. He counted off every ten steps to a hundred, then began counting again. "Haththu, ippaththu, muvaththu, naluvaththu..."

My petticoat began to stick to my thighs. I pulled the end of my sari tightly over my head. Between keeping the hem off the steps and concentrating on each one, I barely heard him after a while. At four hundred, he stopped and turned, but I refused to stop. He chuckled when I passed him. Soon, he passed me again. At seven hundred and fifty, he vanished.

I hurried past a clump of neem trees and found a road. Then I gasped, "Nandi!"

There are many nandis in India, as many as there are temples to Lord Shiva, but the bull on Chamundi Hill is over fifteen feet high, perhaps twice as long. It rests with its forelegs tucked under it and stares patiently up the winding road like a jet black sentinel. It's as black as coal, colourless but for marigolds draped around its neck by the attending priest. Three white horizontal stripes mark it as a devotee of Lord Shiva, stripes repeated on the priest's brow and upper arms.

I thought it must be the heat rising from the road: the Nandi began to blur.

Appa waited on the far side of the road. After I joined him, he asked, "What is it, daughter?" and I wiped my eyes. He gave me his kerchief, checked in blue and white, to blow my nose.

"All the time I was growing up and learning about India," I said, "I used to think I'd give anything to see the Taj Mahal by moonlight. But this..."

He nodded in his Indian way, tilted his head from side to side. He led me up to a terrace. We half-sat, half-leaned against its far wall so as not to interfere with tourists. All of them were Indian. All of them fussed with cameras.

"I come here alone always," Appa said. "I never even brought Shiamsundar." He spat out, "Sam! What is this fetish you people have for shortening even simple names?"

"We people?" I teased.

"Always colossal," he mused. "Nothing we Indians do is on a small scale. Perhaps as a Hindu I should not say this, but . . . to the priests, this bull may be a vehicle to be passed while approaching a god, but to me it is a tribute to man also. That is a rather Christian idea, but we Hindus have survived so long by adapting well. I feel sometimes we are more Buddhist than the Buddhists themselves." He looked serious, almost grave, and his cheek bulged where he prodded at a tooth with his tongue. Finally he said:

"My first wife left me my daughter, whom you will meet when you finally visit Cochin. I remarried because every Indian wants a son. Your husband was born to my second wife after I passed forty. Even she abandoned me. She finds it easier to live with my daughter, her step-daughter, than with me. That is why there is such a gulf between us. Your husband and myself."

I wanted to say, "If you ask me, Sam goes out of his way to please you," but I didn't. Just as Indian sons don't like to be reminded how much they long to please their fathers, so Indian fathers pretend they have no hold on their sons.

"It would pain me if he were to be hurt," Appa said.

This time I had to say, "I wouldn't—" but he kept on:

"It would pain me even more if anyone were to be hurt because of him." He turned from the Nandi at last and tilted his head at me. "Tell me truthfully," he said. "This is a love match, your husband claims, but are you in love with him, or are you in love with India?"

I'd often wondered that since I'd changed my name — not to Mrs. Gurudev, but to an Indian version of my own. "Both," I said.

"I feel sometimes," he said, "that you know everything about India and nothing about your husband."

"I know I love him," I insisted.

"Hah!" Appa's voice startled two parakeets. They took flight from trees behind us. "One learns to love one's mate after one learns to know him. Such is the value of properly arranged matches."

"I do know him," I said. "It's as if I've known Sam, Shiamsundar all my life." It sounded so lame, yet Appa stopped prodding at the tooth.

He smacked his lips and smiled. "I think you may have been Indian in your previous life," he said, "and that is why so much of this appears familiar to you. But you did something wicked and were reborn in a foreign land. Even an old man, one full of what you youngsters mistake for wisdom, must be permitted his fancies. I thought when you first arrived that you were my first wife reborn. You are very much like her in looks. The cheekbones, especially, but you have a fire she lacked. I think sometimes —" He looked angrily at a crow, which circled the Nandi before the priest shooed it off. "I think she died only because she grew weary of my bullying. I was in my late twenties then, too young for courage. I was afraid of her because she came to know me so well, and I had always prided myself as being a difficult man to please. Only she realized how kindhearted I could be when kindness is not demanded. So, I bullied her. Do you know the saying? Mahatma Gandhi said to understand India, one must—"

"—talk to the women," I said.

"Yes, they are tigresses within the home and large tamed cats without." He tried to dispell his sadness with a chuckle. "That is India also: fierce and bold while within her boundaries, fawning while abroad."

"I have something to tell you," I said. "Something we were saving for the right moment." I didn't know how to tell him, though, in words all my own. When I took his hand, he resisted. I pulled it toward me until it brushed my sari where the pleats were gathered and tucked.

He pulled his hand free, blinked rapidly, then looked toward the steps. "You should have told me," he muttered. "You must be very strong." He looked at the Nandi again as I first had, through the heat rising all around us. He bit the inside of his lip and bobbed his head lightly. I thought he looked sad for his first wife.

I glance at the old man seated next to me, and understand now: Appa looked sad for me.

When the old man tilts his head as though waiting for me to say something, I finally do: "Nanna holenadi, nanna ganda." My river, my husband.

It makes little sense to him, but he grins and bobs. He thinks I'm practising my Kannada. He's incapable of understanding the intimacies of our dance.

3

It must be raining. No, not yet, though the sun has vanished. The river swells, my belly swells with clouds. I wish I could rain my flesh into upturned mouths, plaster prying eyes shut, scatter bodies like flies. I hear my voice: "Get away from me!"

"Yenamma?" asks the autorickshaw driver. It can mean anything from, "What is it, woman?" to, "What is wrong with you now?" He clutches the top of the half screen protecting me from him. He looks so twisted. The roof of the autorickshaw shudders in a gust, rumbles like a drum head.

A guard complete with beret and braid peers into the autorickshaw. He looks eager to step in beside me, force me out the other side, watch while I tumble onto the dust.

A hand peels him away finally to admit the light. It must be Sam. No, not yet. His voice is more rhythmic, more mellow than this, even when angered: "Togalu!" Get lost. The hand reaches toward me, and I take it, allow the man to bear my weight when I step out of the autorickshaw. Black with yellow bands, it's metal below, canvas above; has two wheels behind, one in front; and steers by means of handlebars, not a steering wheel. It's a bumblebee turned inside out.

Beyond the man, who cups my elbow, stand peons in khaki shirts and short pants. Beyond stand more men, in trousers and white shirts. They mutter, "Ondalla oudu goolu," and, "Ayoo paapa." Some trouble or other; poor thing.

"Pay the fellow, Raghu!" the man calls, and the youngest lecturer dashes past us.

"Let me," I mutter. Even after the autorickshaw roars away, I search for money in my cloth bag.

"You must take rest," the man insists. He leads me through the open gate into the college compound. "Ladies should not travel by autorickshaw in such conditions."

How could he know of my condition? He must mean the heat. In the first office past the gate, I collapse into a creaking leather chair. The ceiling fan swirls dust through the room and ruffles mounds of paper under weights.

The man calls for water, then bends over me. He offers me a kerchief, brown and white checked, rumpled but clean, to wipe my brow. "I am extremely pleased to meet you at last," he says. "I am Dr. Srinivas."

So this is the bloody fool. He squints through thick glasses until I tell him, "I'm all right, thank you." Still, my hand shakes when I take the stainless steel tumbler a peon has handed him. Lecturers stand in the doorway and gawk without pretending to at the maharani slouched in state.

"Give the lady some privacy," he insists. "Can you not see she must rest?"

The peon straggles from the room and brushes at grime on the ceiling fan switch. The lecturers drift away from the windows and door. Dr. Srinivas wipes his high forehead with his sleeve. The armpits of his shirt sag with sweat. Spidery hair covers his balding head. Smallpox scars, darkened with the years, mottle his dark face. His only distinguishing feature is the plastic liner in his breast pocket, one that holds a mechanical pencil and a fountain pen — a liner with BROWN BOVERI printed on the ink-stained flap. From Sam I know the firm makes ceramic insulators for power lines, and more. The effort of giving orders seems to have drained Dr. Srinivas of energy. He falls back into a nearby chair, and the cracked leather cushion sighs beneath him. He fans himself with a dusty notebook, then brightens as though he has thought of a cure. "Thank you for the house," he says.

How could he know?

Sam and I were to have moved into a bungalow near the college, barely a block away. It was the principal's residence. Dr. Srinivas was living in it with his wife and two children because there hadn't been a principal for nearly a year. There likely wouldn't be one for at least another; it would take that long for the board of regents to act. Dr. Srinivas agreed to move so Sam could have a house that matched his rank.

"Even if you're special because you studied abroad," I asked, "why would the board turn out someone who needs the space more than we do?"

"I asked for it," Sam said. I must have looked shocked, because he added, "Don't worry. Srinivas is moving out to a farm south of here. It was either that or a renovated garage near the racecourse."

Appa's ayah, who waited to serve us, returned to her kitchen. Our masala dosas were growing cold.

Appa lowered his favourite newspaper, the *Star of Mysore*. He shrugged at me as if to say, "These things happen."

"How far south?" I asked.

"Near Nanjangud Town," Sam replied. "That's on the way to Ooty."

"Do not concern yourself," Appa said. "There is a commuting train, and the fellow can read on the journey. Your husband is correct. The arrangement will be more convenient." For a moment I thought he would say, "More efficient."

"For whom?" I asked.

"This is India, remember?" Sam said. "Do you know how long the waiting list is for preferred accommodation? We can't impose on Appa for two, maybe three years. And I'm not about to live in a renovated garage."

"Don't I have any say in this?" I asked.

"It's you I'm considering," he said. "There's no running water on that farm. No flush toilet. Be sensible."

"We'll go and see this Dr. Srinivas tonight," I said. "Tell him we'll take the farmhouse, and you'll commute."

For the first time since our arrival, Sam looked to Appa for help. He said, "She is your wife, not mine." He told me, "It would perhaps be better if you did not go to Dr. Srinivas. If you let your husband deal with this matter." Then he chuckled. "A tigress in the house."

Sam slapped the arms of his chair and strode past the curtain in our doorway. Appa shrugged and went back to his paper. I followed Sam and found him lying on his cot. He pounded the ends of his bolster until it bulged in the middle, looked like that classical two-faced drum the mridangam. He stopped when I murmured, "Oh, Sam."

Dr. Srinivas asks, "Madam?" He is filling the tumbler with water from a jug.

I drink before asking, "How did you know about the house?"

"What is there to know?" he asks. "Mr. Gurudev merely mentioned you wished to experience rural life. To improve your knowledge of Kannada." Sweat beads above his lip. He wipes his shirt sleeve across his lips and nose in one pass. Only then does he allow himself to hiss a laugh through his nose. "In Mysore you would be quite noticeable. On Debur Road, you must be something of a local attraction."

From Sam, even from Appa that would be a compliment. From Dr. Srinivas, it's merely a comment. I like him; his uncertainty puts me at ease. Behind him on the wall hangs an old chart, a cross-section of a motor with its armature, its coils and iron cores, exposed. Sam would resent having to explain the workings of such an outdated motor to students. I want to ask about the lab schedules, but that would embarrass Dr. Srinivas. I barely know the man, but I can guess what really happened. His only sin was in making a mistake so soon after Sam's arrival, in appearing to test the new dean's ability to bring order. Dr. Srinivas isn't as ineffectual or as absent-minded as I'd imagined him. He simply looks like a man with many worries.

"Mr. Gurudev?" I ask, looking about.

"Of course," Dr. Srinivas exclaims. "You did not come to visit us. How thoughtless!" He rises and goes to the door, squints at the second-floor balcony ringing the compound. "He is resting in his rooms."

"I wanted to surprise him," I say, rising.

When Dr. Srinivas turns, his glasses magnify the uncertainty in his eyes. He seems no more able to understand my confusion than I can understand his. "Not in his office, Madam. His rooms. It is only one large room, a garage in fact, which has been renovated for use as accommodation. That is where Mr. Gurudev takes his afternoon rest, when it becomes too hot to work. I myself retire to my house and return after taking my own nap and my afternoon coffee."

What is he talking about, afternoon rests? "I'm afraid you've lost
me," I say. When he asks, "Pardon?" I explain, "This is all too
confusing."

"I could drive you," he says. "However, it might be better if one
of the others—"

He means it wouldn't do for him to be seen currying favours
from me. Especially by Sam. I wish people would say what they
mean here, that they could be honest with strangers. Perhaps it's
not a matter of honesty, though. Many things simply aren't
discussed in India except among families and friends. Elsewhere
too, no doubt, but here it smacks of deceit.

"I'll take an autorickshaw," I say.

"In this heat that would not be advisable," he protests, "and a
hired car would be extravagant—"

"I have money," I tell him. Not enough to squander, but
surprising Sam will be worth spending a few rupees.

"Of course," Dr. Srinivas says.

I wonder whether he assumes I come from a wealthy family. I'm
weary of all this second-guessing and inability to read signals
correctly. I'm likely not the woman he imagined; he's certainly not
the man I expected.

By the time I finish using the toilet and washing my face, the car
arrives from the nearest western-style hotel. The sky has filled with
clouds, grey clouds that mesh to form a shroud. Soon it will rain,
and the rain will bring relief from the dust thrown up by passing
vehicles, from the air as clammy as the palms of men. The lecturer
named Raghu opens the back door for me, and I climb into the car.
I refuse his offer to accompany me, and he grins away his disappointment.

Dr. Srinivas pokes with his fountain pen at a map he has
sketched on graph paper. He adds more crosses and squares and
makes the driver repeat the instructions. Then Dr. Srinivas leans
through the still open back door. "You please give me sixty
rupees," he says. "That will cover two hours of the car. Will that be
sufficient?"

I nod, take three brown twenty-rupee notes from my bag and
give them to him. The driver seems about to ask for more. He
shrugs when Dr. Srinivas glares at him.

"Could I ask you something?" I say.

Frowning, Dr. Srinivas nods.

Now that I have the chance, I don't know how to phrase the question. I begin obliquely: "You're familiar with my father-in-law?"

"Everyone in Mysore is familiar with Professor Gurudev," Dr. Srinivas says with a broad smile. "He is a landmark in his time. A legend, as you Americans might say."

"Did you ever meet his wife?" I ask. "My husband's mother, that is."

"I believe all the time your father-in-law was at our college," Dr. Srinivas says, "he had few close friends. I know only that he was considered a terror by his subordinates, for he was extremely demanding. As for his wife, I know only that he had two. He invited no one to his house. He is what you Americans call a man of mystery."

"I'm Canadian," I say. "There's a difference."

Dr. Srinivas laughs at his mistake. "If so, it is merely one of degree," he says. "You please watch your sari."

I draw the hem from the doorway, and he closes the door. In trying not to startle me, he fails to close it properly. I open the door and pull it shut.

After I thank him through the open window, he says, "Think nothing of it. I am only too happy to be of service." I'm glad he doesn't add, "To the dean's wife." Instead of pressing his palms together as the peons do, instead of saluting as the guard does, Dr. Srinivas touches the plastic flap of his pocket liner in a mixture of farewell and good luck. What began as a surprise visit to Sam, a gift in the form of a new way of looking at a bridge, has become a test of patience. It will be a long time before I leave my life at Debur Road again.

I ignore the driver's eyes on me in the rearview mirror. He swerves to avoid hitting a truck, its racks full of empty soda bottles: Fanta, Limca, Thums Up. I drink only the local soda, bisleri, nothing more than carbonated water and sugar. It costs thirty paise instead of the three rupees for Fanta or Limca. Bisleri bottles are capped with a marble in the upper chamber below the mouth, and the marble rattles when I tilt the bottle. I keep the glass mouth from my lips. Sam drinks Fanta or nothing, and he always uses a straw. Why, I wonder, wouldn't he take his afternoon nap in Appa's house?

On our second day in Mysore, Sam, Appa and I discussed the upcoming holiday in Cochin, on the west coast. There I would finally meet Sam's mother and his sister, step-sister. When Appa mentioned Sam should visit the college before leaving, I suggested Sam begin work immediately. I worried he would grow bored if he didn't begin work for another month. I worried he would grow bored with me. "Appa won't mind if we stay here till the house we're getting is ready," I said. "Will you?" I asked Appa.

"My house is yours," he said, "except for the kitchen."

Sam frowned at us when we laughed. It never occurred to him that Appa and I might already have our private jokes. When Appa had been showing me his house on that first day, he had shown me the kitchen last. When I tried to cross the threshold, I found his forearm blocking my way. Just as quickly, it dropped. "The ayah is extremely orthodox," he said. He knew and I knew the ayah wasn't the only orthodox person in that house. Though Appa ate from the usual stainless steel plates, he'd acquired a set of china dishes for Sam and me. We had eaten meat, what Appa jokingly called flesh.

"It becomes hot even here," he now said. "Cochin will be cooler from the seabreeze."

"You may know a lot about India," Sam added, "but Indian summer here isn't the same as Indian summer in Canada."

"You'll keep it pleasant," I said. I squeezed his shoulder while I stood beside his chair. "So will Appa." He's modern enough that he doesn't mind if we touch in front of him. Kiss, no. He likely thought we rarely lay on the same cot because we didn't want to offend him, but it was the threat of perspiration that came between us, not impropriety. Later that evening, Sam lay in his cot, and I lay in mine. Unable to sleep in spite of the ceiling fan, we talked while holding hands across the gap between the cots.

Appa had apparently resisted Sam's plan to study in the west. "The days are long gone when a boy must leave India to make good here," Appa had told Sam during their debates three years before. "Go north if you must, but why leave India? Do we not have computers now?"

"Yes, and red tape by the yard," Sam had told him.

That was the evening I realized Sam couldn't tell Appa he didn't want to live under his roof. That was why Sam had gone to Queen's after finishing his degree at UBC: not simply for the commerce degree but also to delay his return. Perhaps forever, until he found himself in love with a woman in love with India. The sooner we left for our own house, the better.

I clutch the strap dangling above the open window and close my eyes. Car horns beep, autorickshaw horns honk, bicycle bells ding, police whistles shrill. Compared to Bombay and Bangalore, Mysore is pleasant yet still too much the city. The child within me sloshes below my navel as I rock within the car, while the black leather seat tries to sweat through the nylon of my sari. I grip the edge of the seat with my left hand, feel the leather strap bite into my right palm.

"You are wanting tour?" the driver shouts above the noise. "Maharaja's Palace. I am knowing the guides. Chamarajendra Art Gallery. I am knowing the director. Chamundeswari Temple. I am knowing—"

"I've seen them," I reply.

When he continues with, "Only hundred and fifty rupees half day," I open my eyes and tell the back of his neck:

"Mathu beda." Keep quiet.

His shoulders tense. He casually massages the back of his neck while watching me in the rearview mirror. He wipes the back of his hand across his brow and nods when I add:

"Nanagoskara ninenu madabeda." You need not do anything for me.

After that, he drives in silence while I eat some Gluco biscuits. In my hurry to leave the house, I also forgot to bring a water bottle, but I will be eating lunch soon. I will take Sam to the Lalitamahal Hotel for a late lunch. It is on Chamundi Hill but lower than the Nandi and is reached by a different route.

We are now east of the zoo and headed for the racecourse, what people back home call a racetrack. People in Canada; I am home. The streets are like warrens, barely wide enough for the car to pass the occasional bicycle. The driver makes wrong turns. He has to stop twice and ask shopkeepers for directions. The second time, a

crowd gathers around the car. Men and boys hang back to discuss
me. The women are too busy working to stop. Girls peer at me
through the open window and whisper with hands pressed ver-
tically against one side of the nose, many pierced. The girls mean
no harm. Simply by looking at me, they hope to gain favours, as
one would by looking at a shrine. That was the mistake the young
woman made, the one who circled my bodhi: she kept her eyes
closed. With her eyes open, she would have seen me approach,
wouldn't have been so startled. She might even have gained what
she most desired.

At last the car turns into a new layout. I can smell the horses at
the racecourse, the hay and manure, the roasting of groundnuts,
the constant frying of snacks. No wonder Dr. Srinivas didn't want
to move here, in spite of the view of Lalitamahal Hotel. It spreads
its wings like a great white bird on the north slope of Chamundi
Hill.

After the driver opens my door, I step out. When I go no farther,
he reassures me with, "This is truly the place, Madam." When I
still don't move, he shrugs and takes his place behind the wheel.
He leans back, crosses his arms and closes his eyes. He has nowhere
to go. The longer I make him wait, the more he will earn.

The house has two gates, one in front of an empty driveway,
another in front of the door. The driveway leads to a garage. The
pleated metal doors, not quite held closed in the middle, radiate
heat. I hear indistinct voices above the whir of a fan. None belongs
to Sam.

One voice rises in a nasal American twang: "— real computers,
not these antiquated adding machines hooked up to video screens.
Ya can't even play games on 'em." Among the laughter, I hear
Sam's rhythmic guffaw. I'm interrupting an Indian version of what
people in Canada call a bitch session.

I choose the second gate, sheltered by a stunted coconut palm.
Over the doorway, mango leaves dangle from twine. They've been
left up since the last festival, likely the one celebrating Buddha
Purnima, and are now shrivelled. Even as I reach for the doorbell, a
woman opens the door. Few cars likely stop at her house.

Her midriff rolls, slack, over the tucked pleats of her sari. The
arrival of the car has woken her. Seeing me wakes her further. She

makes namaskar by joining her hands in front of her blouse. Then she massages her double chin as though, had I given her more notice, she could have made it vanish.

"I'm Mrs. Devi," I say. The name means nothing to her. "Mr. Gurudev?" I ask.

Shading her eyes, she looks at the empty driveway. "Garage," she says. When I take a step down, turning back toward the garage, she steps back into the veranda and gestures. "Banni," she says. Again, come.

In the main room, we pass an old man lying on a cot and an old woman on a mat. Both of them are trying to sit up. "Nanna mava, nanna aththe." Her in-laws.

I raise my hand and say, "Please don't get up," but they do. They look embarrassed at having been caught sleeping by a visitor. The old woman looks away and covers her head with the end of her plain cotton sari.

The curtain in a doorway to our right pulls aside to reveal a girl. A boy lies on a cot, one of four in the room.

"Ninna hesaru eenu, magu?" I ask the girl. What is your name, child?

"I speak good English," she declares. "My name is Manju." She gestures behind her at her brother. "This is Raju. He does not yet know English."

On the wall behind their cots hang pictures of film stars cut from magazines. A calendar, CUORTESY MODREN PRINT-WORKS, has other misspelled words. It's three years old. I'm too tired to frame compliments in Kannada, so I tell the woman, "They're beautiful children."

She pretends to scoff, but she betrays her delight. "Mrs. Saroja," she says, laying her hand on her own chest. "Nanna ganda laayaraa." Her husband is a lawyer. She has likely guessed who and what my husband is.

We pass doors leading to the kitchen, the bathroom and the toilet. All of them are closed. She opens the double back doors and leads me out. There's barely room to turn in front of the granite block on which she washes clothes. Beyond it rises a high wall topped by rusted barbed wire and broken glass. She points at two narrow doors, also closed, and turns to re-enter the house. I lean against the washing stone and listen to the voices coming from the garage.

I can make out at least three. "Yenappa, so what is your complaint now?" one man asks.

"Ten thousand rupees for capitation fees!" a second whines. "On top of which I must also bear his tuition? Am I to bleed so the boy can attend a decent secondary school?"

"Welcome to India!" a third man exclaims. "Didja forget what this country's coming to?" It sounds like Sam, but it can't be. It must belong to the American visitor. "Never mind the overpopulation," he says. "We'll strangle in red tape long before that." It is Sam.

I knock on the door and one of the men says, "Must be Bharata finally. Yenappa," he calls, "what took you so long? My nose runs more quickly."

"It's open," Sam calls when I knock again. "C'mon in!"

I push the narrow double doors open.

Two men slouch in wicker chairs. The nearest chair, likely reserved for the latecomer Bharata, is empty. In front of them on a low wicker table is an ashtray. It's made from the brass anklet of a dancer and is full of cigarette butts. A portable fan near the pleated doors, padlocked on the inside, throws up ash. Grey flecks whirl above the ashtray, then settle on computer magazines: *PC World* and *Byte*.

The man closest to me has a packet of Flairs in his breast pocket, but he's reaching for the packet of Wills Gold Flake on the table. When he sees me, he draws back, holds an unlit cigarette in mid-air. He's nearly forty and looks fifteen pounds overweight. His shirt is unbuttoned to his navel; he wears three gold chains and four silver rings. His perspiration smells of cologne and smoke.

The man beyond him is younger and less pudgy. He has been seated with his feet propped on the table, his head tilted back, and a long cigar held idly between his index and middle fingers. When he finally lowers his chin and sees me, he coughs a startled cloud of smoke and snatches up a glass of beer. Bottles line the far wall behind his chair. Some stand half full, others lie empty: quart bottles of Kingfisher and UP Export, even a squat rectangular bottle of Old Monk rum.

A half-full bottle of Kingfisher stands next to the ashtray, within easy reach of the man who looks most at home. The glass in front of him is full of water. He reclines on a cot which doubles as a sofa. He looks like Sam in a dhoti and without his shirt. On one foot is a Birkenstock sandal; the other lies on the floor. He even sounds like Sam when he calmly announces, "Why Bharata, you've gone and changed your sex."

The others laugh at my limp smile. The cigar smoker chokes on his beer now, and his friend slaps his back too hard to do much good. They stop their antics when I tell the man on the cot, the man who watches me with his head propped on one hand, "I would've thought the dean of engineering would prefer better accommodation than a renovated garage."

The end of a dry cigar sizzles while it burns. The fan clacks like a train crossing a bridge. The cot shrieks when Sam sits up. "My wife," he tells his friends. "This is Mr. Hanumanthappa Rao," Sam says, nodding at the cigar smoker. "Hello There Rao to friends, H. Rao to others."

He nods uncertainly at me and says, self-consciously, "Hello there."

"And this is my trusted assistant," Sam says, "Mr. Lakshman."

"One day to be Doctor Lakshman," the man with the rings and chains says. He finally lights his cigarette.

"Perhaps you will actually get the doctorate next time," Sam scoffs. "Then you won't be relegated to AIISc."

Lakshman blows smoke rings at the ceiling. "I prefer to think of myself as PhD bracket failed, close bracket."

H. Rao cackles and slaps his thigh. The front legs of his chair fall forward onto the concrete floor.

"We were waiting for our colleague Mr. Bharata," Sam explains, "to return with some cool drinks." He nods at the empty chair.

"Yes, it gets so hot here even now," I tell him. I take the empty chair. Lakshman half rises and moves his chair toward H. Rao's. It wouldn't do to sit too close to the dean's wife. "Cochin would be cooler from the seabreeze."

With his head pressed back against the wall, Sam watches me as if to say, "So that's the way you want it."

"This looks very cozy," I say. He knows I mean this refuge, where he holds court like Rama, King of Ayodhya, with Lakshman playing the devoted brother Lakshmana; H. Rao playing the monkey god Hanuman; Bharata playing the half-brother who acted as regent while Rama searched for Sita. I will not play Sita, languishing in her captivity. Too quickly for the others to understand, I mutter, "Ask them to leave, or I will." He can take that any way he chooses.

"Pardon?" H. Rao asks.

"I was just talking to my husband," I explain.

"You seem to have adapted well to our style of life," Lakshman tells me. He nods admiringly at the sari and my Indian-made Walker sandals, black with white braid. "I say, sir," he tells Sam, "there is something particularly becoming about a western lady in Indian dress."

I tighten my hold on the bag, squeeze until the brocaded mouth swallows my knuckles. "If you'll excuse us?" I tell a spot above Sam's head. "I'd like to have a word with my husband."

"Of course!" H. Rao exclaims. He leans forward to butt his cigar in the ashtray, looks disturbed by the sudden pall of smoke, and takes the cigar with him. He leaves his glass on the table. "Let us see what is keeping Bharata," he tells Lakshman.

Mr. Lakshman, PhD (failed) rises with his belly inches from the side of my face. I can smell his sudden discomfort. "We shall return to the college," Lakshman announces. He begins saying, "It was indeed a pleasure," but H. Rao pulls him up the step. Each of them closes one of the narrow double doors.

Only then do I allow myself to lower my eyes to meet Sam's. Only then do I allow the tears to begin.

"Sara, Sara," he croons. He rises to stand beside me and pulls me to him. I hold him tightly with my bangles dug into the small of his back, press my face into his taut belly.

I tell him, "I wanted to surprise—"

He bends to kiss the top of my head, lifts my braided hair and kisses the hollow in the back of my neck. "You certainly did that," he says.

Under the flimsy cotton of his dhoti, I can feel him growing hard against my throat. I push him away, savour the feel of his skin against my palms before I drop my hands.

"I suppose I owe you an explanation?" he says. He backs when I rise, watches me sit on the cot.

I lie on my side and will my strength to return. He thinks I'm weeping from disappointment; I'm sure I am weeping from exhaustion. If only the clouds gathering outside would burst, even if then unpaved roads would turn to mud. If only it would rain; then the sun could return. I'm too tired to feel angry at him; I'm simply angry at myself for feeling the heat. Summer is beginning early: that time when people drive one another mad here. I will not let that happen to us.

While I lie there, revolted by my weakness, he clears the low table. The bottle of Kingfisher joins its companions against the wall. Brass grates on concrete when the ashtray joins the fan on the floor. He tosses the magazines onto a stack in one corner, under a shelf. It holds toilet articles, a towel, spare shirts. His trousers hang from one of many nails protruding from the edge of the shelf. How could Dr. Srinivas live here with his wife and children? Yet I know why Sam doesn't rest at Appa's house. Here he has privacy, even if it means invading the privacy of the woman who lives in the house, the lawyer's wife with her two children and her aged in-laws. Privacy here is worth more than gold.

Sam finally sits in the chair vacated by Lakshman, the one directly across from me. He tries to light a cigarette with one of the matches from a box. When the match breaks, he tries another and another, then tosses the matchbox and cigarette onto the table.

I pick up the matchbox. Two birds perch on a branch within a radiant red circle. "WE TWO SAFETY MATCHES," the yellow label reads. "Saraswati Match Works, Peraiyur." At last I say, "We'll leave Debur Road. We'll stay with Appa till we can find our own place." When Sam says, "That might take years," I interrupt with, "At least it's a house. We'll be in the city. You'll have things to do in the evenings. We can go to movies, films."

There are films in Nanjangud every week, outdoor ones shown on the maidan where, by day, boys play cricket. Every Friday night, people from Debur walk into Nanjangud for the films. At two and three o'clock on Saturday morning, they return to Debur. Sometimes they wake me with their singing, with voices amplified by toddy, a liquor so raw it scratches the throat like cane fibre. So Mr. Kempe Gowda claims.

"You'll have your friends," I tell Sam. "You'll be closer to the college."

He snorts. "The more distance I can put between them and me, the better. Do you know what type of fools we turn out? Lakshman was one of our most distinguished graduates. All the bribes in the world couldn't get him a job as a real engineer. There aren't any jobs, but we get students anyway, by the droves." He muses, "Doesn't cattle come in droves?"

I ask, "Then—?"

"Why do you think?" he says. "So their parents can find them good brides. Doesn't matter if the boy won't become an engineer. He's got a degree, that's what counts. We're not turning out engineers for India. We're increasing the market value of bridegrooms."

I know what he's trying to say. I simply wish he would say it. "I thought you were happy being dean," I tell him softly. "You said you'd have that place in shape in no time. Appa says so, too."

Sam slaps the arms of his chair and rises, paces from the table to the padlocked doors, turns and paces back. "I'm not living under Appa's roof," he says. He stops with the knuckles of his fists digging into his waist, a waist with little flesh to pinch. Love handles, Jenny calls them. "I know you like him," Sam says, "but you don't know everything."

I tell him of the visit to the Nandi, of Appa's confession about his first wife, who died young.

"Very nice," Sam mutters. "Very nice." I know he's passing judgement on Appa, and I resent the mocking tone. "You know the four stages of a high-caste man's life," Sam says. "Tell me." When I purse my lips, he sounds less belittling: "There is a point."

I raise my head to drink from his glass, then lie back. "The first stage is bramacharaya," I say. "Studentship. If a boy is brahmin, he studies the *Vedas*. The second stage is the householder. That's you."

"Not that I'm doing much of a job," he says. I ignore that. He's being hard on himself to prevent me from being hard on him.

"The householder raises a family," I say. "He pursues an occupation fit for his caste, and performs rituals. Vedic rituals to keep the world in balance."

"Something else I don't do," he says.

That's true. There's no god room in our house, not even a platform with images and fresh flowers as there is in Appa's house. There's only the pipal leaf of Goddess Saraswati above the radio.

"In the third stage," I say, "a man becomes a hermit. He leaves his home and lives in the forest, sometimes with his wife. He continues the rituals and meditates."

"I'm not old enough to start that yet," Sam tells the empty bottles. "Not that Debur Road is a forest, but I sure feel out of it there."

"I know that," I murmur. "In the fourth stage the high-caste man becomes an ascetic. He abandons his wife, stops doing the rituals and wanders like a beggar. He looks for the knowledge to free him from being reborn."

Sam sits down again, wags his head as if saying, "Not bad." Then he does say, "You know what they didn't teach you in grad school?"

He plans to tell me whether I want to know or not. The sliver of light between the pleated metal doors is growing dim.

"There's a really convenient out for Indian men," Sam says. "Bet they didn't teach you that. Appa's using it now to the hilt. Oh, he can be pious and beat his breast about how badly he treated her, his first wife. Even how badly he treated Amma, my mother. But that's the out. Anyone can treat his family like dirt here, and when he grows old, all is forgiven, all is sweetness and light."

I try to say, "Don't you think you're being too—?"

"No, I don't!" he shouts.

I clasp my hands over my ears. I struggle to sit up.

He's pacing again, flinging his arms toward the cobwebs in the corners, flailing in the direction of the metal doors, the wooden doors, the shelf and the empty bottles. "Did he tell you why Amma left him? Why she lives with my sister in Cochin? Why my brother-in-law's family pretends there's nothing odd that the woman my sister brought with her is only her step-mother? It's so Appa can't get his hands on her. He won't dare go to Cochin." Sam stops, leans forward so he can clutch the back of a wicker chair, and glares at me. "Do you know what he used to do?"

I know how to make it rain. I think, "Rain, rain, go away. Come again another day." I think of picnics, of umbrellas left at home. The only way to make it rain is to hope for clear skies.

"He beat her," Sam says. "If his morning coffee wasn't hot enough, he beat her. If there was one speck of grit in the rice, he beat her. If he found dust on the sill above the door, he beat her. He used a broom, a sweeper's broom. Sure, it's soft, but it's so fine it slashes your skin like razors, little cuts you can barely see. He beat her day and night, night and day till she was so afraid of him — I'd find her when I came home from school and she'd be in the back room, the storeroom, chewing her knuckles raw. That's what she did when he beat her, so she wouldn't scream. Because no matter what, our neighbours shouldn't know. No one should ever know."

The fan whispers now, stirs the cobwebs, moves the heat about us.

"That's all in the past," I tell him. "She's free now."

The chair flies against a wall. Bottles clatter. "Sure she is, free! So is he, free! That's the point!" Sam's voice grates along the concrete roof, bounces off the floor, rattles in the corners. "Appa's free to live out the rest of his life contemplating all the evil in the world, and the rest of us are supposed to bend down and kiss his feet?"

That's exactly what I did. When we first arrived in Mysore and Sam saw Appa on the platform at the train station, Sam said, "There he is."

Appa stood next to a lamp post painted bright blue. I went forward and bent to touch his feet. It was exactly what he expected me to do, though he wouldn't have admitted it. I suppose he'd resigned himself to a handshake. He grinned at Sam and said, "It seems you made a good choice after all. Please get up, daughter." Appa laughed and said to Sam, "You will not mind if I call her my red-haired goddess daughter?"

"There's more," Sam says.

"I don't want to hear any more," I tell him. I search in the bag
for biscuits. If I don't eat a proper meal, I will faint. I am no longer
one person.

"Don't you want to hear the best part?" Sam asks.

I hear him say, "Lizards. They'll keep us up all night." I hear
him say, "Look at this." But no tail flops in a spare room now.
We're in a garage in which a family might find itself waiting for
preferred accommodation. There are only bottles and an ashtray, a
cot which doubles as a sofa, a shelf which passes for a wardrobe,
and three wicker chairs.

"Every time he beat her," Sam hisses, "if my sister and I were
home—"

"I don't want to hear!" I shriek.

Sam bends over the table, pulls my hands from my ears. This
man is not my husband; he is an asura, a demon who once lived in
heaven until driven into the nether world. He's the cannibal Baka;
the horse demon Kesin; he's Hiranya-kasipu, plotting to murder
his son.

"Every time he beat her," Sam continues, "if my sister and I
were home, he made us run for the broom. And whichever one of
us lost, my sister or me, we'd have to watch." Sam is pulling me up
off the cot now, bruising my wrists until I can smell the blood on
his mother's knuckles. "And do you know what else?" he asks.

I glare at him. I silently plead, "Don't tell me. I don't want to
know."

"After the first time," he says. "After I learned my lesson? I made
sure I never lost."

He drops me on the cot. I slump sideways, bury my face in a
pillow that smells of camphor, and weep rivulets across the dust.

He looks defeated by his own anger. He sits down, finally lights
his cigarette, and says, "Discover India, Mrs. Devi." He's mocking
one of the many pamphlets I gathered over the years, pamphlets I
left behind with my painted leaves, my books. "It's more than just
temples and elephants and snake charmers," he says. "It's sure as
hell more than the Taj Mahal by moonlight."

4

Debur Road is hushed. On their way back from Nanjangud, from the Ganesha Rice Mill on its outskirts, villagers pass more quietly than usual. I should be afraid, but I'm not. Perhaps Appa was right. Perhaps I really did something so wicked in my previous life that I was forced to be reborn in a foreign land, forced to feel a stranger there until a stranger brought me to my real home. Brought me back. Now Sam is testing me, daring me to spend a night alone in a farmhouse halfway between a village and a town. I know I can pass the test. Boredom is my only enemy, and I'm not easily bored. I've eaten my supper of hotel food, which the driver bought while I waited in the car. The only plate I dirtied is washed; I've filled the buckets from the well.

All-India Radio broadcasts a tribute to Ravi Shankar. A tribute, perhaps, but the announcer can't keep the disdain from his voice. "Some people consider Mr. Shankar's performances of ragas somewhat un-Indian," he says. "Others have suggested he has not so much ravaged the long span of improvisation as he has condensed it." I know what the announcer is trying to say. I wish he would say it: there's no point in wishing westerners could understand the raga; it's enough they're even willing to listen. Enough for now. "To quote the eminent violinist Sir Yehudi Menuhin," the announcer continues, "European music is like a building carefully structured upon constant principles. Indian music is like a river, ever fluid and subtly changing." At last the raga begins. At first it's almost inaudible. The strings of the sitar barely hum, and I turn up the volume. It's a raga appropriate to the time of day, one for twilight, which is brief here. The raga snakes from the main room, slithers into the veranda. It coils around me like the smoke from the sandalwood cone, takes refuge in the tamarind sheltering the house from the road. To the west, toward Debur, glimmers the light from Mr. Kempe Gowda's house.

The light goes out. The music stops. I flick the switch in the veranda. Nothing. Debur Road is darkly silent. Sam would swear, would comment on Indian inefficiency as though the power never failed in Kingston. I'm always prepared. I can find my way through the house even in darkness. There's little furniture to skirt. On a window sill in the kitchen, silhouetted against the light of night, stands a kerosene lamp. The room smells oily and pungent. I place the glass chimney carefully on the sill, reach for the matches beside the lamp, and light the wick. My shadow flickers on the wall beside me. The matches aren't from a box. They're from a book, a glossy white matchbook stamped SAM AND SARA in gold above a golden date: MAY 6, 1989.

Sam and Sara, Sara and Sam. Samsara. In some of my books, it's defined as the realm of existence; in others, rebirth according to the nature of one's karma. But even karma must be defined. It's the moral law of cause and effect, the law according to which a person reaps what she sows. Sam would scoff, remind me the problem with Indian philosophy is that each idea is defined by another, which also needs definition. This is also our problem: he sees life as a maze. I see life as a river, a raga. One of many rivers, one of many ragas. If he could only see my bridge through my eyes, even through those of our child, he would understand.

In the main room, the lamp casts a shadow of its chimney on the pipal leaf; on the painting of Goddess Saraswati with her four arms, her veena older than the sitar, her book of poetry, her swan rising from the lotus. I know from Mr. Kempe Gowda there's a shrine to Saraswati on the river bank, but it's east of Nanjangud, not on Debur Road. One day I will search for the shrine. For now I have my own: my bodhi, my nagas, my bridge. My god room is the river; my god is a ferryman.

I leave the lamp burning in the veranda, leave the doors un-locked for Sam. The asphalt patches on the road are oily pools of rainbows flecked with stars. I walk barefoot along the bund, place my feet carefully to avoid roots and twigs. The paddy on my left has been thinned; the one to my right is now full. Both paddies are a dark green brocade, embroidered in grey with silhouettes of paddy birds lancing their prey. The women who transplanted seedlings are home and so is the man with his plough; the bullocks have settled outside his hut. I take my time; it passes so slowly here. My feet pad on the planks of the footbridge, a narrow path darker than the path along the bund. Someone sings among the sugar cane. Not the watchman. He sleeps curled to one side while a figure twirls beneath the stars, a figure clad in red, a man in a sari

who chants at the stars. He twirls toward me with his arms
upraised, passes through me as though I don't exist. Then he stops
and smiles, pulls the end of his gold-embroidered sari over his
head. When I reach out, the man raises a finger to his lips, gestures
at the sleeping watchman, and twirls away through yet another
field. He sings a bhajan, a devotional song.

Lizards chuckle and clack. We-too birds corkscrew like swallows. They call, "We-too, we-too." My tree rises darkly on the
river bank; the slabs of nagas, naginis huddle in the dark. I sit
beneath the tree and unbraid my hair, comb it free of tangles with
my fingers. Beyond the temple, the pylons of my bridge wait to be
spanned: four pylons, three spaces between them, one at each end
reaching for the banks.

Many things come in ones, still more in twos, but patterns begin
with threes. There's the triad of Brahma the Creator, Vishnu the
Protector, Shiva the Destroyer. There's the fourth aim of a man,
after he grows old: moksha, the liberation from this cycle of death
and rebirth, of samsara. Then there are the fives like the brothers
called the Pandavas: Yudhi-shthira, Arjuna, Nakula, Saha-deva,
Bhima.

Someone calls, "Mrs. Devi?" It's Mr. Kempe Gowda. He hurries along the footbridge.

"Sara?" This time it's Sam.

I still don't answer. They can find me.

At the edge of the field, Sam nudges Mr. Kempe Gowda aside
and steps in front of him. After Mr. Kempe Gowda returns along
the footbridge, Sam approaches as though unsure he should. He's
wearing his trousers now, and a shirt. He looks more like the Sam
who leaves in the morning for his workday journey.

"I can't think of anything that comes in sixes," I tell him.

He watches, puzzled, while I gaze at the unfinished bridge;
while I hope he sees what I see.

The four pylons and three spaces between them equal seven.
There are seven rivers and seven oceans, seven mountains and
seven stars, seven sages and musical notes; there are seven mother
goddesses. There are many eights and nines and tens: eight regions
resting on the backs of eight elephants; nine planets and nine
emotions; ten incarnations of Lord Vishnu, one of them as Rama.

"Nine is the perfect number," I say. "There'll be five of us, though. We'll have two boys and a girl. I'll name them Krishna, Mohan, and Janaki."

He sighs and sits under my bodhi, my tree of enlightenment. He chuckles at the calls of the we-too birds. When I look downstream and ask, "What do you see?" he says:

"An unfinished bridge." What else would he say?

"Remember what happened after Rama finally built his bridge," I ask, "and rescued Sita?"

"They lived happily in Ayodhya," he says.

"In some versions, yes," I say. "In others, he couldn't believe she'd remained faithful to him, and to prove her virtue she nearly threw herself into a fire."

Sam touches my cheek, brushes aside strands of straying hair. "I didn't mean to yell at you like that," he says. "It's just—" At last he says, "I wasn't sure you'd want me back right away."

I want to tell him, "Don't be such a fool." I want to say, "You know I love you." Instead I say, "The very ending's always the same, though. After Rama and Sita died, they went back to being Lord Vishnu and Goddess Lakshmi, which they were in real life, in heaven." Then I say, "There's a story in one of my books, the ones I left behind. It's an old Hasidic story."

"In a book about India?" he asks. After he edges closer, I begin: "Once there was a poor Rabbi named Eisik, the son of Rabbi Jekel, in a ghetto in Krakow, in Poland. He dreamt he should go to Prague, which was then in Bohemia, where he'd find a treasure buried near the bridge to the castle."

When Sam smiles, I ask, "Have you heard this one?" He shakes his head as if to say, "How could I?"

"Only after he dreamt the same dream three times did the Rabbi leave for Prague. The bridge was guarded day and night, he didn't dare start digging, so he spent days watching it, wondering where the treasure might be. At last the captain of the guards, a Bohemian and a Christian, asked the Rabbi what he wanted. After the Rabbi told him his dream, the captain laughed. 'It's a good thing I don't believe in such things,' he said, 'because the same thing once happened to me. A voice said if I went to Krakow and found the house of a man named Eisik, whose father's name was Jekel, and if

I dug up the corner behind the stove, I'd find a treasure.' The captain laughed again. The Rabbi thanked him and hurried all the way back to Krakow. He dug in the corner behind the stove. He found a treasure. He was no longer poor, and he built a prayer house. The story doesn't say, but I suppose he could never leave his ghetto, could he?"

Sam frowns at me, smiles patiently as though he finds the story quaint.

"We can only find the treasure by going far away," I explain. "Even then, it takes a person of another race to show us the treasure was in our own house the whole time. He may even be a person who doesn't believe in voices, and he certainly doesn't reveal the lesson on purpose. He does it while making his own point."

Sam looks up at the branches of my tree, across at the far bank, even at my bridge. "When are you leaving?" he asks.

"Oh, you!" I scold him. "I'm not the Rabbi. You are."

He nods, then, as though he finally understands. I'm not sure he does, but he will one day. "I guess you know more about India than I thought," he says. He means I know more about him than he thought. Perhaps it's never discussed even among family and friends: how much we know of one another, about some things. One day he will recognize the treasure he unearthed, and it's not a woman who will refuse to die young or refuse to leave him. I may have been Indian in a previous life, but he found me elsewhere. This is the treasure: unlike Appa, Sam gives kindness freely even when it's demanded. Our child and I will demand much.

He puts his arm around my waist and squeezes me toward him. I lay my head on his shoulder.

"There's a Sanskrit word I've been trying to think of all evening," I say. That's not quite true. I've only been thinking of it since he arrived, but it still hasn't come to me. "I can think of lots of words when I want to, but this one's just too slippery."

He kisses my cheek, then kisses the spot between my temple and my eye.

I recite, "It's the inability to fathom the workings of a marriage except through the five senses and pain." Then I say, "Maybe I don't need to find the word, though. I know what it means."

"I'm not like Appa," he says at last. The word pain has pained him.

"I wouldn't have said yes on Valentine's," I tell him, "if I thought you were." That sounds silly, since I hadn't met Appa then, but Sam knows his cue:

"I don't remember you saying yes on Valentine's Day," he says. "Seems to me you were the one who proposed."

"I never did."

"Did too."

"Didn't."

"Did."

When I turn to kiss him, I find the moon forming a horned halo behind him. He also turns. The moon is rising over Debur Road, over the distant lights of Nanjangud. It's a silver-white crescent, but not like the moon I left behind. This one lies on its curved back with its points up like the moon trapped in the matted locks of Lord Shiva. He's called the Destroyer, but the world must be destroyed so Lord Brahma can recreate it, so Lord Vishnu can once more protect it. Sam tilts his head until his left ear approaches his shoulder.

"You're not going to spend the rest of our lives here walking around like that?" I ask. "Wishing you could see the moon the way it looks —" I can't say, "back home," so I say, "— back there."

His head straightens, then tilts again. I hold it straight, tightly, until he laughs. I clasp my arms around him from behind, and we sit like that while the moon rises even farther. When it casts faint shadows among the nagas and naginis, I rise and offer him my hand, lead him to the landing. The ferryman has tied his raft of doors to a neem tree, left his pole leaning behind its trunk. He knows he will find them there each morning. Who would take his ferry? Where would they go except across the river? When I bend to lift one edge of the raft, Sam motions me aside. He pushes the raft fully into the water, where it nudges the bank. He steps aboard, and I untie the raft. I hand him the pole, and he helps me on next to him.

"What if we're caught?" he asks.

I point at midstream. "Shoulders back, head up," I say. "Now, pole."

"Ay ay, Captain," he says and pushes off.

I sit on the raft with my knees drawn up, with my arms clasping my knees. Our journey to midstream follows the uneven line cast by the moon. He stops and anchors the pole in the river bottom. When a car approaches the road bridge, its headlights flare on the bluff overlooking the far bank. The stars gleam except near the moon. Fireflies twinkle among neem along the banks. If I blink rapidly, freeze their flight, they form wavy bands.

In less than four months, we will celebrate Dassehra. There will be a parade in Mysore, performances of the *Ramayana* on the maidan in Nanjangud. People will build effigies of Ravana, the demon-king who abducted Sita. Then they will light fireworks and burn the effigies. But the most spectacular fireworks, hundreds and thousands, will come at Deepavali, a month before our child is born. The people of Nanjangud and Debur will light clay lamps, their wicks burning oil, to show Rama and Sita their way home, back to Ayodhya. A single firework explodes over my bridge. It begins red and white, turns saffron, white and green. People are lining the banks of the river with their lamps. We drift between lines of light, wavering lines that look like bands of silvery gold, light that flickers in the water while the river banks glow, while the wavy light of the moon reaches for the far shore.

I know it's only an illusion, most of it, but just as Sam sees what he chooses to see, so I can see what I choose to imagine. The farther east we drift, the more complete my bridge looks, for the spans of the bridges beyond it, the road and rail bridges, rise in the palm of some giant invisible hand. Now my bridge is complete. The moon floats downward; stars retrace their paths; the sun rises behind us, in the west, before it once more begins to set. My bridge is gold and pink. Young women bearing bundles, men bearing firewood, children leading goats — all cross my bridge. Old women bear nothing yet walk bent.

They have finished for the day.

They will soon be home.

Notes

Garuda. A half-man, half-bird (sometimes eagle, sometimes vulture), Garuda is fiercely loyal. He is the enemy of all snakes except Sesha because Sesha also serves Lord Vishnu. Depending on the occasion, Garuda's many epithets include king of birds, lord of the sky, and he who goes where he will. Garuda despises evil and is allowed to devour all bad men unless they are brahmins.

Lord Vishnu. Also called Vishnu the Protector, a member of the Hindu triad. (The others are Brahma the Creator and Shiva the Destroyer.) Vishnu is very popular because he can visit earth as an avatar, or incarnation, to restore the balance between good and evil. Sometimes his consort Lakshmi, goddess of fortune, descends as his earthly wife. His thousand names include deliverer and he who sleeps on the waters (of the primordial sea). It may even be that mortals are merely characters in one of his dreams.

Sesha. The king of serpents on whom Vishnu lies between creating and recreating the universe through Lord Brahma. Sesha is said to support the world, and his yawns cause earthquakes. With his tail in his mouth (like the Ouroboros of alchemists), Seshsa is called Ananta, meaning endless.

Brahma the Creator. Like Vishnu and Shiva, Lord Brahma is a member of the Hindu triad, but he is not as widely worshipped on earth as the other two gods because he once told a lie. His consort is Saraswati, goddess of music and poetry, and his vehicle (the animal associated with a god) is a swan. Brahma once had five heads, but Lord Shiva burned one of them off with his third eye.

Mysore. A city in the South Indian state of Karnataka (formerly the state of Mysore). The city was the seat of the Wodeyar dynasty, whose palace is one of Mysore's main attractions. It is also famous for sandalwood and incense, for carvings of rosewood and teak.

Srirangapatna. An island city, once the fortress capital of Tipu Sultan, a Muslim ruler. Tipu, called the Tiger of Mysore, tried to halt British expansion in South India by usurping the Wodeyar throne. The British defeated him in 1799 with a traitor's help. They installed a puppet Hindu king from whom later, more enlightened Wodeyars descended.

Cauvery River. Named for the Goddess Kaveri, the river flows down from hills called the Western Ghats. Its birthplace is a sacred spot, for Goddess Kaveri literally rises in the form of a water spout. This happens at the very moment the sun enters the astrological house of Libra.

Goddess of dawn. Named Ushas, she rides a chariot drawn by seven ruddy cows and brings light to all men, whether humble or great. She is like a bride who, each morning, seems more beautiful. Forever young, she makes men grow old.

Goddess of night. Named Ratri, she is Ushas's sister. Ratri's dark robes gleam with stars. Men welcome her just as they welcome her sister, for Ratri allows them to rest while she guards them from harm until Ushas's return.

Racket-tailed drongo. About the size of a thrush, the drongo is an exhibitionist and a mimic. Its long tail feathers are shaped like rackets. They hum in flight and look like bumblebees constantly chasing the bird.

Babul tree. Also called the gum Arabic, a substance earlier used in medicine and sweets, the babul is a type of acacia. Its thorns prevent cattle from eating its lower branches. The thorns also protect animals and birds, like the striped squirrel and weaver bird, from predators. The grey shrike or butcher bird stores its prey on the thorns, impaling insects and lizards so it can eat them later.

Yama. Once a kindly god who welcomed souls to heaven, Yama is now a fearful god who passes judgement on the dead. He has coppery eyes and green skin, and his robes are blood red. While his councillor keeps the great register (of dead men's virtues and sins), Yama keeps the Book of Destiny, which records every human's allotted span of life. At times, instead of sending messengers for the soul, Yama himself rides out on a buffalo and drags the victim into his hell with a noose. And yet Yama can be compassionate, as in the tale of Satyavan and Savitri, Hindu lovers more fortunate (in the end) than the Greek lovers Orpheus and Eurydice.

District of Nanjangud. Some twenty-five kilometres south of Mysore, Nanjangud is, in fact, a town within Mysore District. Since the town has a railway station, it is a focal point for nearby villages. Nanjangud is also on a river, so its temples and shrines attract pilgrims.

Bangalore. The capital of Karnataka state and about 140 kilometres northeast of Mysore. Bangalore began as a small mud fort built in the mid-16th century by a chieftain named Kempegowda. It is called the Garden City of India and, by Indian standards, has a pleasant year-round climate. It has become one of India's fastest growing cities and even has a nightlife. Bangalore comes from Bendha Kaluru, meaning town of boiled beans.

Debur Village. Debur is about three kilometres west of Nanjangud on the way to a town called H.D. Kote for short.

Bengal. An area in the northeast part of the Indian subcontinent, Bengal runs from the Himalayas down to the Bay of Bengal. In the 19th century, Bengal became a centre of intellectual and artistic leadership. Then came Independence and Partition, in 1947. One half became (Hindu) India's West Bengal state; the other half became the eastern part of (Muslim) Pakistan and, still later, the separate nation of Bangaladesh.

Surendranath Bannerjea. Born in 1848, Bannerjea became one of the first Indians allowed to join the Indian Civil Service but was unfairly dismissed. A brilliant orator, he began the tradition of welcoming imprisonment, a tactic Mahatma Gandhi later used to render the British powerless.

Bhagavad Gita. Also called the *Song of the Lord,* the *Gita* is a sacred book like the Bible and Koran. The *Gita* is a dialogue between a legendary warrior, Arjuna, and his charioteer, Lord Krishna, which follows from Arjuna's asking why he should fight in a civil war. Among other things, Krishna offers a solution to a dilemma in Hinduism: whether to serve society and ensure its stability or to renounce society and pursue personal salvation. The *Gita* is a self-contained part of the epic *Mahabharata,* somewhat comparable to Homer's epic *Iliad.*

Homeopathy. Founded in Germany during the late 18th century as a response to traditional western medicine (allopathy). In homeopathy, a disease is cured with small doses of a drug which, if it were given to a healthy person, would cause the disease. The principle is that like cures like. Homeopathy spread to Britain and then to India, where it is still widely practised. Some homeopaths claim allopaths merely suppress the symptoms of a disease instead of curing it.

Anna. Just as the pound sterling used to be divided into twelve shillings, so the Indian rupee used to be divided into sixteen annas. After India adopted the decimal system for currency, the rupee was divided into one hundred new paise. Even now, especially in markets, one may still hear half a rupee called eight annas instead of fifty paise.

Veena. Veenas are lute-like stringed instruments older than the sitar familiar to westerners. The most versatile is the Saraswati (South Indian) veena, named for the goddess of music and poetry. A veena player sits cross-legged on the floor. In earlier times, the veena was associated with the dawn. My late uncle, the musicologist B. Chaitanya Deva, wrote this in *Musical Instruments* (National Book Trust, India, 1977):

> Once the demons imprisoned the sage Kanva in a dark room and blindfolded him. The condition for his release was that without using his eyes in any manner he should be able to tell the coming of the dawn. Hours passed and then the sage heard the gentle sound of the veena and he knew that day had dawned. He told his captors— without, of course, revealing the source of his information — and he was set free. (p. 79)

Tabla. A two-piece drum vaguely resembling bongo drums. One of the drums is the tabla proper and can be tuned. The other drum, the dagga, cannot be tuned. Both are struck with the hands, and the tabla player also sits cross-legged on the floor. According to my uncle, again:

> Bharata in his *Natya sastra* tells a tale of how these *pushkaras* [drums in general] came into being. According to the story, Svati, a great saint, went to a pond . . . in his hermitage for a wash. When he was there Indra, the god, sent a downpour of heavy rain and the drops made sweet and rhythmic sound as they fell on the lotus (*pushkara*) leaves. The sage listened to the sound enthralled and came back to his hut with the music still ringing in his ears. He then had the various *pushkaras* . . . made with the assistance of the heavenly craftsman, Visvakarma. (p. 26)

Yakshagana. Based on both epics and local histories, Yakshaganas are melodramas incorporating music, dance, song, and mime. They originated in rituals of worship. As in Japanese Kabuki, Yakshagana costuming and make-up are elaborate. The preparations are considered integral to the performance. The gilt costumes, mainly green, red, and yellow, are made from ordinary materials like cloth, paper, and straw. Also as in Kabuki, all Yakshagana performers are men. Most performances climax in a battle, in which good defeats evil, and end with a wedding.

Banyan. Likely the most common tree in India, the banyan is a type of fig tree. As its roots grow down from branches, the tree spreads sideways to cover large areas. Because it gives so much shade, it is often used as a meeting place for villagers. The name banyan is thought to have come from the banyas, or merchants, who traded under it and used it for shelter. The banyan is also called a strangling fig because, if its seeds are dropped in a palm tree, the banyan will grow so fast it will kill the palm.

Ondu, eradu. The numbers one and two, respectively, in Kannada, the language of Karnataka state. Muru means three.

Krishna, Radha. Lord Krishna was the eighth avatar of Vishnu the Protector. Krishna is often portrayed as having blue skin to symbolize his divinity. As a youth, he was a cowherd who enjoyed playing his flute and dallying with cowgirls, each of whom thought he loved her alone. His favourite cowgirl was Radha, who was already married, and they are often portrayed as seated on a swing. Later in life, Krishna fell in love with and married a princess named Rukmini (an incarnation of Vishnu's consort Lakshmi); still later, Krishna taught the lessons contained in the *Bhagavad Gita.*

Sannyasi. When a man renounces his possessions and even his family, he becomes a sannyasi. This is traditionally the last stage of a high-caste Hindu's life. He spends this stage wandering in search of the knowledge that will free him from almost certain rebirth.

Dal Lake, Vale of Kashmir. Dal Lake is, in fact, a series of three lakes separated by floating gardens. A 19th-century ruler would not allow the British to own land in Kashmir, so they built the houseboats for which the lake is now famous. The Vale of Kashmir is in Jammu and Kashmir, India's northernmost state. Its snow-fed lakes, green rice fields, meadows, and orchards make Kashmir an earthly paradise.

Toddy. An alcoholic drink made from juice tapped from the palmyra or toddy palm tree. Toddy was a common drink among rural people, who could afford to drink nothing more refined.

Tilak. The red dot often placed on the forehead of a person. In shops and markets, one may find a paper tilak pasted onto photographs of Indian leaders and American presidents.

Kathmandu. Nepal's capital is a jumping off point for viewing Himalayan mountains like Everest. Some claim its drug culture is still irresistible to modern hippies.

Charpoi. A cot with a surface of woven rope to support a thin mattress or bedroll.

Sadhu. Men who have renounced their possessions may become sadhus. Many are followers of Lord Shiva and thus carry his symbol, the trident. They often wander half-naked, with their skin smeared with dust or ash and their hair and beards matted. Many mortify their bodies to heighten their spiritual awareness.

Ganga River. India's largest and holiest river begins in the Himalayas and flows east (passing through Varanasi, once called Be-

nares), then south into the Bay of Bengal. The river is a personifica-
tion of the goddess Ganga and, like a deity, has many epithets—
108 of them. The first is Ganges, the second is born from the lotus-
like foot of Vishnu, and the last is a light amid the darkness of
ignorance.

Hindi. A North Indian language, Hindi is one of India's fourteen
major languages. It is spoken by half the population, but South
Indians do not appreciate efforts to promote the use of Hindi in
their four states.

THE EVIL EYE

Saraswati. The goddess of music and poetry and the consort of
Brahma the Creator. She enables him to realize what he conceives.
She is thus the goddess of all creative arts including learning and
science and is also identified with the goddess of speech. Watery
and elegant, Saraswati is graceful, but she is also haughty and given
to disputes.

Brahminy kite. A chestnut-coloured, water-loving hawk, the
brahminy kite feeds on fish, crabs, and small reptiles. Kites are
members of the hawk family, which includes eagles and buzzards.

Coconut palms. As opposed to date palms. The coconut palm is
among the most useful of Indian trees. Around the nut is a fibre
called coir, used to make rope and mats. The ribs of the long,
fringed leaves are used for brooms and paper kites. The sap
produces a wine. The white inside of the nut, called copra, can be
eaten or crushed into oil, used to make candles and soap. The
water in the nut is sterile so, during World War II, doctors gave
injured soldiers who needed body fluids transfusions from coco-
nuts.

Delhi. A common name for New Delhi, in the northern plains of
India. The walled city of old Delhi was India's capital under the
(Muslim) Moghuls until the 19th century. In the early 20th
century, the British decided to move their imperial capital from
Calcutta, in Bengal. One should not read too much into such
things, but British architects created New Delhi out of a wilderness
inhabited by animals.

Bombay. Located halfway up the west coast of the Indian subcontinent, Bombay was once a string of seven swampy, malaria-infected islands. The Portugese received them from a local sultan under a treaty. A century later Mumbai, the largest island, went to England as part of Catherine of Braganza's dowry when she married King Charles II. He, in turn, leased it to the British East India Company for ten pounds a year. Like Manhattan Island, which once went for twenty-four dollars, Bombay is now a centre of high finance.

Kulfi. An Indian version of ice cream made of sugar, almonds and pistachios in milk, which has been reduced by boiling. The mixture is poured into terra cotta cylinders which are, in turn, cooled in earthernware vats full of ice.

Kannada. One of four South Indian languages. The Kannada alphabet contains nearly twice as many letters as the English alphabet. People who speak Kannada are called Kannadigas. In 1956, state boundaries were redrawn on linguistic lines; what was once known as Mysore State became Karnataka.

Sambar. Eaten with rice, sambar is a soupy mixture of tomatoes or other vegetables, lentils and spices. The essential ingredient is the spicy sambar powder.

Curds. Meals end with curds, which cool the palate and aid digestion. Curds may be mixed with rice or served diluted with water and a fragrant coriander leaf. Each night, a bit of the day's curd is added to warm milk to make the following day's curds. According to a Kannada proverb, an eloping daughter will forget to add the curd to the night's milk.

Autorickshaw. A three-wheeled hired vehicle, often yellow, with a canvas top, often black. The driver sits in front and steers by means of a column and handles like a scooter's. The passengers — usually two but sometimes three or more — sit in the back, separated from him by a low panel. In top gear, autorickshaws sound like radio-controlled model airplanes.

Jaipur. The capital of the state of Rajasthan, once controlled by warriors called Rajputs. (Largely barren, Rajasthan lies on India's northwest border with Pakistan.) Jaipur was built in the early 18th century by Jai Singh II — soldier, astronomer, prince — who had the buildings of his new (now the old) city made from blocks of pink sandstone.

Kankanam. A talismanic wrist-ornament made of lac and covered with tinsel. A marriage may not be consummated until a kankanam is tied around the wrists of the bride and groom.

Furlong. An imperial unit of distance used in daily conversation. One furlong is roughly 200 metres (220 yards).

Dhoti. A long, loose cloth (typically white) worn by men. It is tied at the waist and allowed to hang free about the legs. Its ends can be pulled up and tucked for ease of work or riding a bicycle. Everyday dhotis are made of cotton; ceremonial ones are made of silk.

Slaked lime. When water is added to lime (the white powder used for fertilizer or covering walls), the water changes the chemical properties of the lime and makes it safe to consume.

Sanskrit. The ancient tongue of migrating Aryans who settled in India, Sanskrit is closer to Latin and English than modern Indian languages. Texts like the *Bhagavad Gita* were composed in Sanskrit, which is still used in rituals.

Agni, the god of fire. Agni appears in heaven as the sun, in the atmosphere as lightning, and on earth as ordinary fire. The sacrificial fire into which priests pour ghee (clarified butter) is thus a mediator between gods and men, who must together strive to maintain the creative and life-sustaining powers of the world. Among the earliest of Hindu gods to be worshipped, Agni is present at significant events like weddings.

Pan supari. A betel leaf wrapped around ingredients called pan is chewed after a meal to aid digestion. It can even be mildly intoxicating. The ingredients include slivers of betel nut, lime paste, and cloves. After they are well chewed, they are spit out. Over time, pan will turn a person's lips, teeth, and tongue reddish black.

Heating coil. A simple immersion heater for water. The instrument is hooked onto the edge of a bucket with the coil in the water —and only then plugged into a wall socket.

Jamuna River, Agra, Taj Mahal. The Jamuna begins in the Himalayas and flows south; it passes through New Delhi and Agra, then flows east to join the Ganga River. After Shah Jahan built the Taj Mahal as a tomb for his beloved wife, Mumtaz Mahal, he planned a tomb for himself—identical, but made of black marble instead of white. He was overthrown by his son, who imprisoned Shah Jahan in a palace called Agra Fort, across the Jamuna from the Taj Mahal. The deposed king spent his final days nearly blind, with his arms wrapped around a pillar and his back to the river. On the pillar hung an emerald, and in it he could gaze at a reflection of his monument to his wife.

HONESTLY, AS IN THE DAY

Koran. Also called Qur'an, the Koran is to Muslims what the Bible is to Christians and the *Bhagavad Gita* is to Hindus. The Koran contains the infallible word of God as revealed to the Prophet Mohammed, who founded Islam in the early seventh century. Muslims treat the Koran with respect because it is an earthly copy of the eternal Koran, inscribed in heaven.

Kabini River. The Kabini flows through southwest Karnataka to join the Cauvery River at a town called T. Narsipur for short. Both Debur and Nanjangud are on the Kabini River.

Monsoon. This may mean either the season of heavy rain or the wind that brings this rain. The summer monsoon, which lasts from about June to September, moves from southwest to northeast. The winter monsoon, from about October to December, moves from northeast to southwest. While the monsoons bring much-needed rain, they can also cause floods.

Holi. A Hindu festival of spring, during February-March, which marks the rekindling of the spirit of life. Revellers throw coloured powder and balloons filled with coloured water on one another and on passers-by.

Deepavali. Also called Diwali, this festival of lights marks the beginning of the year, in October-November, on the Hindu lunar calendar. Deepavali is celebrated for five days by lighting lamps and fireworks and by exchanging sweets.

Lancashire cotton. Cotton milled in Lancashire, England; thus considered superior to Indian cotton. During the freedom struggle, Mahatma Gandhi convinced Indians to wear homespun cotton to defy the British. He received unexpected support from even unemployed millworkers in Lancashire.

Sankranti. This largely local festival, celebrated in January, marks the sun's return to the northern hemisphere.

A PROMISE WE SHALL WAKE IN THE PINK CITY AFTER HARVEST

Neem. Called margosa in English, the neem is one of India's most medicinally useful trees. The end of the twig, when chewed, can be used like a toothbrush. The leaves are used for treating boils, and oil from the seed is used in treating skin disorders and leprosy.

Jatayu, Ravana, Sita, Rama. Characters in the Hindu epic *Ramayana*, also called *Song of Rama*. In a famous early scene, Ravana, the demon-king of Lanka, abducts Rama's wife, Sita. When Jatayu, the vulture king, tries to save Sita, Ravana cuts off Jatayu's wings. Before the vulture king dies, he tells Rama what happened. Jatayu was an earthly incarnation of Garuda, the king of birds; Rama was the seventh avatar of Lord Vishnu; and Sita was an incarnation of his consort, Lakshmi. Somewhat comparable to Homer's epic *Odyssey*, the *Ramayana* is beloved among Indians. However, it was also used to legitimize the superiority of Aryans from the North over darker-skinned Dravidians of the South.

Wallah, Chai. Hindi for person and tea respectively. Wallah is useful for creating English-Hindi terms for occupations, e.g., autorickshaw-wallah (sometimes synonymous with a fellow who will drive like a madcap and cheat you blind).

Ayah. A female household servant who may do one or more tasks like cooking, cleaning, and even caring for children.

Red dust. The name Kannada comes from kari, meaning black, and nadu, meaning land. Thus Karnataka is a land of black soil, yet only the soil north of the Tungabhadra, a major river, is black. Soil south of the Tungabhadra is red.

Naleba. Kannada for come tomorrow.

Mangalore tiles. These are smooth, rectangular, red-orange tiles originally made in Mangalore, on the west coast of South India, following a process imported from Europe.

Ghat. The stone steps or landing at a river, often near a holy place, on which bodies are cremated.

Seer. A basic unit of Indian measure. For liquids, one seer roughly equals one litre (about one quart). For dry goods, one seer roughly equals one kilogram (just over two pounds).

Namaste, Namaskaara. Hindi and Kannada respectively for good morning, or an equally respectful greeting and farewell.

Idu nanna mane. Illi irabeda. Nimage eshtu halu beku? Kannada for the following: This is my house. You should not be here. How much milk do you require?

UNDERSTANDING MAYA

Fakir. Applied to Hindu sadhus and other ascetics, a fakir is more correctly a Muslim who has taken a vow of poverty.

Somnipath. One who practises mesmerism, loosely called hypnotism, based on the work of Franz Anton Mesmer, a German physician of the late 18th century.

Khajuraho. The temples of Khajuraho, also called the City of the Gods, are among the finest examples of medieval Hindu architecture. Khajuraho is best known for its erotic sculptures — couples demonstrating the worldly aspects of principles in the *Kama Sutra* —but other motifs include animals, flowers, and gods.

Rajiv Gandhi. The son of Indira Gandhi and grandson of Jawaharlal Nehru, India's first prime minister, Rajiv studied engineering and became a pilot for Indian Airlines. After Indira's as-

sasination in October 1984, he became Prime Minister and held
the post until the elections of November 1989.

Sixty Thousand Sons of Sagara. Impudent young men who were
burned to ashes for angering a sage. They were eventually brought
back to life by Ganga, a goddess who fell to earth as the Ganga
River. Lord Shiva broke her fall with his matted locks to check her
unruly and unpredictable course.

Ramadan. The ninth lunar month of the Muslim calendar. During Ramadan, from sunrise to sunset, Muslims abstain from eating, drinking, smoking, and all forms of pleasure. They refrain
from quarrelling and try to settle outstanding differences. It is also
a month of festivities, which occur once the sun sets. Ramadan
ends with the sighting of the new moon, and the next day is Eid-ul-
Fitr, the joy at the end of the days of fasting.

MOSAIC

Caste. The caste system is the ancient but still persistent social
structure of Hinduism. There were four castes, among which
marriage was not encouraged, and each caste was said to be
descended from a different part of a supreme being, Purusha. The
brahmin (priest, scholar) was at the top because he came from
Purusha's mouth. The kshatriya (noble, warrior) came from Purusha's arms. The vaishya (landowner, merchant) came from Purusha's thighs. Last came the shudra (artisan, serf) from Purusha's
feet, but shudras were still above outcastes or untouchables. Caste
comes from the Sanskrit word varna, which means colour; the
lighter-skinned Aryan invaders of India placed themselves at the
top and relegated the darker-skinned Dravidian inhabitants to the
bottom. Over centuries, the caste system became complicated by
the jati system. In this, people are divided into some two thousand
occupational groups, which are more or less important depending
on where each jati lives.

Ashram at Pondicherry. An ashram is a religious retreat or self-
contained community — in which people live part or all of their
lives, or to which people retire. Pondicherry, on the east coast of
South India, was once a French colony. It is now the site of the
popular Sri Aurobindo Ashram.

Shakuntala. A masterpiece by the sixth-century playwright Kalidasa based on events from the epic *Mahabharata*.

Satyajit Ray. The first great Indian director whose films reached the west. Many Indians consider his films too serious because they present Indian life realistically.

Rama. One of many names by which Hindus call upon God.

Goondas. Ruffians, who can be hired, and all too often are — even by candidates for political office.

Apsaras. Heavenly nymphs called the daughters of pleasure, apsaras are skilled in music, song, and dance. When they were created, they were so beautiful that neither gods nor demons wanted the apsaras as wives, so they became wives to all.

SAMSARA

1

Bund. An embankment made of earth built up between fields. A certain amount of standing water is needed in a rice field, especially while planting and transplanting.

Sword tree. An informal reference to the gulmohur, a popular roadside tree. After its seed pods harden, they turn black and remind some people of curved swords. Westerners call the gulmohur the Pentecost tree, because it flowers about the time of Pentecost, which is on the seventh Sunday after Easter and marks the descent of the Holy Ghost to Christ's apostles. The gulmohur is also called the fire tree or the flamboyant, because its flowers are bright orange and red.

A Midsummer Night's Dream. One of the many plots of this Shakespearean comedy concerns a lovers' quarrel between Oberon and Titania, the king and queen of fairies. The explanation, given by Puck, properly reads as follows (act 2, scene 1):

> For Oberon is passing fell and wrath,
> Because that she as her attendant hath
> A lovely boy, stolen from an Indian king;
> She never had so sweet a changeling.

> And jealous Oberon would have the child
> Knight of his train, to trace the forests wild.

Felix Mendelssohn-Bartholdy, a 19th-century composer, wrote an overture and incidental music for the play.

Bodhi tree. More commonly called the pipal, a type of fig tree like the banyan. While the banyan has aerial roots, the pipal has roots growing from its trunk, so they look like pillars. It has medicinal and other uses. A reddish dye comes from the bark. Pipal leaves can be fed to camels and elephants or dried and painted for decoration.

Madeleine Slade, Meerabehn. The daughter of a British admiral, Madeleine Slade was in her early thirties when she left London society to serve Mahatma Gandhi in 1925. He renamed her Meerabehn. She, in turn, took vows of chastity and poverty and wore saris made of homespun. She became his constant companion and even fell physically ill when separated from him. She died in 1982, thirty-four years after Gandhi's assasination. He once admitted she haunted his dreams.

Naga. Female, nagini; a serpent demon. Nagas have human bodies to the waist, below which they have serpents' tails. Most nagas personify evil and guard the nether world, but many are worshipped as gods. These include Sesha, the king of serpents, on whom Vishnu lies. Nagas own the very best jewels, worn on their hoods to light the darkness of the nether world.

Ooty. Short for Ootacamund, in the state of Tamil Nadu. Called the Queen of the South, Ooty is a hill station some 150 kilometres south of Mysore via Nanjangud. (Ooty can also be reached from the surrounding lowlands by a miniature, cog railway.) In the mid-19th century, the British found Ooty's climate more pleasant than the climate on the east coast, so they transformed the hill station into one of their summer capitals.

2

Beedi. Essentially a rolled-up tobacco leaf, a beedi is a small brown cigarette. It is less expensive than the white tailor-made.

Punjab. Also called the Punjab, this largely agricultural land is in the northwest part of the Indian subcontinent. It is home to most of India's Sikhs and was partitioned between India and Pakistan. The name Punjab comes from panch, meaning five, and ab, meaning river. Which five is sometimes debated, but they include the Indus, Chenab, and Sutlej.

CIDA. The Canadian International Development Agency.

Yudhi-shthira, Bhima, Arjuna, Nakula, Saha-deva. The five Pandava brothers, also called the Pandavas, in the epic *Mahabharata*. They were born to two wives of the same king but fathered by five different gods.

> Yudhi-shthira, the eldest, was the son of Dharma, the god of justice (or Yama, god of the dead). Yudhi-shthira was trained as a warrior but became renowned as a ruler. His selection as heir apparent began the protracted civil war between the Pandavas and their cousins, the one hundred Kauravas.

> Bhima, meaning the Terrible, was the second Pandava brother and son of Vayu, the god of wind. Bhima was huge, strong, tempermental, and fearless; he was prone to cruelty; and he ate half the food allotted to the Pandavas. He was also called the large-armed, and his weapon was a club.

> Arjuna, meaning White, was the third-born Pandava. He was the most prominent of the brothers and a great warrior. His father was Indra, god of the firmament, the atmosphere personified. On the eve of battle, Arjuna's charioteer, Lord Krishna, related the teachings now found in the *Bhagavad Gita*.

The fourth and fifth Pandava brothers were fathered by the Aswins, or Horsemen, who were twin sons of Surya, the sun. Riding a golden car drawn by horses or birds, the Aswins herald the appearance of Ushas, goddess of the dawn.

> Nakula, the son of the Aswin called Nasatya, learned the art of training horses. Saha-deva, the son of the Aswin called Dasra, learned astronomy and the art of managing cattle.

Rama's bridge. To reach Lanka, where his wife, Sita, was being held captive, Rama had to cross the Gulf of Mannar, possibly at shoals now called Adam's Bridge. Rama's bridge, built by his army of monkeys and bears with the help of other animals, was made of everything from stones to sticks to mud. Even a lowly squirrel contributed a pebble. When Rama bent to stroke the squirrel's back, his fingertips left stripes, which some squirrels bear to this day.

Ayodhya. One of India's seven sacred cities, Ayodhya was founded by a grandson of the sun and became the capital of the Solar race. Some seventy kings including Rama ruled from Ayodhya — among them, Bhagiratha, who brought the Ganga River to earth.

Hasidic tales, Heinrich Zimmer. The Hasidim, also called Chassidim from the Hebrew for pious, are Jewish mystics. They believe in the ability of all men to reach God and are known for their tolerance. The sect was founded in the 18th century. Heinrich Zimmer was a 20th-century German expert on India. He applied the work of Swiss psychologist Carl Jung on archetypes and the collective unconscious. Zimmer's work influenced the American mythologist Joseph Campbell.

Maharani. From maha, meaning great, and rani, meaning queen. (Maharaja thus means great king.)

Lord Shiva. Also called Shiva the Destroyer, a member of the Hindu triad, Shiva gained his power through his ability to perform austerities. Though feared, he is widely worshipped, for he must destroy the universe (by dancing) before Brahma can create it and Vishnu can protect it. Shiva is thus, paradoxically, an auspicious god of fertility. His weapons include a trident, a club with a skull at its end, three serpents which twine about him, and his third eye. His vehicle is the bull called Nandi. His consort is Parvati, also called Devi or Mahadevi, the great goddess. His many names include moon-crested, bearer of the Ganga River, and lord of beasts.

Cochin. A port city on the southwest coast of India in Kerala state, Cochin was settled at different times by the Portugese, Dutch, and British and influenced by many other cultures. It contains such unlikely sights as Chinese fishing nets, introduced by traders from Kublai Khan's court, and a synagogue, built by descendants of Jews who settled there in AD 1000. According to legend, St. Thomas the Apostle visited Cochin in AD 52.

3

Peon. Originally meaning footsoldier, peon can refer to one of many useful and necessary positions: attendant, orderly, messenger, office boy, and (under the British) native Indian police constable. The term sounds derogatory to westerners because, in Latin America, a peon was once a debtor kept in servitude until his debt was discharged.

Mridangam. Long and barrel-shaped, the mridangam has a bulge off centre and a face at each end. Like a tabla player, the mridangam player sits cross-legged on the floor. The mridangam is one of only two drums used in South Indian classical concerts.

Fanta, Limca, Thums Up. Indian soft drinks sold in capped bottles. (Bisleri is also the brand name of a soda water sold in capped bottles.) Fanta tastes like orange and Limca tastes like lemon-lime. Thums Up is one of many Indian substitutes for Coca-Cola. Another is Double Seven, which commemorates 1977, the year Coca-Cola was forced to stop selling in India because the company would not register its formula. A highly acclaimed novelist soon had India's top secret agent, Janu Bond, in pursuit of the formula.

Mango leaves. The mango tree is sacred to Hindus because it is a manifestation of Prajapati, the lord of all creatures. (In some texts he is Brahma the Creator.) Thus, mango leaves — leathery, lance-shaped and smooth — are used in celebrating festivals. According to legend, the daughter of the sun god once found herself chased by an evil spirit. To escape it, she dove into a lake and changed into a lotus. A king, passing by, fell in love with the lotus. The spirit was so incensed it burned the lotus to ashes. Out of these ashes grew the mango tree.

Buddha Purnima. The holiest day of the Buddhist calendar. The appearance of the full moon in April-May is especially sacred to Buddhists because of a triple coincidence: on this day Buddha was born, later achieved enlightenment, and still later achieved nirvana when he died. Hindus respect days holy to people of other faiths, so even if Hindus do not celebrate such days, they mark Buddha

Purnima just as they mark Christmas and Eid-ul-Fitr, the end of the Muslim month of Ramadan.

Mava, aththe. Father-in-law and mother-in-law, respectively, in Kannada.

Capitation fees. The fees parents pay to gain their children seats in good secondary schools or colleges. Some Indians make little distinction between capitation fees and bribes.

AIISc. Associate of the Indian Institute of Science, a graduate degree, much like a master of science.

Maidan. A flat, open space with many possible uses: fairs, sporting events, military parades, and political rallies.

Vedas. Indo-Aryan scriptures which form the basis of Hinduism. The best known are the *Rig Veda*, composed about 1200 B.C., and the *Upanishads* (dialogues between a teacher and student), composed as late as 400 B.C. There are three forms of Vedic literature. *Samhitas* are hymns praising various gods like Indra, god of the firmament, and Agni, the god of fire. *Brahmanas* are descriptions of rituals such as maintaining the sacrificial fire. *Aranyakas* and *Upanishads* are philosophical, metaphysical texts on the quest for ultimate reality, or the truth that will make men free.

Asura, Baka, Kesin, Hiranya-kasipu. Originally gods, asuras were driven from heaven. They became demons who live in the nether worlds below the ocean but remain as powerful as the gods, who can only outwit asuras by trickery or by gaining more power through austerities.

> In return for not eating the people of nearby villages, Baka received a daily tribute: cartloads of rice and vegetables and a man. One day Bhima, the gluttonous Pandava of the *Mahabharata*, went as the human sacrifice. On the way he ate all the food. Bhima killed Baka, and the asuras promised not to harm humans.

> Kesin was a sworn foe of Indra, god of the firmament, and often led attacks on the gods. In another tale, Kesin took the form of a horse to attack Lord Krishna, who thrust his hand down Kesin's throat and made it swell until Kesin burst.

> Hiranya-kasipu performed such austerities he received this boon: that he would be immune from beasts, men, and gods and could die

neither by day nor by night, neither inside nor outside his palace. He grew so arrogant he forbade the worship of gods and became incensed when his own, young son remained a devotee of Lord Vishnu. Hiranya-kasipu tried to have the boy put to death in numerous ways until Vishnu at last came to earth as his fourth avatar, Narasinha, a man-lion — neither beast nor man nor god. Narasinha killed Hiranya-kasipu on the threshold of his palace at twilight— neither by day nor by night, neither inside nor out.

Camphor. Distilled from the wood and bark of the camphor tree, camphor has a penetrating odour and pungent taste. It is used to make mothballs (as is naphthalene, a petroleum distillate). Though mothballs are carcinogenic, they are still widely used to preserve clothes and bedding from moths.

4

Ravi Shankar. The artist largely responsible for introducing westerners to Indian music. His compositions include ballets, two concertos for sitar and orchestra, and music for films like *Gandhi* and Satyajit Ray's *Apu Trilogy*. Shankar's recordings include three albums called "West Meets East," which feature artists like tabla player Alla Rakha and violinist Yehudi Menuhin. (The radio announcer's comments are paraphrased from *The Music of Man* by Yehudi Menuhin and Curtis W. Davis [Methuen Publications, 1979].)

Raga. Literally a mode of music rather than a scale or a melody (though ragas often appear to contain both). Since ragas are appropriate to the time of day, a raga of the evening is introspective and serene. A raga has four formal sections. The soloist sets the raga's mood in the first section, which has little rhythm, and moves into a slow, meditative exposition in which the soloist gives each note full attention. In the second section the soloist introduces some rhythm, while the tempo of the third section is fast. The percussionist enters only in the fourth section, in which rhythm becomes important. This final section is a structured composition with both the soloist and percussionist improvising; they play sometimes in unison, sometimes in counterpoint, and sometimes in echo of the other.

Sitar. A lute-like stringed instrument like the veena, the sitar is to North Indian music what the veena is to South Indian music. As with the veena, the sitar player sits cross-legged on the floor. According to my uncle, B. Chaitanya Deva, writing in *Musical Instruments*:

> The *sitar* gained importance and prestige not very long ago; prior to about a century from now it was not even considered "respectable." It was the *Rudra veena* which was the highbrow instrument. Indeed, the traditional *ustads* [masters] of the *veena* rarely, if ever, taught it to anyone outside their fold; [it] was a family prerogative! "Aliens" who knocked at the doors of their citadels of knowledge were initiated into "despicable" instruments such as the *sitar*.   (pp. 99-100)

Bhajan. A song arising from bhakti, the tradition of fervent devotion to a personal god. Bhakti includes singing bhajans, congregational hymns in the form of love songs to the god.

The Rabbi from Krakow. A retelling of the version in Heinrich Zimmer's *Myths and Symbols in Indian Art and Civilization* (Princeton University Press, Bollingen Series VI, 1946), edited by Joseph Campbell. Zimmer first read the tale in a 1928 book by the theologian Martin Buber.

Dassehra. Held in September-October, the most important festival in Karnataka state. Celebrations in Mysore include a parade led, on elephantback, by descendants of Mysore's maharajas. The battle between Rama and Ravana lasted ten days, and so does Dassehra. On the last evening, huge effigies of Ravana and his followers — all filled with firecrackers — are set on fire. Good once more triumphs over evil and restores harmony, perfect balance, to the world.